star crossed

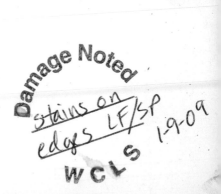

To my brother, Ben

MARK SCHREIBER

star crossed

Woodbury, Minnesota

First Edition
First Printing, 2007

Cover design by Kevin Brown
Cover image © 2006 Photo Alto

Flux, an imprint of Llewellyn Publications

The Cataloging-in-Publication Data for *Starcrossed* is on file at the Library of Congress.
  ISBN-13: 978-0-7387-1001-3
  ISBN-10: 0-7387-1001-6

This is a work of fiction. Names, characters, places, and incidents are either the product of the author's imagination or are used fictitiously, and any resemblance to actual persons, living or dead, business establishments, events, or locales is entirely coincidental. Cover models used for illustrative purposes only and may not endorse or represent the book's subject.

Flux
Llewellyn Publications
A Division of Llewellyn Worldwide, Ltd.
2143 Wooddale Drive, Dept. 0-7387-1001-6
Woodbury, MN 55125-2989, U.S.A.
www.fluxnow.com

Printed in the United States of America

part One

A pair of starcrossed lovers take their life
Shakespeare

Corpse Blue Tattoo

How did a sweet girl of destiny like myself, far along the road to recovery from youthful mistakes and misfortunes, in love—really—for the very first time, find herself one stormy, ominous night in a death embrace with her stricken Romeo, holding a nine iron defiantly on Life's eighteenth hole, while the dark clouds of our destruction rolled overhead?

It all started when I got Benjamin scraped off my chest.

It was an expensive correction, since insurance companies don't pay for tattoo removal. But fair enough, I didn't want anyone to know anyway and I had some money stashed under my bed. But every office I called wanted my life history. I even thought of doing it myself with carbolic acid and a Q-tip. But then I called a plastic surgeon that gave me an appointment just like that—reason for visit, name, you'll have to pay at the time of service—she didn't even ask my age. Cool.

I'd never been to a doctor alone before. This unwelcome thought came to me as I entered the medical building and stood alone waiting for the shiny elevator doors to open. My mom always took me to the doctor, or Benjamin. Once I wanted him to take me to my gynecologist because my mom didn't know I was on the pill and I didn't want to go alone. He refused until I told him a lot of women have affairs with their ob-gyn. Mine was a woman but Benjamin never paid attention to details.

So I was feeling anxious standing there alone waiting eons for the damn elevator—there are only three floors, where could it be? The Sears Tower was faster! I wanted to be comforted at a time like this, distracted—I wanted someone to talk to, to take my mind off the fact that I was about to get ink—ink that's seeped into my breast scraped off with a needle or a razor or burned away with carbolic acid on a Q-tip. It's like waiting for a roller coaster but with only misery ahead and no thrill.

And what if someone I knew saw me? Someone who knew my parents? I looked at the building directory. I'd tell them I was seeing Stephen Wilde, M.D., allergist, also on the third floor, for my hay fever. But what would happen when I was actually in Dr. Dobrowski's office itself—the point of no return? What if my dad's secretary also happened to be there, waiting to get her eyelids lifted?

I crept past the allergist's door and paused casually in front of Dr. Dobrowski's office like I was looking for the drinking fountain. There was a sliver of glass next to the door through which I could see several people. Plastic surgeons shouldn't have waiting rooms. They should have doors with peepholes and buzzers like crack houses.

My throbbing heart told me to leave. But the line of blue ink with that cursed name an inch or two away from my heart said *stay*. Besides, it took three weeks to get this appointment and they'd probably bill me anyway.

Inside were a couple fat women, a couple old women, and a guy about my age. A guy! Maybe he was waiting for his mother or grandmother, back there becoming thirty again. The nurse behind the counter told me to sign in and pushed some forms on a clipboard my way. She had an expensive nose but could have used a smile.

I'd give them my name, rank, and serial number but I wasn't signing in or filling out forms. I put my purse on the counter on top of the clipboard to prove I was a serious patient—I was going to pay—in advance! But the nurse didn't care. She was put on earth to make sure people filled out forms and if a blank form should happen to slide through it could mean the end of the universe as we know it. I patiently explained—whispering of course—that who-ever I talked to on the phone said everything was cool. Who did I talk to? How should I know, I'm not the one making the appointments! She went to consult with a woman in the back, her supervisor—the woman I talked to?—and when she returned said I didn't have to sign in or give them my insurance info but they needed my medical history for their records. I answered the medical questions truthfully but I put down a false address in case they decided to send me coupons, and where it said person to contact in case of emergency I wrote God with a question mark above phone number. If my plastic surgeon didn't have a sense of humor it was better to know before his sharp instruments descended on my naked flesh.

I took a seat beside a table piled with magazines and flipped through a tattooless *Vogue*. But who did these mags think they were kidding? These models had tattoos, they were just concealed or Clearasiled over. If I were in *Vogue* no one would be wiser. You'd have to see me in a Victoria's Secret catalog modeling one of their lace bras to catch a glimpse of my secret. And even then you'd only see the traces of blue ink; you wouldn't be able to read the name. Maybe I was overreacting. Who had to see my breasts any-way? By the time I was ready for a husband they might have stretched or sagged enough to make it just a blue blur.

"What are you here for?"

It was the guy, sitting on the other side of the table. I looked everywhere but at him, but I was alone. The fat women and old women who would surely have supported me against this rude offender were gone. I went to the ends of the earth to protect my privacy and a complete stranger—a guy—at the point of no return—asked me why I was here!

I couldn't ignore him since we were alone so I sneered back like his worst nightmare. "Excuse me?"

He was smiling but I could see he was nervous—this was his pick up line, maybe he'd hung out here preying on girls with crooked noses. "What are you in here for?" he repeated.

Now I looked at him full force—cringe and die, and he did shift back a little. "Don't you know that's a question you never ask in prison or a plastic surgeon's office!"

He became flustered, but to his credit persisted in annoying me. He was scared but courageous. "I just wanted to tell you if you were getting a breast augmentation it isn't necessary."

Now I was the one who was flustered and it wasn't so much because of what he'd said—although that was bad enough—as the fact that I couldn't help noticing he was sort of cute. He had a nose that didn't need fixing—I never looked at noses until I stepped into this office—perfect white teeth—long blond-streaked hair, and murderous ice-blue eyes. He was taller than I was, which was tall enough, and was wearing tight jeans, a Northwestern jersey, and a gold earring.

"If I want a tit job that's my business!" I told him loudly

to show him he couldn't embarrass me. "Not that that's what I'm here for."

"I just couldn't think why someone like you . . ."

"It could be a thousand things." And I immediately regretted my big mouth as his eyes widened imagining those thousand things.

"What's wrong with a tit job anyway?" I asked to keep him from thinking about all the hideous flaws I could have been hiding. "It's because of men that the women in these magazines starve and inflate their bodies."

"But women buy these magazines," he said, trying to be too logical. And then he looked too serious for this conversation. "I don't think the same substance inside a PC should also be inside a woman."

"And I suppose you've had personal experience with silicone?"

"Well . . ."

I laughed. I went back to my *Vogue*.

"You want to know what *I'm* here for?" he said after a while.

"Some kind of augmentation?"

"I'm getting a tattoo removed."

I turned some pages. But it *was* a coincidence.

"What's your name?" he said when I still ignored him.

"I don't give out my name."

"I could look at the sign-in sheet," he said cleverly.

"I didn't sign in," I said, more clever.

"I only want your first name."

I thought about it. "What's your sign?"

"Why do you want to know my sign?"

"I'll tell you my name if you're the right sign. What's your birth date?"

"February twentieth."

"A Pisces."

"Is that good?"

"Could be better. Christy."

"Really! With a *C* or a *K*?"

"With a *C*."

"Wow."

"What's the matter?"

He rolled up his left sleeve and turned his shoulder toward me. There in dark blue letters on his upper arm was my name!

"Too bad I don't like you," I said. "You could have saved a hundred and fifty dollars!"

I thought this would devastate him, but the coincidence only made him bolder. He looked at me with his ice-blue eyes. "If you don't like me, why did you sit next to me?"

"I didn't sit next to you. I sat next to the magazines."

"There are magazines over there."

"It isn't considered sitting next to someone when there's a table between them!"

"You're the astrologer. You should know it was fate that made you pick this chair out of all the chairs in the room."

"You'd need a lot of stars in your corner to stand a chance with me. I'd blow you away."

"My name's Ben."

But I was the one who was blown away. "Is your real name Benjamin?"

"Yeah, but I never use it. It either sounds like a little boy or an old scholar. Why?"

"I hate that name," I said.

⊙ ⊙ ⊙

I sat on the exam table, my legs dangling above the floor. The nurse told me to take off my shirt and handed me an ugly green gown. Without examining the tattoo herself—thank God—she asked me a zillion questions and wrote my answers on her clipboard like I had just been convicted of murder and she was from the *Sun-Times*. Where did you get the tattoo? I don't know, I was wasted at the time. How long ago was it? Before the arrest. Was it a professional or amateur job? I didn't ask Michelangelo for his diploma. Describe the tattoo. Benjamin—do you know how to spell it? And which breast is it on? Over, not on. My left. What color is the ink? Corpse blue. Do you know the number of the ink? How many corpse blues are there? Were you ever bitten by a bat in the Amazon Rain Forest?

Tense minutes later Dr. Dobrowski smiled at me through a silver beard. His face had plenty of wrinkles, his eyelids were as heavy as an elephant's, and he had a virgin nose. Maybe plastic surgeons are like hair stylists, the worst advertisements for themselves because they can only work their magic on others. He asked me to pull down the strap of my gown. He smiled again when I hesitated. "Don't be embarrassed . . ."

"It's just that you're the first non-felon to see it," I confessed anxiously.

He looked at it for only a second.

"How long will it take?" I asked.

"Two sessions should do it."

"I mean today."

"The surgery itself will only take about three minutes."

"Surgery? Do you use a knife?"

"We use lasers," he said with another smile, but this smile said, *Kids today know the latest dance tunes but when it comes to cosmetic surgery they're still listening to the Bee Gees!* "It's modern and painless. You'll feel a sensation like the flick of a rubber band. That's all."

"Really?" I said with cowardly relief.

"First Roberta will apply a topical anaesthetic and then you'll have to wait a few minutes for it to take effect. You may want to get a magazine."

He was about to leave when I thought of a practical question. "Oh doctor, does the $150 cover both sessions?"

"No, that's just for today. But the follow-up will cost less."

"What kind of car do you drive?"

He smiled, a proud smile this time as if to say, *Even though I have eyelids like an elephant's I can still impress high school girls!* He had opened the door when I thought of a second question, a crazy romantic question, because the Northwestern guy had just flashed through my brain. "Would it be any cheaper if I just got the end of the name removed, the *j-a-m-i-n*?"

"No."

My heart sank. Not meant to be, I thought.

"But next time you might want to look for a boyfriend named Al," he joked as he left.

Everyone's a comedian. After Roberta rubbed some cream on my chest she asked if I wanted a magazine. I said I would get it myself—it would give me a chance to talk to Mr. Silicon some more. Anyway, I had time to pass and why should I be self-conscious wearing their puke-green gown in an office of flawed humanity?

But when I peeked out he was gone.

Spinning My Wheels

My life continued to tumble in its dizzying course through the universe. Earth, sun, planets, and yours truly were cosmically and gravitationally bound together in the Creator's great race toward some ominous black hole that would suck us all into eternal oblivion. But until then it was party time and I struggled heroically to enjoy the summer despite having to contend with two parents, a zit from Outer Mongolia, letters from prison, and enormous figures on my credit card.

I drifted through the Windy City like a kite without worry or care, twisting to the celestial hands that were holding the string. I rollerbladed through Lincoln Park, shopped at Field's, gossiped with my closetless hairdresser on Clark Avenue, read my horoscope in Starbucks, and watched the Cubs lose to everybody with my dad and his yuppie cigar-smoking friends. And at night when there weren't clouds I rode my soon-to-be-stolen bike away from the city lights and communed with the stars. And when it was raining—which seemed to be every night that summer—I went with a group to a death and destruction flick at the super-duper plex or scoffed at dance-impaired boys at Reflections. When I wasn't alone I hung at the fringe of one of those masses of youth you see at theaters or shopping malls, those pockets of America's future that have nothing in common except the same high school, dangerously low IQs, and a religious reverence for Thai sticks. I had completely forgotten about my tattoo mate who had appeared and vanished like a ghost that one long, far-off day in Dr. Dobrowski's office.

OK, it had only been a week, but I wasn't marking the days off a calendar. I wasn't the one in prison. And then I saw him! I was with a group of friends at the U2 concert—50,000 people and I see *him*! He was wearing the Northwestern jacket but I would have recognized him anyway—his hair, that nose—I had become a connoisseur of noses. I was standing in line for the bathroom when I saw him come out from the next gate. I only saw him for a couple seconds, long enough to know for sure, before he disappeared into the crowd. He wasn't looking my way and it was too noisy to call out. Besides I wouldn't have called him, even though I wanted to. I walked after him but it was intermission and the place was body to body. When I found a clearing I ran like OJ, afraid I would lose him and at the same time thinking that I'd have to slow down before I reached him and make it look like we bumped into each other by accident—I'm not the kind of girl that runs after boys. But he was nowhere, and then the music started. I went back to the gate I saw him come out of, but this was field level and he could be anywhere. I spent the whole second set and encore squeezing through the dazed and confused youth of Greater Chicago, getting pushed, stepped on, groped a couple times, almost tripping in vomit—all for a boy I'd completely forgotten.

I never did go to the bathroom.

I spent the next week in the prison of my heart, counting the cruel days of eternity throughout which I was destined never to see him again. I even had a dream. I was getting my tattoo removed, strapped on a table like James Bond beneath a monstrous laser. It started burning off the *n-i-m-a* and I screamed "Stop! Enough!" But it kept going, erasing it completely. And then I saw it was *him* pointing the laser! Laughing ominously, wearing a Northwestern hat, bare-chested, and where his own tattoo had been there was now a simmering flame.

The next clear night the stars weren't twinkling but laughing at me—at their most inept descendant who'd just rolled two gutter balls in life's dark frame. I longed for the days before we met, or just after when I had completely forgotten him—but now he would haunt me forever, out of reach. Why did I have to scare him away? Why couldn't I just be nice? It wasn't the harmless laser that caused him to flee Dr. Dobrowski's office but my vicious tongue.

And then at the Cubs game I got an idea. What if life wasn't bowling but baseball and instead of two chances you got three? I'd still be at the plate. Maybe like some players who hang in for eons knocking off foul balls I could survive the curve balls of fate and hit my true pitch far over the fence! I was so inspired I looked for him then and there, expecting to meet his laser-blue eyes behind every program. When I saw a Northwestern jersey I almost fainted, but it was a woman.

I was a kite miles out to sea. I was soaring without a string.

⊙ ⊙ ⊙

Meanwhile the letters from prison came fast and furious. It made me wonder if convicts got free postage like congressmen. It was almost enough to force a pang, the thought that he was paying for all those stamps, working extra hours in the laundry, breaking rocks in the juvenile chain gang, trading precious cigarettes for a roll of self-adhesives. But I'd had enough of *that* life. I didn't even know what the letters said because I refused to open them. To put my parents at ease I told him early on, when I was still writing him, to send his letters in care of my friend Miranda. I made her swear not to open them, and personally burned them in her ashtray, stamps and all. Once I found an envelope that had been crudely resealed and nearly scratched her eyes out. You think you know someone! I was sorely tempted to read it since it was already opened—since *she'd* read it, but I put it to the flame. I thought he would eventually stop writing, take up with some muscular cell brother, but some guys can't take a hint. I mean, it wasn't like I was pressing my lips to the glass on visiting days. I never saw him in the Big House, I didn't even go to the trial. It wasn't like I was wearing a ring. Just a stupid tattoo over my heart and that was off for good—almost.

I rose and fell, slept and woke, wore my blackest lipstick in symbolic mourning for my starlost Northwestern lover. Everything tasted like plain oatmeal—I even stopped watching television. My mom grew worried. "Are you taking drugs again?" she asked, looking for dilated pupils. "Are you taking drugs again?" I shot back, staring at *her* pupils.

And then my bike was stolen.

It was like the coming of winter, getting my bike stolen, except it happened more than once a year. It always caused a fight with my parents, as if I were responsible for humanity being the way it is. They should have expressed some sympathy—my bikes were like pets to me—I even named them. I named them after dogs because I was allergic to real dogs. The latest casualty was Frisky. Fido and Rover were dim memories. My parents always wanted to replace them with a cheap bike—why invest in an expensive bike when it was destined to be stolen? But I ask you, did any parent ever try to soothe a child whose German shepherd puppy had just run away by getting him a frog? So if you want a better bike get a job, my mom always said. And leave the magic cocoon of childhood? I'd be entering the faceless labor force soon enough. Besides, why should I compromise my ideals for five dollars an hour when my dad, whose ideals had been gored to death by the bull market, could earn enough to buy a Cannondale with a phone call to a client? Sometimes I felt I was sent to my parents as a karmic tax collector. Someone had to make sure they paid for the irresponsibility of their youth—all that Day-Glo and blotter. And they were getting off cheap. I mean, I didn't even have a car.

So there I was at O'Shannon's Cyclery on Fullerton where I was on a first-name basis with the management when who do you think walked in? I heard the bells clang over the door and glanced up and there he was! The bells made me think of *It's a Wonderful Life* where every time a bell rings an angel gets its wings, and I thought every time a bell rings a twisted girl gets her third swing at the plate of destiny. I was spinning the wheels of a Trek bike and my fingers nearly got severed by the spokes. But I was cool enough to look the other way.

"Hi!"

The voice I thought I'd never hear again. But it was a lukewarm exclamation. I wasn't the only one trying to be cool. What a pathetic species we are! Other animals prance and bite and we spin bicycle wheels. But maybe his lukewarm greeting had ominous overtones. Maybe he'd reconciled with his Christy. Maybe I'd driven him back to her.

I looked up slowly, theater time. "Oh, hi."

"Remember me? From the plastic surgeon's office? The guy with your name still on his arm?"

"Oh . . . yeah. I didn't recognize you without your Northwestern shirt, and you're wearing glasses." Come to think of it, how *did* I recognize him?

He raised his glasses, revealing those tragic blue eyes that had haunted my dreams.

"Buying a bicycle?" he asked awkwardly.

"No I'm looking for a car but I find bike salesmen easier to deal with." What was I doing? But what an inane question—was this the man of my dreams?

"So am I," he said, as if he hadn't heard. "Mine was stolen."

"Mine too. Maybe they were stolen by the same thief."

"I doubt it. Where do you live?"

Clever, gets points for that. "Lincoln Park." But I didn't ask where he lives. I was colder than his eyes.

"Well I'm in Evanston, so it's probably not the same thief."

"But was it stolen in Evanston?"

"I didn't think of that. It was stolen in town."

"There you go. So was mine." More clever again. The heavens had definitely sent me a project.

At this point Tom, the salesman, stepped in and I think we were both glad for the space. He shifted between us like a referee at a boxing match. He thought he was pitching bicycles but he was really pitching that high fastball I'd so hoped for, allowing us to look at each other through spokes, behind seats, across handlebars without having to say a word.

By the time he'd finished we were almost a couple and Tom had made a hefty commission. Ben bought a jade green racer, after asking my approval. I picked a black mountain bike.

"Why black?" he asked.

"It's ominous. Besides, I want to call him Shadow."

We pushed the bikes outside and walked together on the sidewalk. I followed him without thinking where we might go, or when we would part.

"Can I give you a ride home?" he asked, back to the nervous voice now that we were alone again.

"You mean you have a bike *and* a car?"

This must have given him encouragement because he then asked if I wanted some coffee.

"Why would I want to have coffee with you?"

"Because I'm paying."

He stopped beside a black BMW! Without asking, he put my new bike on the rack next to his. "They'll be harder to steal, locked together," he said.

"They'll just take the car," I told him, familiar with the inner workings of the criminal mind. But the sight of our shiny new bikes locked together gave me a pang.

⊙ ⊙ ⊙

There was a Starbucks around the corner, so we walked. I was out of gum, so I popped into a drugstore. I also got a *Rolling Stone* and *People* magazine and a couple tabloids. I'm easily overwhelmed and always buy more than what I go in for.

We ordered cappuccinos and sat by the window. "Do you name all your bikes?" he asked, licking his whipped cream seductively.

"You should pick a name for yours. It's as expensive as a yacht, it deserves a name."

"You name it."

I thought about it. "Colin."

"Colin?"

"It's a British racer, sensitive and snooty. Colin."

He was struggling to think of something to say, or maybe he was just thinking what a crazy chick I was. So I asked the next question, whether he'd been going to Northwestern long.

"How do you know I go to Northwestern?"

"You were wearing a jersey at the doctor's office."

"Everyone wears football jerseys."

"Everyone wears Bears jerseys. Or Notre Dame. The

only people who wear Northwestern stuff are the people who go there."

"You know nothing about football."

"I know plenty about football and even if Northwestern wins the Rose Bowl it won't erase their reputation as a geek school."

"I'm supposed to start in the fall," he admitted. "If I don't kill myself first."

At the time I thought he was joking, although he didn't smile. And he quickly glossed it over by telling me he wanted to be an astronomer. "And what about you? Are you in school?"

"Actually, I'm going to take a year off," I said. "Do some traveling. You know how some rich kids do the European tour? Well I'm going to backpack all through Milwaukee. Do you want some gum? I quit smoking so I chew a lot of gum. You don't mind? You're not worried about the effects of passive bubbles?"

I was rambling, rambling, rambling. Why did he have to be so quiet? Why couldn't he just talk about himself like most guys? Instead he just stared at me like I had landed in Roswell.

"How can you chew gum while you're drinking coffee?"

"Haven't you ever sucked on coffee-flavored candy?"

"Yeah."

"There you go." I blew a coffee-flavored bubble. "So you didn't get it taken off?"

"The tattoo? Not yet."

"Can you tell the court why you left the doctor's office that day?"

"I couldn't wait. I had to be somewhere."

"I should warn you perjury is a felony in this state. I speak as an expert on felonies. So are you still in love with her?"

"No." This time it sounded like the truth.

"Can I see your wallet?"

"Why?"

"Because if I find her picture I'll know you can't be trusted."

"Only if you show me your purse."

I dumped the contents of my Esprit purse on the table. Makeup, assorted lipsticks, brushes, combs with broken teeth, gum wrappers, keys, loose change, tampons, Q-tips, mace, U2 ticket stub, sunglasses. I opened my wallet—a few dollar bills, Blockbuster card, starter Mastercard, my astrologer's card, fake ID—make sure he sees that—photos of my parents, my granny, me and my friends Miranda, Jasmine, and Stacey drinking Hurricanes on Bourbon Street during spring break.

I quickly put it all away.

"So you were at the U2 concert?" he said. "Me too. Where were your seats?"

"In Iowa. And yours?" I asked, very curious.

"Third row."

The one place I didn't look!

He took out his wallet, just a plain brown wallet. He flashed through his driver's license, bank card, insurance card, student ID, library card, museum membership, organ donor card, gold Amex! tens and twenties. No pics.

"You should at least have a photo of yourself."

"Why?"

"Say you're in a horrible accident and your face is completely disfigured. How are the plastic surgeons supposed to know what kind of face to reconstruct?"

"Speaking of plastic surgeons, you never did tell me why you were there."

"It wasn't silicone, that's all you need to know. Why are you so hung up about silicone anyway?"

"I told you."

"You know what I think? I think your girlfriend got a tit job and afterward she attracted a whole new league of boys, leaving you in the dust."

He didn't say anything. I couldn't figure him out. I knew he wasn't shy after the way he talked to me in the doctor's office, but when I taunted him he usually just took it without a fight. But he didn't seem offended by anything I said either. Sometimes he just smiled, sometimes he just looked at me through those Pacific-blue eyes.

"So tell me what she looks like."

"Oh . . . I don't know."

I looked out the window, at the eternal parade of addicts, whores, gangsters, and stockbrokers—the pride of Chicago. "Does she look like her?" I asked, pointing to a statuesque blonde in a pinstriped suit.

"No."

"What about her?" This time a pink-haired punk on rollerblades. "Or her?" An Asian girl in overalls. "Or her?" A gray-haired street lady pushing a shopping cart filled with all her earthly possessions.

He laughed and stared out the window. "Like her," he finally said, and I saw a short, homely girl with eyebrow rings and dark, shaggy hair.

"Her? She's nothing special. Maybe you're better off." But I didn't believe him. "Probably more like her," I said, looking at a tanned blonde in red hot pants.

"What about you?" he asked, trying and failing to be casual, still staring out the window. "Are you seeing anyone?"

"I don't answer personal questions."

He seemed surprised, and disappointed. "I answered yours."

"That's you. Me, I don't tell my life story to freshman wannabes with murderous eyes."

"What's wrong with my eyes?"

"Nothing. They just look like the eyes of someone who might kill someone."

"Maybe they are." And I thought he was just joking, trying to hold his own against my relentless attack.

I began to feel sorry for him—or for myself, because after all I was pushing him away, and right about now his homely, ragged-haired ex probably seemed to him like the Playmate of the Month. "But you know," I said, "you have a good sign. I'll answer your most prying questions if you get your horoscope read."

He wasn't expecting that! But he didn't put astrology down, like I thought he would. He called my bluff. "Now?"

"You can't do it now. You have to make an appointment with my astrologer, Svetlana. Then if she says everything's fine, I'll talk."

"Horoscopes are expensive, aren't they?"

"She takes gold cards. Besides, you saved all that dough at the plastic surgeon's." I gave him Svetlana's card and we walked back to his car.

"Can I give you a ride home?"

"That's all right." I didn't want him to see my still-married, liberal, sickeningly cheerful parents. I didn't want him to see my room. I didn't want him to find out this early in the game that I was only sixteen.

I felt a pang as he unlocked our bikes from each other, as if it was a portent.

Pisces Ascendant

What a moron I was! I rode home in the clouds, and it didn't hit me until I was washing my hair that night—I didn't know his last name! I didn't get his number, or e-mail address! I could have at least memorized his license plate. I imagined him throwing Svetlana's card into the trash the moment he got home and giving his ex a ring. It was strike three.

I never felt more helpless in my life! I tossed and

turned all night, my dreams filled with fleeing figures and fading faces. I was lost, lost, lost!

In the morning I looked like a corpse. My face was pale and my eyes red—if my mom saw me now she'd definitely think I was on drugs. But then heroin has nothing on love. I mean heroin only wastes you away, but love makes you a raging moron! Love makes you do crazy things, like forgetting to ask your starmate's last name or phone number! Who ever shot up heroin and then woke up the next day with a guy's name tattooed on her breast? There isn't a drug illegal or not that holds a candle to love when it comes to completely fucking up your life!

Miranda stopped by. Mousy Miranda with her pointed ears and rat nose. I wasn't in the mood for company, but then I didn't want to be alone either. She was all exuberance and smiles, which only made things worse. She was going to the Rock Gym with her Blues Brothers boyfriend and wanted me to come. He was out in the car, what did I say?

I guess I didn't say no because the next thing I knew I was riding in the back seat of her boyfriend's rusted Impala. And there just happened to be another Blues Brother in the car, more Belushi than Aykroyd, conveniently sitting beside me.

"Rick, this is Christy, my best friend," Miranda said. "Christy, Rick."

"Uh, do you climb a lot?" Rick asked.

I stared out the window. When I'm really feeling hostile I say nothing.

When we got to the Rock Gym I pulled Miranda aside. "You didn't say anything about this other guy!"

"Oh didn't I?" she said, all false innocence, lighting a cigarette. "He's a friend of Mike's."

"I've told you not to fix me up. You keep doing this to me—every week a new ditz."

She took a long drag and blew the smoke through her nose. "Hey, there's nothing wrong with these guys. They're a lot better than your prison pen pal."

"I'm just not interested."

"Hey, it's one thing to do celibacy as a phase, you don't have to make it a career."

"What makes you so sure I don't already have a boy-friend?"

Miranda pulled her cigarette out of her mouth with-out inhaling. "You have a crush? Since when? How come I haven't seen him?"

"Maybe I don't want you to."

"Hideous huh? You're embarrassed," she said, remem-bering her cigarette and taking another drag.

"Sure I'm embarrassed, but not of him."

"I think you're lying. What's his name?"

"Ben. Not Benjamin," I added when she began to smirk. "And that's all you need to know."

She patted my arm as if to remind me we were bud-dies. "So tell me all about him? How old is he? Is he tall? Where'd you meet?"

I couldn't very well tell her that. Miranda never knew

about the tattoo, thank God. That was one thing I was able to keep from her. She may have been my best friend, but that was only because my other friends were that much worse. Besides, the tattoo was a private thing between my ex and me. I even made sure no one saw it in the locker room at school by Clearasiling it over or showering last.

"Do I know him?" Miranda asked. "You have to tell me if I know him. Ben . . . Ben . . ." I could see the wheels spinning. "Does he go to the Academy? Does he live in town?"

"No, he lives in Evanston and he's going to Northwestern." I was angry at myself that she got that much out of me. "Now are we here to climb or what?"

I wanted to climb alone. I didn't want to race, or socialize, or find out who Brother Belushi's favorite bands were. When he kept trying to talk to me I just stared down at him—I was a head taller with my shoes on—and crushed him with my eyes.

I took off my boots and let the spotter strap me in. Bare feet, bare hands, I was a child of nature and it was just me and the polyurethane mountain. I grabbed onto the small jagged rocks, ignoring the plastic holds. I liked to climb, but today it all seemed futile. I didn't go fast— what was the point?—but just lingered like a lizard on a wall, wondering where I would go from here.

I kicked myself for telling Miranda. Now I'd never hear the end of it and after a while I'd have to imagine some reason for our break up. The last thing I wanted to do was talk about him. He was history as far as I was concerned—

or rather I was history. He would meet some pleasant anti-New Age babe with her own BMW who didn't name bicycles and didn't put him down every thirty seconds. Not that I thought he wasn't attracted to me. I mean, I knew I turned heads. Every time I walked down a street I could feel the lusting eyes of boys too young to do it to, men too old to remember what it was like—and all those untrained amateurs in between. But there's only so much ridicule a guy will take from a girl—even an eighteen year old at his sexual peak on the rebound—before tossing an astrologer's card in the trash.

And I wouldn't blame him, I would do the same thing if I were a guy and met someone like me. I'd cover my ears and run, run, run. Oh why couldn't I just be nice?

Suddenly I realized I'd reached the top. I looked down at my spotter, holding the rapelling rope, probably wondering how many more hours I was going to cling to this wall. The only worthwhile part about the climb was letting go.

⊙ ⊙ ⊙

And then the next day my phone rang—and another angel must have gotten its wings because it was Svetlana! I was convinced God must have a Russian accent and squeezed the receiver as if it were Ben's hand. He had called her after all—the idiot, the fool! And now his chart was done and could I meet them in her apartment at four o'clock? But that was an eon away! I wanted to know now, I pleaded with her—sometimes I thought Svetlana took this professionalism of hers too seriously. I mean, there isn't a lawyer-client privilege in astrology—she wasn't a shrink for Christ's sake! But it was his chart, his gold card, it wouldn't be fair, etc., etc.

I hung up. I cried. I said a New Age prayer to the Creator, and then the Lord's Prayer just to be safe.

⊙ ⊙ ⊙

And there he was! Sitting in the wicker chair, nervous as a bridegroom. I was probably blushing like a bride as I hugged plump Svetlana, who always reeked of Chanel. I didn't hug Ben or even shake hands, but just pulled up another chair. We looked at each other awkwardly, not knowing what to do or say. It felt more like a divorce than a wedding.

"Well now if you're ready . . ." Svetlana said dramatically. Spread out on the glass table were crystals, a samovar, fresh flowers, complicated charts and graphs, a map of the heavens, and a white folder with Ben's name and birth date on the cover. The first thing I did was memorize his last name—Penrose.

Svetlana opened the folder and laid out a hand-printed drawing of the twelve houses of the zodiac with Pisces, Ben's sign, highlighted in blue. The symbols for the sun, moon, and planets were written in the appropriate houses, with their longitude at the time of Ben's birth.

"First, I remind you astrology is an art," Svetlana said pouring three cups of tea, Russian-style with the strong brew first and then watered to taste. "The human soul is no less complicated than the weather, and the astrologer, like the meteorologist, can only look to the sky and predict events in the broadest terms. Tomorrow it might rain in the Sahara or snow in Florida. But each person is like a geographical area, and a good astrologer, like a good meteorologist, can tell you with reasonable accuracy what your climactic—or in the case of astrology, celestial—characteristics are, and whether you are in the Gulf Stream of life or living on the San Andreas Fault.

"Pisceans, as I'm sure Christy already knows, are patient, generous, and extremely friendly. They make loyal, faithful lovers and often care more for their partner's needs than their own." Here I believe I sighed. "They can be indecisive, easily discouraged, gullible, and sickly—but their weaknesses rarely cause harm to others. Pisces' triplicity is water, its quadruplicity is mutable, its quality is negative, and it is ruled by Jupiter. What this means for your horoscope, Ben, as well as the lunar modes, the planetary aspects, and the solar sign and house at the precise moment of your birth, I will now explain in detail."

I was rapt—why couldn't they teach *this* in school? But every now and then I stole a glance at Ben, who looked like someone who'd watched too much MTV. I could see he wasn't really following her, the way I never followed my chemistry teacher, and that several times he wanted to talk, probably to challenge her, but he kept quiet to please me. Some men fight duels to get their girl, others have their chart read, and judging from Ben's reaction I think he would have picked the duel.

Two glasses of herbal tea later we were ready for the part I'd come for—the compatibility guide.

Svetlana smiled, looking at us both. I took this as a clue and grabbed Ben's hand. It was the first time we'd touched since coming here—it was like Svetlana's smile was a kind of permission.

"As a Capricorn, Christy, I don't see how you could choose a better match than Pisces. His watery nature perfectly compliments your earthy soul, and his wandering, emotional spirit will take root in your sensible soil. His romantic, sympathetic character will sweep you off your feet, though you may find his disregard for material wealth frustrating."

"But I don't care about that. Besides, he's the one with the BMW."

"All in all, Christy and Ben, the heavens are solidly behind you. But the heavens can't make dreams come true without our help and hard work."

I squeezed Svetlana goodbye and gave her a ten dollar tip. Ben submitted to a hug from our Russian matchmaker. He was smiling now. He'd gotten his money's worth, after all.

⊙ ⊙ ⊙

It was a nice enough day, breezy and cool, so we went for a walk in Lincoln Park. We walked toward town, the John Hancock building where my dad worked with its fang-like antennae looming ominously ahead. To our right, wannabe

Mario Andrettis raced along Lake Shore Boulevard like it was the Grand Prix, while on our left wannabe Columbus' discovered America on gray Lake Michigan. And on the plaza around us swirled well-bred dogs, cyclists wearing helmets, rollerbladers, fat joggers, speed walkers pumping weightless weights, tourists wearing windbreakers pointing cameras—the cream of yuppie culture.

"Wave!" I said, waving at the Hancock.

"Who am I waving to?"

"My dad. He works on the 43rd floor."

"Do you think he can see us?"

"Maybe he has a telescope."

"Maybe he's influencing your life from above like the stars," Ben teased.

"Dad knows better than that. You need to be fiery gas, light years away to tangle with me!"

We walked for a while without talking. I knew I was here to explain my past—it was payback time—but I wasn't about to volunteer anything. We were no longer holding hands—any discussion of my recent history required a certain amount of distance.

"What did you think of Svetlana?" I asked. "At least you liked the tea, didn't you?"

"Great tea. What was it?"

"I don't know. Some herbal blend. I think it's Russian. I'll ask her next time. Want some gum?"

"No thanks."

"What did you think of her reading? Was her interpretation accurate at all?"

"Her interpretation of me or her interpretation of us?"

Us—a magic word. Just having him say it put all my doubts to rest.

"So what really happened with your ex?" I asked instead. "You must have really liked her, to get a tattoo. Why did you break up?"

"I thought we were going to talk about you?"

"We have a long way to walk. Don't you want to save the worst for last?"

"There's not much to say. We grew apart. The tattoo was just a stunt, and I got tired of wearing the name of someone I knew I'd never see again."

"Unless her name was Christy!"

"Yes, unless her name was Christy."

"Admit it—I'm the reason it's still on your arm."

"Yes. You're the reason," he said, looking into my eyes.

I felt like one of the fat joggers, wanting to stop and catch my breath. But I kept my cool. "Then why didn't you wait for me that day? Why did you leave?"

"I planned to look you up. I went to the desk when no one was up front and your chart was there, and I memorized your address."

"But I gave a fake address."

"I know. I ended up at a brewery!"

We both laughed—it was so funny, but it was also so touching. He had wanted to see me after all. And if only I'd written my real address . . . But then he might have met my parents, who kept few secrets, and found out about my ex and my age before mad infatuation had a chance to break the blood-brain barrier. No, it was better as it was, left to fate.

Clouds were rolling in over the lake and the wind was blowing Ben's long blond hair. It looked like it was going to rain, but we kept walking.

"Have you had a lot of girlfriends?" I asked.

"How many is a lot?"

"Two."

"Yes."

"Are you into double figures?"

"Are you talking about dates, or girlfriends, or what?"

"You know what I mean."

"Then no."

"What about guys? If you're bi I want to know now."

"Couldn't Svetlana tell you that?" he said with a grin. "No."

"Have you ever committed a violent crime?"

He laughed, glad to be asked an easy question. "Of course not."

"I don't mean convicted of a violent crime. I mean have you ever committed one?"

"Do I seem like a criminal to you?"

"No. But I've been wrong before."

"Ah! And what was his name?"

A few raindrops were falling. We stopped to look at each other. "Benjamin."

"Ah!"

"What does your astronomy have to say about that?" I challenged him.

"Life is full of coincidences."

"Like our each having our ex's name? And meeting at the bike shop? And at the . . ." But I wasn't about to mention the U2 concert. And I certainly wasn't going to tell him about my tattoo with his name on it, fading as we spoke.

"So Svetlana made a mistake. Or didn't you consult her the last time?"

"I was using another astrologer. I won't go back to *her* again!"

"So where is he now?" Ben asked. He couldn't bring himself to call my ex by name, especially since it was his own.

"He's languishing in the joint," I told him.

"He's in jail? For what, drugs? Stealing bicycles?"

I started to walk again. "Murder."

"Murder!" He froze. He grabbed my arms like our nice little developing romance had gone from Barbara Cartland to Stephen King with a turn of the page. "You were in love with a murderer!"

"I knew you wouldn't understand!" I shouted back. "It's not like he's Manson! He only killed one person!"

"Oh well, that hardly counts, one person." And he glanced around as if Benjamin were hiding in the bushes ready to pounce. I could see the fear in his eyes, and not just of my murderous ex, but of me.

"He's not violent by nature."

"Only in practice."

"It's not what you think. He got into a fight with some gang punks. It was self-defense."

"Then why is he in prison?"

"Because he was the only one with a gun."

It was raining steadily now, but I could see the disapproval in his eyes. Like my parents, like my friends—just like everyone. "Oh I knew you wouldn't understand!" And I walked faster to break away from him.

He followed me, and when my legs were too tired to walk any farther I stopped and cried. It was pouring now. He put his arms around me. He didn't speak or kiss me, but just held me as the rain drenched our clothes and hair. I clung to him—a final embrace. Oh, why hadn't I lied when I lied about other things that didn't matter half as much?

I jumped at the sound of thunder. Ben held my hand and we watched the lightning flash over the lake. "Doesn't it frighten you?" I asked, seeing how calmly he was standing, like he was watching a sunset and not a storm.

"Do you know what lightning is?" he asked, staring at the lake and not looking at me at all.

"Sure, it's electricity."

"But why does it strike down and not up?"

"Gravity I guess."

"But a helium balloon rises. Why not a bolt of lightning, which is lighter than helium?"

"I don't know," I said impatiently, beginning to feel the rain soak through my clothes. "I'm not a scientist."

"It's because the earth has a negative charge. Sometimes this electro-magnetic charge escapes into the atmosphere. Lightning is nature's way of restoring the balance."

I was feeling cold and clammy from my drenched clothes sticking to my skin, but it was interesting, what he was saying, kind of mystical, I thought, and the lightning striking over the lake was beautiful in a dangerous sort of way—the way a haunted house can seem beautiful.

"Sometimes I feel I am a bolt of lightning," Ben said.

"But what are *you* supposed to return to?"

He didn't reply but kept staring over the lake. The storm was getting closer, but I think he would have stood there until it passed despite the danger, or because of it.

But the thunder and the flash were coming almost together now and I was really scared. "I think we better go!"

But he just calmly held my hand like we were admiring some seagulls and not standing in the path of electro-magnetic destruction.

"Have you ever wondered what it would be like to be struck by lightning?" he said in a strange and serious voice.

I could only think of the *Tom and Jerry* cartoons where Tom is burnt to a crisp after sticking a paw in a socket. "I hope I never find out."

"I think it would be the ideal way to die."

To die? I didn't understand what he was talking about. Was this just part of the Piscean irrationality Svetlana had talked about? Or was it something more ominous?

"Would you feel anything?" I said, praying the next bolt didn't come straight at us for daring to ask.

"Nothing at all," he said, as if in a trance.

Rockin' with the Jaundiced Eyes

I was getting dressed the next night, stumped over whether to wear the red vinyl skirt or my black mini, when my mom knocked on the door.

"Ben is here!"

Damn! He was early. Guys are never early, and now he was out there pinned to the sofa by my prying parents like a butterfly on a piece of styrofoam, ready to be examined under a microscope. And I wasn't even dressed.

He had asked me out yesterday as we were leaving the park, two soaked survivors of the storm. He wanted to drive me home, but I refused. So he asked me if I wanted to go to Cagney's tomorrow night. The Jaundiced Eyes were playing. We had the same tastes in music, another good sign. I said I'd meet him, but he insisted on picking me up, and I couldn't very well say no without making him think I had more terrible secrets waiting at home.

And now here he was! I threw on the black mini, sprayed my hair and hurried out. Were my parents asking him a bunch of embarrassing questions? Were they telling him about Benjamin's arrest? About sending me to the Academy? That I was still there?

To my relief my dad and Ben were talking about the Cubs. Ben seemed very relaxed, sitting in the brown leather chair with his legs crossed, drinking a soda.

"I'm ready to go!"

"Let Ben finish his drink," my mom said, playing the grand host.

"But we'll be late," I said, looking at my Swatch.

"You know concerts never start on time," my mom said annoyingly. "Why, I remember when I saw Jefferson Airplane—when they were still the Airplane—and—"

I took the drink and pulled on Ben. "Don't wait up."

"Have a nice time," my mom said, as we rushed toward the door. "Oh, and Ben, if you're not doing anything tomorrow night we'd love to have you for dinner."

"I'm sure Ben has plans," I said, pushing him out the door. But I was too late.

"No, that would be great, Mrs. Marlowe. What time should I come?"

"How is seven?"

"I'll be here. Nice to meet you."

"Nice to meet you!" I snarled, as we walked to his car, parked several blocks away. "Did you have to be so friendly with my parents?"

"What's the problem?"

"I just don't like it. It's our first date and you're already sitting in the brown chair shooting the breeze about the Cubs. Before you know it you'll be smoking cigars! And you didn't have to say yes to dinner."

"Don't you want me to come?"

"No! I mean, not so soon, not for dinner. It'll be so awkward, they'll give you the third degree—remember, my last boyfriend was a killer. They don't want me to repeat *that* mistake."

"Neither do I. But don't worry. I like your parents."

"It'll be so embarrassing! They think because they got high at Stones concerts they're still cool!"

"Well it doesn't bother me. I think you're the one who's hung up. You shouldn't be so rude to them."

I was surprised. I thought my parents would turn him off and here he was defending them against me. "Who made you an expert on parents?"

"I'm not an expert," he said. "I don't have any."

"Oh. You're an orphan?"

"Not exactly. My mother died in an auto accident when I was a baby. My father died two years ago."

I walked the rest of the way with my foot in my mouth. It was a rule of mine never to break up *before* the concert, especially when he had the tickets. So I kept my mouth shut. But now I'd made him think about his dead parents—just the right mood for the first date.

There was a line outside Cagney's. The show was sold out, but I didn't ask Ben how he got tickets. I figured anyone who sat in the third row for U2 could afford broker prices for the Jaundiced Eyes. The Eyes were one of my favorite new bands and I thought it was so cool Ben liked them too. I hoped our tastes in other things would jibe as well. We were poles apart when it came to astrology and astronomy but I hoped he'd eventually come around.

Cagney's held about a thousand people and it was open seating at long tables. Ben and I sat next to each other, facing the stage near one of the exit doors. He kept asking if the seats were all right, but I wasn't the one used to the third row. We ordered nachos and Cokes—my fake ID was for eighteen, not twenty-one—and talked while the rest of the crowd filed in.

"I like your shirt," I told him. He was wearing black jeans, boots, and a black polo shirt. He was also wearing a gold chain, which I hadn't noticed before, and the gold earring, which I had. "Does your chain say 'Christy' too?" I asked.

"No, it's just a chain."

"But it's nice," I said, fingering it. "Fourteen karat?"

"Eighteen."

"Really? You didn't buy this for yourself."

"Yes. Yes and no."

"Well you did or you didn't! It's from that Christy, I know it. Don't lie! You might hate her now, but gold is gold."

"You're half right," Ben admitted. "She did give me a chain, but I pawned it in a moment of anger. But later I thought—who was I punishing, her or me? So I bought another one to replace it, that didn't have her fingerprints on it."

I started unbuttoning his shirt. "Let me see the tattoo."

He started to speak but then thought better of it. I mean, it wasn't like we were at the art museum. He couldn't very well claim modesty when the couple across from us were burning cigarette holes in their beer cups.

CHRISTY

"How old were you when you got it?"

"I don't know. Fifteen."

The same age I got mine! Another non-coincidence, I thought. I ran my fingers across it, like it was braille.

"Feel anything?" he joked.

"It's mine now," I told him.

"Until I meet another Christy."

"You won't. Two Christys are all you're allowed."

"One is more than I can handle."

I tousled his hair with my fingernails. "Just remember, I'm not like lightning. You'll feel plenty if you dare me to strike!"

Our nachos and drinks finally came. I was thirsty as hell from all the smoke, dying for a cigarette myself. I settled for cheese dip and gum.

"What are your plans for the summer?" he asked, after ordering me another coke. I took out some bills, but he wouldn't let me pay.

"Plans? Why should I have plans?"

"You're not going to college this fall."

"Not right away," I said, quite honestly.

"Then what are you going to do?"

"What am I going to do about what?"

"About your life. Are you looking for a job?"

"Jobs can come looking for me, as far as I care. I caddied for my dad last summer and I'm still spitting out sand. Right now it's enough just to keep my life unscrewed up."

"I see."

"No, you don't see. I didn't mean that—I was exaggerating. I can chew gum and recover from my past at the same time. It's not like I'm one of the pathetic walking wounded that keep Oprah and Sally in the millionairesses club—I'm not in therapy or anything. I got involved with a murderer—I'm not a graduate of the Betty Ford Center."

"You didn't do drugs?"

"It's not what you did but what you do that gets you

elected president, and right now I chew gum. I don't even smoke cigarettes anymore."

"I didn't mean anything. I wouldn't have asked you out if I thought you were screwed up."

"Why not? That hasn't stopped anyone else. But why shouldn't you hold out for the best? You have a lot going for you."

He certainly wasn't fishing for compliments, or maybe he didn't hear me with all the noise in the place, because he continued to ask about me. "You should have some plans then," he said. "Some goals."

"Goals are for soccer players," I told him. "The rest of us have the stars."

"You think the stars care at all about you?"

"They better."

"Christy, how can balls of gas light years away make any difference in your life?"

"If I knew that I'd be the one wearing Chanel, making the big bucks!" I shot back defensively. I did know a lot about the theory of astrology, but I feared a wannabe scientist like himself would pick it all apart.

"These stars that you think control your life are more numerous than all the people who have ever lived on earth! So even if there are other worlds with intelligent beings there must be stars in the universe that spend their entire existence without their heat being felt by anyone, or their light being seen! Now if a massive star can have such little impact on the universe, what is to be said for us?"

"Exactly!" I agreed angrily. "So what's the point of making plans?"

For two people with so much in common, why were we talking about the one area where we were polar opposites? He certainly could be depressing at times. Scientists might build better bombs and mousetraps, but when it comes to being cheerful they have nothing on astrologers, who can even manage a smile when they're warning you about an approaching catastrophe! But at least his death-of-stars speech got me in the mood for the graveyard rock of the Jaundiced Eyes, who now came onstage in ghoulish makeup beneath a blood-red strobe.

I was in heaven, or maybe a sweet kind of hell—considering it was the Jaundiced Eyes—with the booming music and Ben's arm around me, the arm with my name on it. When they played "Dead, Deader, Deadest" we got up and danced, and I would have danced on the table if there had been beer in our cups instead of Coke, but even I have inhibitions.

After the first set we ordered more drinks and cooled down. The place was thick with smoke and we were sweating from all the bodies and the dancing. I guess Ben thought my defenses were down because he started asking me about the murder.

"I don't know all the details," I said. "I mean, I wasn't there, and I didn't follow the trial. He wasn't in a gang, but he ran with people who were, and one night he got into a fight with someone over something—I think it was over a dope deal, or it could have been over me, I don't know."

"You!"

"It's pure speculation. You know, some remark the other guy made. Or it could have been drugs, or anything. The other guy pulled out a knife and Benjamin pulled out a gun and shot him."

"Did you know he owned a gun?"

"Yeah, I knew. But it wasn't like he ever used it before. Chicago is a rough town. And we were in public school at the time."

"How could someone as smart and strong as you get involved with someone like that?"

"You should have seen the guys I turned down! I was only fourteen when we met. He was my first real boyfriend, though it doesn't seem so real now, kind of like temporary insanity. But I didn't know anything then, and he wasn't all bad. I mean, he had some good qualities too."

"Like what?"

I was surprised he asked. "I don't know. You want me to tell you off the top of my head? Just take my word for it."

"Was he better looking than I am?"

"You're jealous! No, but he was all right. I mean, I wouldn't pick someone who was a loser *and* ugly, even at fourteen!"

"He was a tough guy."

"No, the tough guys carry knives. He was a scared guy. Scared guys carry guns."

"Was he ever violent with you?"

"Of course not! Do you think I'd let someone abuse me? I mean, he may have pushed me a couple times, but only because I pushed him first, and harder. He was a little boy—I frightened *him*. But that's what I learned from all this—it's the scared people in the world who are the most dangerous."

"What did your parents think of him?"

"They hated him at first, then later they really hated him. After the arrest my dad wanted to have me deprogrammed. I tried to explain Benjamin wasn't the Moonies."

"Do you ever visit him?"

"No! I told you, I didn't even go to the trial."

"But if you thought it was self-defense why didn't you support him by going?"

"The trial was only two days. We're not talking about independent prosecutors here. Besides, he didn't consult me when he bought the gun, or got involved with those people. He deserves to be locked up just for being stupid. Anyway, I was under house arrest myself."

I threw down another Coke, sweating more than ever. "We were practically split up when this whole thing happened," I explained. "We were fighting all the time and I was tired of his temper and his stupidity and his jealousy. I had outgrown him. So you see when he shot that guy it was the last straw, the perfect opportunity to break up."

Ben seemed to get a little comfort from that, but his face was still too serious. "Does he write you from prison?"

"Of course not," I lied. "Even if he did I wouldn't open his letters," I said honestly.

"Is he still in love with you?"

I laughed my best bluffing laugh. "He probably doesn't even remember my name," I said, secretly thinking that jealousy must be a hereditary disease for all guys named Benjamin.

"Was he sentenced to life?"

"I wish! But he's a juvenile."

"A juvenile!"

I realized I hadn't mentioned this particular fact before, and from the shock on Ben's face I could see it was important information.

"He's younger than you are?"

I did the math as quick as I could. "Yeah, by a year."

"So he's not in prison at all," Ben said.

"Not a real prison. They have bars there but it's not like San Quentin or anything."

"And he'll be released?"

"Not until he's eighteen."

"Eighteen!"

"It's not for a whole year! And then he'll probably get life probation. He certainly won't stay in Chicago. The last thing he'll think of is to come looking for me. Besides, he might get off'd by some reform school Dillinger or kill someone else himself and get tried as an adult this time."

But I could see these assurances didn't make any difference to Ben, whose shocked face was like that of the painted singer of the Jaundiced Eyes, staring into the haze as the band crept back onstage to the spooky rhythms of "Silver Bells and Cadavers."

⊙ ⊙ ⊙

"Great show!" I said, as we headed out.

"We could go visit a cemetery now," Ben said.

I thought it was a cool idea, but he was joking. He was very quiet in the car.

"I hope you're not still thinking about him," I said.

But I could see Ben had been thinking of nothing else since the beginning of the second set. "I just don't understand how you could fall for a murderer!"

"Well, who the hell ever thinks some boy with a name like Benjamin is going to kill someone?" I said. "It's like someone named Winnie the Pooh taking hostages!"

"I just hope you're right about him now, that he doesn't come looking for you."

"He's got another year to go. And for someone who stands up to lightning you sure are scared of a little punk who's history and behind bars. Scared and jealous!"

But maybe also disgusted, I thought. Fed up with me completely, pushed over the edge.

He was driving around the block, looking for a place to park.

"You can just pull up in the driveway," I said. I opened the door but didn't move to get out. "Thanks for the concert."

"Sure, it was fun," he said, looking like someone totally miserable.

"Guess I'll see you tomorrow for dinner then."

"Yeah, tomorrow."

I waited. Hello? Hello? But he was so panicked by that other Benjamin he forgot to kiss me goodbye.

Never take a first date to the Jaundiced Eyes.

The Cleavers Entertain

I was in pure agony! Like Svetlana would say, the stars could put you in sunny California with not a cloud in the sky, but if you pee on yourself you're going to get wet. Well, she wouldn't put it exactly that way, but that's how I felt. I thought Ben deserved to know the truth about my ex, after going to all the trouble of getting his chart read, and I had been confident—too confident. I should have just told him Benjamin was in prison for drugs and saved the part about murder for our diamond anniversary. And then it had stormed during our walk, and I had agreed to see the Jaundiced Eyes for our first date, and I'd forced him to think about his dead parents. The stars were wasting their time with me, pure and simple. And so was Ben.

I couldn't sleep forever. And then I had a dream—I was in Cagney's during the concert but it was storming through the roof, or there was no roof, and everyone had umbrellas but me, and I couldn't find Ben because of all the black umbrellas and it was dark—only then lightning flashed and I saw his face far away but in that same moment he was burnt to a crisp like Tom—or Jerry?—when he sticks his paw in a socket—and all that was left was the skeleton of the umbrella.

I woke up in tears. I spent the day in a daze, bonding with my dad and my team at Wrigley Field. If misery loves company I had plenty that day because we lost nine to nothing. But what else should I expect? I was feeling pretty shut out myself.

And when I came home and saw four plates on the dining room table I felt a pang. I looked into the fourth plate like it was a crystal ball and I would see Ben instead of my own reflection—would see him wherever he was in the world, at Starbucks with that other Christy, who seemed pretty together right now, or visiting his parents at the cemetery, or pounding on Svetlana's door, demanding a refund, or at the airport with a one-way ticket to Tibet.

"Why don't you get ready for dinner, dear?" my mom

said, as if we were the Cleavers and not the Addams' family—with no sense of impending catastrophe.

"You might as well put that extra plate away," I said. "He's not going to show."

"Oh, why?"

"Because I'm me. Anyway, it's after seven."

"Don't worry, dear, he'll come. He seems like a nice boy," my mom said in that cheerful voice that still believed in nice boys. "Why don't you help me with the salad?"

But I was restless, I needed air. Grating cheese and chewing Bubble Yum didn't exactly kick in the endorphins, so I thought I'd take a walk, curse and spit, stare at the rising moon.

But all my feelings of self-pity quickly turned to horror. I was halfway down the block when a figure came around the corner. Benjamin. But it was the wrong Benjamin.

"Benjamin!"

I think he would have thrown his arms around me, hugged me, grabbed me, assaulted me if I hadn't stepped back as quickly as he came forward until finally he stopped and we stood looking at each other, much too close for my comfort.

"Hey, what's up?" he said, as if I had seen him only yesterday, as if he had never pulled that trigger.

I had left my purse inside—my mace. I listened for the barking of police dogs. I looked for the broken shackles on his legs. But he was wearing baggy jeans and a White Sox hat, not prison rags. Shirt tucked in, clean-shaven, a regular civilian.

"How's it going?" he asked, as if we were best friends, taking a step forward, which I matched with a step back. At this rate we would soon be in front of my house, and I certainly didn't want to lead him in that direction.

"What are you doing here?" I asked. Where were the sirens, the helicopter searchlights?

"I just thought I'd come by," he said, as if it were the most common thing in the world to escape from jail and look up your old girlfriend at dinner time in uptown Chicago. "I got out today."

"But they'll be looking for you," I said, picturing a SWAT team careening around the corner, slaughtering us both in a hail of bullets.

"It's good to see you again."

"You have to get out of here. You'll be seen."

"Seen?"

"You have to turn yourself in. It was stupid to escape, with only a year—"

"What are you talking about? Didn't you get my letters?"

"Letters?"

"I wondered why you didn't write. I thought probably your parents, you know."

"Yeah, and if they see you they'll call *America's Most Wanted*, so you better split."

"But I was released today," he said, like he was talking to someone underwater.

"Released?"

"It's my eighteenth birthday."

Shit! Shit, shit.

"So I thought maybe we could go somewhere and . . . you know . . . celebrate."

I didn't have time to die on the spot, which certainly would have been the best thing. I didn't even have time to think or even scream—and I wanted to scream because at just that moment the other Benjamin, the good Benjamin, came walking around the corner—carrying a bouquet of flowers!

Benjamin—the Benjamin of my nightmares—stepped forward and I stepped back while the Benjamin of my dreams was gaining on both of us. Soon we were all tangled together and I could imagine three chalk outlines on the pavement as investigators tried to piece together who shot who.

But he didn't have a gun. I didn't see any bulges in his clothes and he wouldn't have a gun anyway, would he, his first day out of the slammer? But knives were plentiful enough, or he could just try to strangle Ben with his bare hands.

I didn't have my mace, and all Ben had to defend himself with were the thorns on his roses.

Saint Benjamin and Sinner Benjamin looked at each other for a moment, trying to figure it all out, while I—who am never lost for words—stammered like a basket case. Actually Ben looked down and Benjamin looked up because there was such a difference in height, and then

Ben, with his eager friendliness that could easily have gotten him killed, smiled like a moron and said, "Hi, I'm Ben."

Benjamin, who hated friendliness more than hostility because he knew how to fight but not how to be kind, immediately became suspicious and scowled back, "So am I."

Now it was Ben's turn to be suspicious, beyond suspicion, because he knew exactly who this punk who had been talking to me was. It was like he was struck by one of his lightning bolts. I think he expected to take lead then and there. Not only were his flowers useless as a shield, they were incriminating evidence.

But Benjamin kept his hands in his pockets. "You a friend of Christy's?" he asked with darting eyes, looking back and forth between Ben and me like his judge had probably looked between him and his lawyer before passing sentence at his trial.

"Not a friend, really," Ben stuttered. "An acquaintance."

"Of my dad's," I took up. "An acquaintance of my dad's, a florist, and these are samples for a banquet Dad's firm is throwing next week." I talked fast, and Benjamin was dumb enough to believe it—anyway, he wanted to believe it. "Ben is active in the gay community," I added for good measure, remembering all those *Three's Company* reruns, "in case you ever need a good hair stylist now that you're a free man. But you better go before anyone sees you."

I pushed out my hand like I was waving away a wasp, but he took it as a sign of affection and briefly held my arm. He was obviously in deep denial. "I'll see you later then," he said, as if he were James Dean, and walked away, looking back once or twice—which James Dean would not have done.

Ben and I kept our distance from each other and didn't even speak until he was well out of sight. I had a feeling Ben would not take this latest development in stride.

"My God," he moaned.

"That's what you get for coming to dinner," I tried to joke.

He shook the flowers at me, probably wishing the stems were rifle barrels. "Why didn't you tell me?"

"I didn't know! It's as much a shock to me! I was out here waiting for you and he suddenly appeared, only a minute before you came."

"How could they let him out?" Ben screamed. "Is he on a pass or something?"

"No, he's free."

"That's insane! How could they let him out a year early?"

"But it's not a year early," I tried to explain.

"You told me it was another year, until he was eighteen."

"Yeah, well I always was terrible with ages. I can never remember, for instance, whether my dad is—"

"You mean he's eighteen *now?*"

"This very day."

"Oh God."

"But don't worry," I said, trying not to tremble myself and to keep the fear out of my voice. "He knows it's over between us."

"That's why he comes over the minute he gets out?"

"For all we know he's been visiting people all day. I could have been the last person on his list. A mere formality. Besides, what's he going to do? I'm sure he's on probation. And next time he goes in with the big boys."

"How could you make such a mistake?" he said, and walked through the open gate to my house and sat on the steps at the end of the walkway.

I didn't know if he was talking about my getting the year wrong, or about my getting mixed up with someone like Benjamin. True, he'd put on weight and, if anything, had become more jealous of other guys. There were other qualities, not all monstrous, that didn't exactly shine through at their encounter. But this was no time to defend the past.

I sat down beside Ben and took the roses. "Thanks for the flowers."

"They're not for you. They're for your mother."

Clever boy. Didn't get into Northwestern for nothing. But then it was my mother who had invited him.

I handed the flowers back. "She'll love them. But what did you bring for me?"

But Ben was in no mood for front porch chitchat. He stood up, probably afraid Benjamin would come back and find us in a compromising position. He was obviously preoccupied.

"I hope you like fettucini. It's the only thing my mom cooks well."

"If you think he's over you why didn't you tell him the truth?" Ben asked, staring past the gate. "Why did you tell him I was gay?"

"Dinner's ready," I said, taking his arm.

"I'm sure your parents won't be happy about it."

I stopped him before the door, glad for the warning. "Promise you won't say a word!"

"But they'll find out eventually."

"No, not for certain."

"When he comes back."

"But he won't come to the house. I mean, he won't knock on the door. He knows my parents will call the police. Besides, I'm sure he'll leave town. Remember, the guy he killed has friends, gang friends. And they're sure to come after him if he hangs around. He's a marked man. Anyway, even if my parents found out, they don't have to find out this exact moment. You don't want to ruin dinner, do you?"

But as soon as we got inside I remembered another promise I had to exact. The moment Ben gave my mom the flowers and she gave him a kiss on the cheek—she didn't have to do that!—I pulled her into the kitchen.

"Listen Ma, whatever you do, don't say anything about my age! And tell Dad. You can't let anything slip!"

"Christina!" she said in that principal's voice, as if she were a model of authority. My mom was a reformed hippie, a reformed amphetamine addict, a reformed alcoholic, a reformed coffee drinker, a reformed smoker, a reformed carnivore, a reformed radical Maoist, so at the ripe age of forty-five—or was it forty-six?—there was nothing left to reform, she was absolutely perfect, and I couldn't stand her.

She had been like my best friend when I was a child. Now that I was a teenager she was like my worst enemy. I got along much better with my dad, who had never bothered to reform himself and loved me unconditionally as long as my troubled life didn't influence the price of corn futures.

"What have you been telling him?" my mom asked, putting the flowers in a vase. She really did look okay for an old girl. I mean, you wouldn't think a human being could drop so much acid and decades later still do credit to a pair of Calvin Klein's. You'd think she'd just be a pile of mush without a brain cell to her name.

"Nothing, it's just what I haven't been telling him," I said. "I think he thinks I'm eighteen."

"You think?"

"Well, I haven't actually told him anything. I mean, it's really none of his business how old I am, right? But I think he thinks I'm eighteen since you have to be eighteen to get into Cagney's and I kind of hinted I was out of school."

"Oh, Christina."

"But you see *he's* eighteen and we just met—"

"How do you know *he's* not lying about *his* age?" my mom said cleverly.

"It wouldn't make any difference to me—he's a Pisces, that's all that matters as far as birth dates are concerned. But he might not take me seriously if he thought I was sixteen."

"He might think you were immature," my mom said with a grin.

"Exactly! So I'll tell him, I promise, eventually, but I want to give him time to get to know me first, and I want to tell him myself."

"When?"

"When I'm your age."

"Well this certainly wasn't the way your father and I raised you," my mom said, correctly enough, shaking her head.

"If I'd turned out the way you raised me I'd be fighting alongside the peasants in some South American jungle!" I shot back, as we joined the boys in the dining room.

I sat across from Ben, who was kind of blocked from view by those damn flowers he'd brought. "Start in," my mom told him, and I breathed a sigh of relief when I saw her whisper into my dad's ear as she poured the drinks, obviously to tell him to keep mum about my age. My dad made a sour face like he sometimes does when reading the *Wall Street Journal* at breakfast and he finds out a stock he's told everyone to buy embarrasses him by dropping ten points. But he quickly regained his composure and asked for the parmesan cheese.

Ben, for his part, wasn't betraying my trust. In fact, he wasn't saying anything at all, still preoccupied with recent events. He kept looking over his shoulder, as if Benjamin were going to crash through the window like a meteor.

"I understand you'll be attending Northwestern," my mom said, sitting down.

"I'll be a freshman in the fall."

"Ben wants to be an astronomer," I said. "Ask him what he thinks about astrology. But be careful," I warned Ben, "my mom's a believer too. She's a Taurus, which explains a lot!"

"I had my chart read," Ben said. "I found out I'm emotional, impulsive, and artistic, which was all news to me."

"I think it's all a lot of nonsense too," my dad said. "Does anyone want the parmesan cheese?"

Why on earth did my mom have to make fettucini? I mean, it's impossible to eat the stuff without getting Alfredo sauce all over your chin, and the pasta doesn't just roll on your fork like spaghetti but hangs like wet laundry. And I can never remember what the big spoon is for. I was beginning to feel glad for the flowers blocking Ben's view.

"So how did you and Christina meet?" my mom asked Ben, as if she couldn't trust me with the question—which, after all, she couldn't.

"We met at the—"

"We met at the bike shop," I interrupted. Man, I should have made a list of subjects not fit for discussion. "Ben had his bike stolen too."

"Oh, I'm sorry to hear that. We keep trying to persuade Christina to buy a cheap bike since the expensive ones always get stolen."

"You should make her work it off," Ben said.

Whose side are you on? I thought.

"Christina has no sense of the value of money," my mom said, just kicking into her "embarrass the hell out of her only child" mode.

"Why don't you make her get a job?"

What's his game? If he keeps talking like this he can let my mom kiss him good night!

"Christina get a job?" And my mom laughed, like I were a strand of fettucini or something.

"Could you pass the asparagus?" my dad asked.

I knew this would happen. My mom would embarrass the hell out of me while my dad, my only ally, would ask for the asparagus. But I had expected her to embarrass Ben too, not for the two of them to gang up on me.

"Christina's still only—" And my mom caught herself, thank God, when I glared at her. "I mean, she's still young, she has plenty of time to find herself."

"My mom's still trying to find herself," I said. "She's down to three personalities."

"Does Christy get her sarcasm from you, Mrs. Marlowe?" Ben asked, enjoying himself too much. I liked him better a minute ago when he was speechless with fear. But my mom's overbearing personality was enough to bury thoughts of just-released jealous murderers in the dust.

"Heavens no. She gets *that* from her father!"

But good old Dad showed no signs of his gargantuan wit, opening his mouth only to shovel in another forkful of fettucini, tuning out our conversation, communing with his parmesan cheese. He didn't care if he made a slob of himself in front of his daughter's starmate, none of this Miss Manners stuff for him. And if his beloved daughter was slowly being embarrassed to death by two people she trusted he wasn't about to come to her aid. It served her right for all that money going down the Academy drain that could have been spent on cigars and Jordan memorabilia. But he was lovable all the same, eating away like Henry VIII at the head of the table, a little mountain bike tire around the middle and not much tread left on top, a born-again capitalist, generous to a fault, wicked with a racquetball racket, a recent convert to the death penalty for juvenile offenders, forty-seven—or eight?—years old, a Sagittarius with Neptune rising.

"Are your parents in Chicago?" my mom asked, and Ben was silent. I would have kicked her if my foot could have reached. I really should have made a list of subjects out of bounds.

"Mom!"

"Well, I don't see what's the matter in asking . . ."

"His parents are dead."

"Oh, I'm sorry. Christina hadn't told me." As if it was my fault! "So you're alone in Chicago?"

"Yes. In Evanston. But my father lived here."

"Your parents were divorced?"

"Yes."

"Ma!"

She finally took the hint. "Would you like some more water?" she asked Ben.

"I'll get it." I had to do something—my mom had been the one who had invited Ben in the first place, made dinner, and was now monopolizing the conversation. I know it sounds stupid, but I felt I had to compete for Ben's attention—at least show him that I was the host too.

So I refilled his water glass, standing behind his chair, looking over his shoulder. I felt more master than servant—it was fun waiting on this guy who risked life and limb for me. It was certainly a new experience—I never waited on Benjamin. First, because he never came over for dinner. Second, because he was one of those people who never eats sitting down. Come to think of it, I never saw Benjamin drink out of a glass. It was always a can or bottle. The closest I ever came to waiting on him was when he told me to get him some ketchup at McDonald's.

Pouring Ben's water also gave me the chance to see the top of his brilliant head. Benjamin had the beginning of a bald spot, his follicles probably had more room to grow inside than out. But Ben had a full head of blond-streaked hair, and no dandruff.

As I replaced the water pitcher I looked at the three of them sitting at the table and I felt like the stranger. Obviously Ben felt more comfortable with my parents than I did. But then he'd just met them.

The weird thing, though, was how the whole situation was turning against me. I had hoped my parents would approve of Ben and that their embarrassing behavior wouldn't drive him away. But by the time I helped my mom serve dessert—assorted sorbets and fat-free finger cookies—I realized I was the one who was being driven away. Even my dad had joined the conversation. *I* was the only one silent, in my ghetto behind the roses. *I* was the one who was embarrassed, not Ben; I was the one my parents disapproved of.

By the time I helped my mom carry out the cappuccino I was resigned to giving up my room. After all, they could cancel the monthly family therapy if *he* were their child. You see, I'd never had a boyfriend my mom had even looked at, and it was strange now watching her giggle at Ben's jokes like a teenager. Sure I was jealous—Ben hadn't just forgotten about Benjamin, he'd forgotten about me. They were talking, the three of them, about intellectual crap, stuff I didn't understand at all. Was it my fault I was the only one at the table who hadn't taken the SATs? Yes, Ben was the child my parents had always wanted. My mom might even have an affair with him, weak woman that she was.

I finally moved the roses aside like an explorer hacking through the jungle with her machete, trying to find her way back to civilization, and forced my way into the conversation, the first words I'd said in years. "Ben, have you seen *Severed Heads Part III*?"

"I'm waiting for the reviews."

Very funny! And then my mom asked him if he'd seen some Japanese film with subtitles I'd never even heard of, so unimportant it was only playing at one theater in the whole city.

And of course he'd seen it, so they talked about Japanese acting for ten minutes while I stirred the bitter dregs of my cappuccino.

I decided everyone was finished and started to clear the table without being asked.

"Maybe Ben would like some more coffee?" my mom asked.

"If he wants more coffee we can go to Starbucks," I answered from the kitchen.

"You're going out then?" she asked cleverly, as a way of making everything public and official.

But I couldn't say yes. Ben was here at my mom's invitation and hadn't offered to take me out. I looked to him for a decision.

"I'm afraid I have to go. I have an early tee time tomorrow."

"So you play golf then?" my dad asked, suddenly the conversationalist. And they talked about irons and bunkers and I thought I might as well move out tonight.

I took it Ben was a good golfer because my dad was asking most of the questions. "You can stay a little while longer, can't you? Would you like a cigar?"

"I'd like a cigar!" I said.

But Dad shot me a look as if to say, "Are you still here?"

"Natalie doesn't like cigar smoke, so we'll step outside," my dad said, taking two cigars from a drawer in his study. "Where are you playing tomorrow?"

"Mohawk," Ben said. "A friend of mine's a member."

"Mohawk!" my dad said, like two potheads talking about Afghanistan blonde.

While they bonded in the cool night air I helped my mom with the dishes. I predict five thousand years from now, thanks to the march of science, women will be able to dunk a basketball and men will be able to give birth. But men will still smoke cigars and women will still do the dishes.

"He's a very nice young man," my mom said. "Where did you meet again?"

"At the U2 concert—no, I mean the bike shop." I was telling too many lies, even for me.

"Well maybe all those stolen bikes were a blessing. He's certainly the first mature, responsible boyfriend you've brought over."

"I've never brought any boys over! You've only met them in courtrooms! And he's not my boyfriend yet."

"You mean you haven't been . . . well . . . intimate?" my mom said, hiding her head behind the cupboard.

I don't care how many love-ins people had in the sixties, when it comes to talking about sex with their kids in the AIDS-plagued nineties, every former hippie is the Pope.

"No!" I answered, peering into the dishwasher. "Not that it's any of your business!"

"You know I think you're too young to be sexually active. But if you choose to be, I insist you use protection."

"If I want politically correct public service announcements I'll watch MTV! Can we talk about something else?"

"Are you in love with him?"

"Oh, that's much better! I guess I should be glad you didn't ask these questions at the table."

"It's just that you never open up to me."

"There's a reason for that, Mom."

"You don't trust me."

"Of course I don't trust you. Did you trust *your* mother?"

"Those were different times, dear," she said, pouring the powder into the dishwasher. "I could never communicate with my mother the way I communicate with you."

"Maybe there's a lesson in that."

"I've always shared my innermost thoughts with you."

"I still have nightmares . . ."

"He's quite nice looking," my mom said, swooning over the sink. "He has gorgeous hair, and he's so articulate, and respectful and well-mannered."

I couldn't bear any more. It was like she was talking about a dead man. I wanted to run after him. I locked the dishwasher door and turned the knob. "I'm afraid I do," I confessed, hoping she wouldn't hear above the water.

"Afraid you do what?" my mom asked, drying her hands. "Love him?"

But I'd already said too much. I could read her mind— she was mentally ordering the invitations. I escaped outside and waited anxiously on the porch, wishing I had a cigar to steady my nerves.

Finally the gate opened and my dad loomed out of the shadows, his cigar now a stub. He was alone.

"Where's Ben?" I saw images of him running away through traffic, of being ambushed by Benjamin. But my dad was too relaxed for any drama to have occurred.

"He went home. I walked him to his car."

"His car? Did he kiss you good night?" Was this it then? Two wannabe dates and my mom gets the flowers and my dad the firm handshake by the BMW? I had been afraid of losing Ben to my mom—but now I saw where the real threat lay. Just when you think your parents can damage you no further!

"Nice kid," my dad said, walking past me. My mom would have gone on and on about Ben—his gorgeous hair, his perfect manners, etc., etc., but my dad summed up everything in two words—and I didn't know which reaction said more.

Actually, there were more than two words. There were two words summing up Ben, and five words summing up me.

"Nice kid," my dad said. "What's he doing with *you*?"

Ouiji Madness

This wasn't getting any easier—it was getting infinitely harder. As I lay awake that night I managed to thoroughly convince myself I would never see Ben again. Why had I been in such a hurry to get the tattoo removed? Why had I gone to U2? Why hadn't I replaced my stolen bike with a Huffy from K-Mart like my mom suggested?

And not even a kiss to remember him by.

I imagined him lying awake as well, in his own apartment, which I would never see, weighing the pros and ex-cons, concluding, after only a few minutes, "She might be worth the risk of a premature, violent death, if only she were more like her parents!"

I was in agony. I had only thought I was in agony before. But this was real agony. Because now I'd reached the point—two wannabe dates and many nights of major obsession—that I knew I could never forget him. And yet what was there to remember? Not even a kiss, not even a red-eye Polaroid.

I wanted to look at the stars, but venturing out at this time of night meant certain death and, besides, the lights of the city drowned out the heavens. So I scoured the net for horoscopes like a drunk stumbling from bar to bar in search of the drink that will knock him senseless.

I wanted something tough but comforting—"The planets are aligned so ominously you'll be lucky to just survive this day so don't even think about love. But hang in there because tomorrow holds great promise."

But all I got was drivel: "This is an auspicious time to take that long-postponed trip." "A career move upward is in the air." "The winds of change are blowing seeds of prosperity, so don't close your window."

My window had bars on it to keep old boyfriends at bay—or to keep me from escaping, and if I opened it the only thing that would blow in would be mosquitoes. Of course I knew the horoscope was just symbolic, but at two a.m. I wanted something more personal than trips and careers and seeds blowing through windows. I turned off my lights and stared at my black-painted ceiling covered with glow-in-the-dark stars and if I ever got to sleep I don't know how.

⊙ ⊙ ⊙

I moped around the house all morning—what was left of the morning after I finally woke up—and then went for a long ride on my new bike through the flat, straight avenues of Lincoln Park, past ethnic restaurants, trendy boutiques, and neighborhood bars where the adult population retreated from life's disappointments. But where was I to seek solace? There was plenty of carbon monoxide spewing my way from the Chicago Transit Authority to put me out of my misery, but it only irritated my eyes—probably red to begin with, and made my throat dry.

By the time I returned home it was dark, and Ben was there. Can you believe it? I was lost for words. Actually, he'd just come, he was standing in the living room talking to my mom, a package in his arms. For me this time? But I didn't have a chance to be curious, or jealous—I was so overwhelmed to see him. It was like he was dead and had come back to life. I wanted to pinch him. With my lips.

"There you are!" my mom said, always the shrewd observer. "I was just telling Ben he was welcome to wait. I even offered him some dinner but he's already eaten."

"Martha Stewart's evil twin," I mumbled, groping at

the tangles in my hair. Why did he have to see me like this? Especially since he looked perfect—his blond-streaked hair shining, his skin newly tanned, his shirt unbuttoned just enough to be sexy without giving away any secrets. And that package, about the size of a dress box, in silver gift wrapping.

"I didn't get a chance to say goodbye last night," he said, smiling with the knowledge that I was completely his—or at least my parents were.

"No you didn't."

"But I hate to say goodbye, so it's just as well."

"Another present for my mom?"

"This one's for you."

But before I took it I cast a spell of disappearance on my mom. It only moved her back a few feet.

"I can't imagine what it is!"

"What does your horoscope say?" he smirked.

"My horoscope says it's time for a career change." I held the package up to my ear. I shook it. I weighed it in my hands. "A Northwestern jersey?" I guessed. "A bicycle tire, uninflated? A mutant box of chocolates?"

"I hope your psychic skills improve as the night wears on."

"Psychic skills?"

"Just open it," my mom said, leaning like a voyeur in the doorway.

I tore the wrapping and gasped. "No way! This is so

cool!" I held up a Ouiji board. "Look Mom! Can you believe it? Is this a joke?" I asked Ben.

"Have you ever used a Ouiji board before?"

"Only at slumber parties. But we never got anyone who spoke English."

"Most ghosts wouldn't," Ben agreed. "If you wanted to play the odds you'd be better off with a Chinese or a Latin Ouiji board. But maybe we'll be lucky."

"Too bad your father isn't home," my mom said.

"Too bad he didn't take you out for dinner!"

I wanted to hug Ben but stopped short out of respect for the dead. After all, spirits might be congregating in the house as we spoke, itching to communicate.

"I'll clean off the table," my mom said.

But I didn't want her scaring away the afterworld and led Ben into my room. My room! I was so preoccupied with the Great Beyond I forgot all the potentially incriminating evidence in my room—evidence of my age. But then eighteen year old girls have unmade beds, panties on the floor, stuffed killer whales, Tweetie Bird slippers, black ceilings with glow-in-the-dark stars. I tossed all the clothes into the corner, peering for more specific proof of my immaturity.

"Sorry about the mess."

But Ben was looking at the Absolut ads on the wall—the only organized thing in the room. Absolut vodka bottles cleverly outlined in swimming pools, or fountains, hidden in watches. Absolut LA, Absolut Brussels, Absolut

Geneva. How else was I supposed to learn geography? And there at the bottom was a picture of me, a goofy birthday photo with the caption "Absolut Madness."

Then he turned to the computer, my dad's old HP—obsolete for explaining to clients why you lost their life savings because a barley truck got a flat tire in Nebraska but just fine for booting up Tamarind Ellerbee's "The Complete Capricorn."

"What are those?" he asked, pointing to a stack of CDs propping up one of the table legs.

"That's my educational software library."

He turned the computer on, without permission.

"Looking for something?"

"Your diary."

"I don't type that fast."

He clicked on the internet icon. "I'll settle for your bookmarks."

"Don't you dare!" And I yanked out the plug.

"Hey, that can damage *your* processor!"

"I'll damage your processor if you read my bookmarks! Not that I have anything embarrassing. It's just the principle."

I wanted to go wash up and brush out the tangles in my sticky hair, but there was no way I was going to leave him alone in my room now. "You can check out my bookmarks next time."

"Sure, after you've purged the revealing ones."

"Right. Like you don't have the Naked Astronomers' page."

"When you come over you can open all the files you want."

This computer talk was getting pretty sexy. His invitation reminded me I still didn't know his address or phone number. But I couldn't ask him now—it would seem too desperate. I would have to wait for a casual moment, when it would seem more polite than important. I just hoped I wouldn't forget—again.

So instead I asked, "I thought you came here to stir up the dead?"

He suddenly stepped over to me and kissed me without putting his arms around me, a quick kiss, as though we were already lovers.

"You owe me that from last night," he said.

"Hey, I'm not the one to make the moves."

He picked up the crystals on my windowsill. "Crystals prefer darkness."

"Then turn out the light."

He flicked the switch and a couple hundred pseudo stars glowed on the ceiling. He laughed. "You're really into this star stuff."

"Look who's talking. OK, I know it's immature, but I hardly ever get to see any real stars."

"Then I'll have to show you some night. But you could have made it accurate," he said, looking at the ceiling like he was peering through a telescope.

"I did, sort of. See, here is the Big Dipper. And here is Polaris."

"Oh yeah. And Orion. Although it's backwards."

"This is the view from the other side of the galaxy," I said, embarrassed. I mean, I'd copied this from maps—I spent a lot of time on this project and now he'd shown it up for what it was—the sloppy work of an amateur. I might as well have thrown paint at the ceiling. But he was standing next to me in the glow of artificial starlight. I could hear his critical breath in the silence as we lost faith in the stars together.

And then I was in his arms. He was kissing me passionately this time—thank God I spit out my gum in the yard. And it was fantastic—or almost fantastic. Because truth to tell it just wasn't the right moment with the Ouiji board on the bed and half the spirit world watching us.

I stepped away. "We're not alone, you know."

"Your mom can't hear us."

"Not my mom. The dead."

"They'll just have to wait their turn." And he kissed me again.

It really was what I wanted, after all, to kiss him beneath the stars, real or mispainted. But Capricorns are creatures of mood, and I was in the mood for bodies that couldn't be touched. "It's your fault," I said. "If you wanted to make out you should have brought a bottle of wine and not a Ouiji board."

He couldn't argue with this and opened the box. "Do you want to do it with the light on or off?" he asked.

"Off, but we have to read the letters. I'll light an aromatherapy candle. Do you want jasmine or chamomile? Jasmine is stimulating, chamomile is soothing."

"Let's go with the jasmine."

I struck a match. Ben unfolded the board on the floor and set the pointer in the middle.

Someone knocked on the door.

"We haven't even started and the ghosts are already rapping!" Ben joked.

"I wish it were a ghost."

My mom peered in with a festive smile, as if we were hosting a party. "Would you like another pair of hands? I haven't played Ouiji since college."

"Thanks Mom, but we don't want to end up with Mama Cass hovering around."

She left, but didn't close the door all the way. Clever girl.

Ben was ready to go, sitting cross-legged like the Dali Lama. I knew he didn't really believe in this stuff, that he was just humoring me, but he sure looked serious.

"We'll need paper," I realized. "Maybe I should have let my mom join us to write down the letters."

"I can remember them."

"But what if we get a long speech or something? I don't want to miss out because we weren't prepared." I tore off a sheet of paper and grabbed a pen from my dresser.

"I'm getting excited!" But was it because of the Ouiji board or because I would be sitting across from Ben with our fingertips almost touching, sharing a spiritual experience?

"It's better if you relax," Ben said, as if he did this every day.

I sat on the floor and made eye contact with him in the flickering candle light before looking down at the board and the rows of letters that could spell out anything anyone—living or dead—could possibly want to say, except maybe for what I was feeling right now. It was such a shock coming home and finding him here, when I really thought I would never see him again. And to bring me a present—and a Ouiji board of all things! And not as a gag gift, not as some kind of critical joke, but with serious intent. It was too much for me to comprehend. It would take me days to sort it out. Maybe I would never get it. He certainly wasn't like other guys.

But one thing I did realize, looking down at the alphabet, was that for all my interest in ghosts, there was no person, alive or dead, I wanted to contact at that moment more than Ben himself. It was unfair, almost, that we would be asking questions of spirits we didn't know, and not of each other. Spirits who didn't matter in our lives, as much as we mattered to each other, sitting so close in my darkened room, and yet not even able to look at each other, forced to follow the pointer and record the results. By the end of the night I might learn all about Cleopatra's love life, but Ben would walk away as much a mystery as before.

"Ready?"

Ben, for his part, had no reservations. His eagerness surprised me. "I didn't think you believed in ghosts?"

"I have an open mind," he said.

"I think you have ulterior motives."

"Who's the cynical one then?"

"Is this your first time?"

"Using a Ouiji board or sitting in a room with painted stars?"

"Both."

"Yes. Are you ready?"

"Wait. Have you ever had a psychic experience?"

"Once I had a premonition my aunt died."

"And she did?"

"Five years later."

"Now you're making jokes."

"I guess you've had a lot of psychic experiences?"

"Yes. A lot! Including real precognitive dreams."

"Like of a plane crash?"

"Not a plane crash, but I had a dream of a bicycle crash and the next day I skidded into a lamp post. OK, maybe that's not so convincing. But when I was little I woke up in a cold sweat with a feeling that the world had lost a great soul. It was the day Nixon died."

"Now *you're* joking."

"No, these things go beyond politics. And I had an out-of-body experience last winter. I was lying on my back, meditating with incense burning and Yanni on the stereo, when I rose out of my body and floated up to the ceiling."

"Did you see yourself sleeping?"

"No, which is the strange thing—because that's what's supposed to happen. I mean, that's what you read about. Now I ask you, if this was just a product of my imagination, why wouldn't I have looked down on my sleeping body? Tell me that!"

"How do you know it wasn't a dream?"

"Because it feels so much more real than a dream. If you ever had an out-of-body experience you would know. There's this whoosh feeling when you leave your body like you're being pulled through a keyhole. And when you wake up every nerve in your body is tingling like you've been struck by—" I was about to say "lightning," but remembering our walk in the storm I decided not to open *that* subject.

"So you just floated on the ceiling and then woke up?" Ben asked. I didn't know if he was really interested or just looking to poke holes in my story.

"No, that was just the beginning. I knew I was out of my body so I decided to do some exploring. I floated around the ceiling and then out the window—straight through the iron bars. But then Chicago disappeared and I was in the countryside with hills and valleys and brilliant green grass, and the sun was shining and I saw cows in the distance. And then I saw this old woman and I realized she must be a spirit guide. So I floated over and said, 'Tell me what I need to know.' And she answered, 'Do your homework.' Of all the luck! My spirit guide turns out to be my third grade teacher! Don't tell me the Creator doesn't have a sense of humor."

"Maybe she'll speak to us tonight," Ben said.

"I hope not. I still have assignments due!"

Ben put the first two fingers of each hand against the pointer and I did the same. "How should we begin?" I asked.

"Just relax."

"I mean, should we let the spirits speak for themselves or get the ball rolling by asking yes or no questions?"

"Just let it happen." The pointer wasn't going anywhere.

"We should ask if there are any evil spirits present."

"You believe in evil spirits?"

"Some days I do and some days I don't. It's an unresolved issue for me." I looked at the ceiling—stupid, I know, and whispered, "Are there any evil spirits in the room?"

I felt my fingertips begin to tingle against the plastic pointer. Jasmine filled the air, which seemed to have grown colder. And then the pointer moved! Slowly, until it covered the word "No."

"That's a relief," I said. "Now we don't have to worry. Does it feel colder than before?"

"Look at the board."

I stared at our fingers on the pointer, still resting on "No," trying to concentrate and relax at the same time. And then the pointer moved again, to the letter *I*.

"I!" I shouted, and reached for the pen.

"No, keep your hands on the pointer."

I let Ben have his way, hoping he had a good memory, because I knew when a Ouiji session really gets hot the pointer can fly over the letters like a secretary after her fifth cup of coffee.

The pointer moved again, of it's own will to the letter *L*. It was real spooky because I could feel my fingers against the plastic, but I wasn't doing anything, it was like watching a movie.

And then *O* and *V*.

"Ilov," I said, trying to make sense of the message. "I think I should write this down."

"Quiet."

"*E*. Of course! I love! One of us has an admirer in the Great Beyond!" But for all my joking I was beginning to get chills up my spine. Nothing like this had ever happened at the slumber parties. I realized this is how fishermen must feel when they get that first tug at their line. "We've made contact!" I whispered, with the awe of a true believer.

The pointer glided. I called out the letters. "*B, E*." The pointer stalled, then slowly moved to *N*.

And then the pointer took off and covered the letter *Z*. "I Love Benz!" I shouted.

Ben let go of the pointer. "No, it said 'I love Ben!'"

"You can see for yourself it's on the *Z*. You're in trouble, BMW man!"

Ben frowned and turned on the light. He'd been outsmarted on both earth and in heaven and it was just too much for him.

Murder at the White Hen Pantry

Now I'm the first to admit I can be my own worst enemy, but what was I to do? Let the boy trample my most deeply held beliefs? It was like blasphemy, what he tried to do—it was like giving the spirit world the finger. And as I gazed at my ceiling of stars that night I worried something terrible would happen to him—one of his lightning bolts would strike him right between the *N* and the *Z*.

Didn't the fool know he didn't need the Ouiji board? That I was his long ago? That he didn't have to bring me flowers or gifts or confirmation from the Great Beyond? That he was the ruling spirit in my life and all he had to do last night was show up and I would have been his in this world and all the others?

I should have just humored him and he wouldn't have marched out like the Iraqi army. I should have just played his game—and I would have if it wasn't of such a serious nature. I still didn't know his phone number. Can you believe it? When was this struggle going to end? Would I be an insomniac for life? But, truth to tell, I did feel a lot more confident tonight. I mean, he had come back, and with an act fit for the circus. Mad infatuation had broken the blood-brain barrier after all. I knew now we were destined for each other, if we didn't tempt fate too far.

⊙ ⊙ ⊙

I was on my way to the White Hen to buy milk the next morning when a black cat crossed my path. "Hey!" it snarled.

I kept walking.

"Where are you going?" Benjamin asked, creeping beside me.

"Where are *you* going?"

"You look the same."

"What are you talking about? My hair's longer, with

red highlights. I got rid of the nose ring, and I no longer wear Guns 'N Roses T-shirts."

"Yeah, but I mean otherwise."

"Don't you have a probation meeting or something?"

He grabbed my arm. "Talk to me!"

We were on the busy corner of Clark and Diversy, surrounded by our fellow creatures—Saturday shoppers, lesbians with dobermans, punks on skateboards. If he shot or stabbed me how long would I bleed on the pavement before anyone came to my rescue?

"I have nothing to say."

"Have you been faithful to me?"

"That's none of your business."

"Tell me!"

"Look, if I haven't had a date in a year it's only because I was afraid of getting involved with someone else like you. Besides, I suppose you didn't have any candlelight bread-and-Perrier dinners while you were locked up? I watch HBO, I know what goes on!"

"I love you more than ever, Christy."

"Let go of me! Do you want to get thrown back in the can for loitering?" And I crossed the street as the light blinked red.

He followed me, of course. But what could I do? I ignored him, looking at the traffic and walking as fast as I could in my Nine West sandals while he told me how much I meant to him.

"You can't love me. You don't even know me," I said.

But he had known me, in what seemed centuries ago. Was it possible we had once been as close as he said? I guess so, considering the tattoo as exhibit number one. But trying to outwalk this little guy with a White Sox hat, it was painful to admit he had once seemed as big as James Dean to me, powerful and sexy, everything I aspired to, everything my parents opposed.

Hard as it is to believe, I wasn't always the ultra-secure girl of destiny I am now. Only a couple years ago I was wracked by inner turmoil, major confrontation on the home front, doubts as to my own self-worth, acne, and an astrologer I should have sued for malpractice.

I first met Benjamin in ninth grade. He was in my Home Ec class, dangerous with a souffle pan but man that kid could sew! Some dufus got the idea that the way to meet girls was to sign up for Home Ec, so there were about thirty boys in my class and two girls. Needless to say, I got a lot of attention. He had flunked a year—one of the reasons I forgot his age—but social climber that he was, refused to hang out with anyone who hadn't been left behind at least twice.

I was still clinging precariously to the honor roll, so for a while our paths didn't cross. He was actually shy with strangers, especially anyone whose vocabulary exceeded a hundred words. What finally brought us together was our Quilts for the Homeless project. You probably think he wanted me as his partner, but in fact it was I who picked him because, as I said, he was quick with a needle, and I wanted an easy ride, sliding perilously from the Everest of my parents' expectations into the Netherworld of terminal adolescence, a nightmare world of alcohol, drugs, and promiscuous calls to the Psychic Hotline.

And he was cute—I mean, I did have some standards, and he was as close to James Dean as I was going to get for a while. Of course, he couldn't kiss like Ben, he knew nothing at all about love, but then neither did I, being only fourteen and conceived, so to speak, in the mud of Woodstock.

We started hanging out—he taught me how to play pool and blow smoke rings, I taught him the alphabet. It goes without saying our quilt never got finished. Every winter when I see a story about some poor homeless man who froze to death I feel like a murderer.

⊙ ⊙ ⊙

"So why didn't you answer my letters?" he asked, following me into the White Hen. "Why didn't you visit me?"

"I told you," I answered beneath the watchful eye of the security camera. If there was a place to be bold this was it. I wouldn't be just another anonymous statistic found dead on the street but "film at eleven." I might even make the national news if he shot me enough times. And my parents would have the video to remember me by: Here's Christy being born—can you believe they did that? Major camera shake from my father. Here's Christy playing soccer. I hated soccer. I was always catching the ball. Here's Christy singing "Yesterday" at her sixth grade play. Fortunately Dad screwed up the audio. And here she is being gunned down by her ex-boyfriend at the White Hen Pantry while an alert and maybe overzealous clerk returns fire with a concealed Magnum. Dig the artistic camera angle, our dying heroine glorious in black-and-white like the star of a Hitchcock film, clutching a quart of two percent to her breast as if it were her child, determined not to let it spill because—moral role model that she is—she hasn't paid for it yet.

"It's your parents," Benjamin said.

"It's a lot of things," I spelled out, getting a quart of milk and a serving of banana yogurt. "I'm not fourteen anymore. I'm not into the same things. We're not compatible now. We never were."

"You think I'm a bad person."

"Isn't that your goal in life?"

"I've never done anything to you."

"Well keep that in mind," I said, roaming through the aisle. Like I said before, it was impossible for me to just buy one thing when I went into a store. I was always overwhelmed—even at the White Hen. I got some Bubble Yum and an energy bar for later.

"You think I'm a murderer," he said, too loud in my opinion for the sensitive acoustics of a dairy mart.

"What's the difference what I think?"

I put my supplies on the counter, along with a copy of *Cosmo*. "Don't follow me out," I warned, speaking to the camera so if anything happened the world would have a record of my resistance.

But of course he followed me out—the only time he ever opened a door for me. "You weren't there that night," he said, playing to a jury of one. "You don't know what happened. I had no choice. It was self-defense!"

I turned on him. "Why didn't you use your fists?" All of a sudden the memories of that night—actually for me the next day when I heard the news—came back in a flash. My shock and disbelief. My anger at my parents for calling him a killer, my anger at the police. It wasn't until a week later that the fog began to lift and my misguided loyalty was buried as deep as Benjamin's victim. It was the worst week of my life, tumbling from one extreme to the other at full volume, I imagine like kicking heroin. I had been like an addict who wakes up one morning and finds the palace he'd been living in is a sewer swarming with rats.

"Did you want me to be killed?" he yelled back.

"With what? A nail file from a Swiss Army knife?"

"I was outnumbered. I had no choice!"

"You had a choice when you went there that night. You had a choice when you bought the gun. You had a choice when you stole your first pacifier in day care!"

"It had nothing to do with us!"

"It has everything to do with us! I feel guilty when I wear wool and you killed someone and you still don't feel any remorse! Tell me the truth, you enjoyed pulling that trigger, didn't you? You enjoyed taking that punk down!"

"Only until the police came."

We were standing on a corner. And speaking of police I noticed a patrol car parked on the opposite curb.

"I'm crossing now and you're going to cross the other way. Or I'll grab a ride home from them," I threatened, pointing to the cops.

Benjamin looked more like an abandoned puppy than a killer and I almost felt sorry for him. The light turned green and I hurried across. He was standing in the same spot when I reached the other side.

⊙ ⊙ ⊙

"What took you so long?" my mom asked, taking the milk for her coffee.

"I stopped to smell the roses," I said, unpacking the rest of the bag.

"Where's my change?"

I handed her some coins.

"This is it? When I give you ten dollars to buy a quart of milk I expect change." She looked at my other purchases. "What do you think we give you an allowance for? I'll deduct the gum and *Cosmo* from next week's."

"Don't you dare! Besides, the *Cosmo*'s for you. I just want the horoscope."

I poured myself a bowl of Coco Puffs and sat across from my dear mom at the table. Quality time.

"So did you make contact with the spirit world last night?" she asked.

"Yeah, some guy in the CIA, but it was all in code."

"You know, now that you have the board we can use it all the time. Give it a real test."

"I don't know."

"But you were so excited last night."

I looked up Capricorn in *Cosmo*. "Romantic possibilities fill the air this month, but you may find yourself being pulled in different directions . . ." Wasn't that right on?

"I've just realized it's easy to be fooled. And today I'm leaning toward the existence of evil spirits."

"By the way, Ben called."

She said it without emotion, and I was still thinking about my encounter with Benjamin, so I thought she was talking about him.

"Did you hear me, Christina?"

I didn't look up. "Benjamin?" My mind was filling with all sorts of crazy thoughts. He had called just after I left, asking for me. Or worse, he had called from a pay phone after the White Hen, threatening to blow up the house. Our whole family would have to move, like in the witness protection program. The juvenile court system would have to give us new identities.

"He said it's supposed to be clear tonight," my mom went on.

But this wasn't like Benjamin, who always came to the point. "Clear for what?"

"For viewing the stars."

"What stars?" And then it hit me—of course, Ben! And I laughed, the way people swimming in the ocean laugh when a shark fin turns out to be a body board. "He wants to show me the stars?" And I grabbed the *Trib* and turned to the weather page. "It's a full moon tonight."

"Maybe he'll bring a telescope."

"But we won't be able to see anything in the city."

"He said he'd take you into the country."

"Really?" My head was spinning.

"I told him to have you home by one," my mom teased—or was she teasing?

"A full moon . . ." I forgot all about Benjamin. My heart was still pounding, but for new and better reasons.

My mom put her coffee down and gave me one of her looks. "Christina, when are you going to tell him you're sixteen?"

"I don't know."

"Christina . . ."

"Before the next full moon, I promise."

"Christina, you can't begin a relationship on lies."

"One lie, just one."

"And what if he's telling lies as well?"

"It wouldn't matter. I wouldn't care."

"Sure you would. And if you thought he really liked you—liked you for who you are—you wouldn't be afraid to tell him your age."

"What do you know about it?"

"He's bound to find out."

"Especially if you tell him I have to be home by one."

"It also puts your father and me in a compromising position."

"Just pretend he's the draft board."

"I insist you tell him tonight."

I poured myself another bowl of cereal.

"Christina?"

"Sure, tonight, now leave me alone." And she left me in peace after that, to look at a picture of an alien toy on the back of the cereal box, and to dream of other worlds.

Alien Abduction

When Ben came over that evening he found me leaning over a map of Illinois spread out on the kitchen table, highlighting rural highways like a general planning an invasion. He didn't kiss me—we weren't exactly in private—but just looked over my shoulder at the places I had marked.

"What's all this?"

"A map of Illinois."

"I can see that. Are you planning a trip?"

"My mom said you were going to take me to look at the stars."

"We don't have to drive to Indiana!"

I looked at him, suddenly worried. "You don't have a place in mind?"

"I didn't think it would be so complicated."

"Good, then we can go here."

"Where is here?" he asked, peering at the map.

I pointed to a back road far from any town, about fifty miles southeast of Chicago.

"Kind of far, don't you think?"

"It won't take long to get there," I said, determined, folding up the map so that our road was still in view.

"Whatever you want. Have you stargazed there before?"

"No, but I've heard about it." Which was true enough, but not the whole truth. Because the real reason I wanted to go to this road in the middle of nowhere was because it was a place where the stars gazed back—yes, a regular O'Hare of alien abduction!

⊙ ⊙ ⊙

"Didn't you bring a telescope?" I asked in the car.

"It's in the trunk."

"I've never looked through a telescope before. None of my friends even own a telescope. The only scientific instruments you'll find in my crowd are scales for weighing pot."

"So why don't you have a telescope yourself, if you're so interested in the stars?"

"What's the use in the city? Besides, my parents are too busy buying me bicycles."

We were nearing a cut off. I looked at my map and told him which way to go. Then I opened the sunroof. Already the stars were breaking through.

"We'll be out of the city in a few minutes. I don't see why we have to go so far."

"It's not that far."

"I told your mom I'd have you back by one."

"She was just joking!" And I thought, this would be a perfect time to tell him I was sixteen—that is, as perfect as any. But I still didn't know how he would take it. We might have a long argument, ruining the mood. He might yell at me when we got there, scaring off the alien observers. He might turn around and take me straight home.

It was too much to risk. But what if he already suspected? "I bet you think my mom treats me like a child?"

"Not at all. It's her house."

"Exactly! And rules are rules, so even if I were forty she would have a right to set a curfew. Can't interrupt her REM cycles." And, hoping that would put any suspicions to rest, I quickly returned to the subject of our adventure. "You know it's a full moon tonight."

"Yes, I know."

"Of course you know." I stared up through the sunroof, the warm air blowing back my hair. The moon wasn't directly above—it was too early still—but there were plenty of stars. "What do you think of moon madness?"

"I think people are the mad ones, not the moon."

"You know what I mean. Like prisoners and mental patients rioting during full moons. Any nurse will tell you full moons are the worst time."

"You're right. Now that I think of it, I always have to shave twice during full moons."

"Very funny! And I suppose you think the tides are psychosomatic!"

"They're two different things."

"Well if the moon's gravity can influence the oceans why shouldn't it influence us? After all, we're mostly water."

"Because the earth presents more surface area for the moon to pull against."

"I think you're just making that up," I said, catching sight of the moon through the back window.

"How does the full moon influence you?" he asked. "You seem no different from any other night."

"That's because I'm not crazy—enough," I added. "Besides, I'm sure it has some influence, I've just never looked into it."

"Well I'm sure you'll find in your theories whatever you're looking for."

Actually, what I should have been looking for at that moment was Rt. 31. And I almost missed it. "Slow down! You want to turn left at the light." And I glanced at the map to make sure.

"We're going to run out of gas soon!" he exaggerated.

I sat back, enjoying the unpolluted air. We were really in the country now. I turned off the radio to listen to the country silence, gazed through the sunroof at the country darkness, the country stars. And I wondered what *he* was looking for. Certainly not anything to do with theories. Or with the sky. What was he looking for in me?

"This was my idea, to view the stars," he reminded me. "But every time I have an idea you have a way of taking over."

"Like last night," I said.

But he didn't want to talk about our Ouiji experience, and I couldn't blame him. Did he have a similar ploy scripted for tonight? And did he think I would sabotage that as well?

We were on a two-lane highway. Ben passed a truck and switched on his bright lights. Nothing but pavement, corn, and stars as far as the eye could see. "Why do I feel you're not telling me everything?" he asked suspiciously.

"Hey, this was your idea, remember?"

"So this isn't some sort of trap?"

"If it's a trap it's not of my devising," I said, certainly true enough.

I started looking at the mileage markers. We were getting close. I told Ben to make another left and after a few hundred yards to pull off the road. We were truly in a desolate spot, the two-lane road stretching as straight and silent as the tall rows of corn behind us. Ben turned off his head-lights and smiled at me in the starlight.

"You almost don't need a telescope," I said, tilting my head back, letting the night sky fill my vision. "The only time I see this many stars is just before the Enterprise goes into warp drive!"

Ben put his arm around me for a moment, not saying anything—in fact, I think looking more at me than at the stars. Then he opened his trunk to get the telescope.

I noticed approaching lights as Ben set up the telescope on the gravel and for a moment my heart stopped, thinking it was a spacecraft. But it was only a semi and, after stirring up the dust, it roared back toward the cities of man.

"The moon looks so three-dimensional out here. You can see the shadows and craters. And look, there's Mars!"

"Venus."

"OK, Venus. I can never get over the fact that we can actually see other planets! It's so phenomenal!"

"Here, look."

I bent down and peered through the lens. Filling my vision was the moon, but like I'd never seen it before, with deep craters and ridges and gray rocks. "Wow! It's like a living thing!"

"I don't think anything looks more lifeless. But it is beautiful, isn't it?"

"Can we see the flag?"

"No."

"But it's still there, isn't it? And the footprints . . . It certainly makes you think."

"Would you like to travel into space?"

"Sure!" And sooner than he thought!

"What would you do if you were on the moon?"

"I'd sit on top of a crater and stare back at the earth. And I'd jump up and down. What about you?"

"I wouldn't go to the moon."

"Come on, you're an astronomer."

"I'm not an astronomer yet."

"But you could see the stars so much better. Like the Hubble telescope."

"I just think the emptiness of space would be very depressing. Earth is empty enough."

"Do you believe in God?"

"No."

"But how do you explain all the meaning in the universe?"

"I don't see any meaning."

"I see meaning everywhere. Isn't it strange that we both love the stars, but when you look at them you see nothing and I see everything."

He readjusted the telescope to view Venus. After the moon, I found Venus a little disappointing—a hazy pink ball without shadows. "Is it too far away to see its craters?" I asked, like the moron that I was.

"Venus has a thick atmosphere," Ben said, like to a three year old.

"Oh, I knew that." But then, to show him how really stupid I was, I said, "I'd like to go to Venus too."

"No you wouldn't. The atmosphere is poisonous and the surface is hot enough to melt lead."

"Just like Gary, Indiana."

"But you might be able to make out some features on Mars." And I waited with growing excitement while he repositioned the telescope.

And there it was—the red planet! And it was red, and beautiful, clearer than Venus, although I still couldn't see any mountains or craters. "Do you think there was ever life on Mars?" I whispered, as if the Martians were close enough to hear.

"There may still be."

This from the boy who didn't even believe in moon madness! "You're not serious?"

"Sure. There could be bacteria in the rocks, or in the polar ice caps."

"Oh, bacteria," I said, disappointed. "I think I read something about that on a cereal box."

I stood up and looked at Mars with my naked eye. "What else have you got to show me? Can we look at Saturn?"

"Saturn isn't visible now."

"Too bad, I wanted to see the rings."

"But I think you'll be interested in this." And he focused his telescope lower in the sky.

I could see two medium-sized stars, one white, one

greenish. "Doesn't look like anything special," I said, expecting something more interesting.

"That's Capricorn."

I took another look. I looked for a long time.

"Only two stars of the constellation are visible this time of year. The rest are in the Southern Hemisphere."

Capricorn. Wow. I'd never actually seen it before—I mean, that I knew. I felt his hand stroking my head, silent while I communed with my natal sign. Suddenly they were the two most important stars in the sky. But when I lifted my eyes they were only two ordinary stars among thousands, barely over the horizon.

And then I experienced a total eclipse, as Ben kissed me. Anywhere else it would have been great, I wouldn't have let him go, but not here, with the sky brimming with aliens and Capricorn peeking over the horizon.

"What's the matter?" he asked, when I pulled away.

"I feel like we're not alone. I feel watched."

He laughed, like he was dealing with a madwoman. And maybe he was. "There's not a person within miles!"

"Not a person!"

He kissed me again, as if my opinion didn't matter. Here we were on a sparkling clear night on a solitary road, our faces lit by the full moon, and all he could think about was sex!

When I pulled away again he adopted a backup strategy and lay down on the gravel. I took the bait and lay next to him, on my back. The view was tremendous. But a minute later he was on top of me, groping.

"I thought we were here to look at the stars?"

"Am I blocking your view?" he asked.

I pushed him off and stood up. "I meant it when I said we're not alone! People have been abducted from this place!"

He looked at me like I was the alien. "Abducted?" And then it hit him and he laughed, but only for a second, because in fact he was too angry to find much humor in the situation. "I knew there was a reason!"

"Please don't shout."

"Did you read about it in some tabloid? Did Svetlana tell you to come here?"

"Channel 11 News had a three-part series. A farmer, a truck driver, and a newly married couple were all abducted here—on different nights."

"I guess someone paid their ransom if they lived to tell Channel 11."

"You can make all the jokes you want, but if there wasn't something to it why would Channel 11 run a three-part series?"

"I knew you had an ulterior motive. Why didn't you tell me?"

"Why do you think? No one else would take me, and when my mom said you wanted to show me the stars it seemed like a perfect opportunity. But I knew if I told you the reason you wouldn't want to come."

"You still should have told me, Christy. To make me drive halfway across the state because you think you'll find aliens here . . . when I thought you wanted to look at the stars."

"I did want to look at the stars. Besides, I'm not the only one with ulterior motives!"

"What do you mean?"

"You know what I mean. You didn't visit Svetlana with an open mind. And that trick with the Ouiji board was criminal, and showing me Capricorn just now—taking advantage of my beliefs while you don't believe in anything."

"Well, since we're here . . ." he said, softening a bit.

"You're the scientist. Isn't it the scientific thing to conduct experiments? You should support me in this. I'm offering myself as a human guinea pig."

"And me."

"If we do get abducted I'll feel a lot safer knowing you're with me. I mean, you have a cooler head, you'll know what questions to ask. That is, if you aren't paralyzed!"

"Paralyzed?" he said, not the least bit scared.

But I was getting goose bumps just talking about it. Who knows, maybe the alien tape recorders were already rolling? It would be stupid of me to give *them* ideas.

"So what are we supposed to do?" Ben asked, giving in. "Is there some kind of incantation we should chant? If you'd told me I would have brought my interstellar landing lights."

"I hope you still have a sense of humor when alien scientists are scanning your brain."

"Oh look, a Pleiadean battle cruiser!"

But it was only another semi, and this time I wasn't fooled. I walked slowly along the middle of the road. "This truck driver said he was driving along the highway, just where we are now, when he was blinded by a bright light and ran off the road. He didn't remember much else, except two spacemen examining him in the cab as he regained consciousness."

"It's always the aliens' fault," Ben said.

"And the farmer was out plowing late one afternoon when he saw the same bright light and then a silver UFO streak across the sky and then rise straight up through the clouds."

"What about the charge of kidnapping?"

"That was the newly married couple. The wife was driving late one night, on this same road, and was also blinded by a bright white light. Then she saw a spaceship hovering above them—and she thinks the whole car was teleported into the ship, although on this point she wasn't sure. The next thing she remembered was being strapped down on an operating table, naked, with her legs spread while an alien penetrated her body with different-colored beams of light."

"A modern variation of the rape fantasy," Ben said. "What about the husband?"

"He was asleep. But he recovered the memories with the help of a therapist. What do you think of that?"

"I think he should have just bought a set of colored flashlights. Some guys will do anything to get—"

"Shhh!"

I stood dead still, but it was only the howling of some animal. Or was it?

"I don't think aliens bark," Ben said.

"It wasn't a bark. It was a kind of grunt." I listened for a moment, but there was only silence.

"So why didn't Channel 11 investigate these claims?"

"They did. They came here with a crew and everything. But what use would aliens have for the Channel 11 News team?"

I turned around and we started walking back toward the car. It was getting chilly and I hadn't brought a jacket.

"Hello?" Ben shouted. "Aliens, are you there? You've come all this way, don't be shy!"

"Quiet!"

"They're not fish."

"If you really had an open mind you'd give this a chance."

"What bothers me isn't that you have such a rich imagination, but that you have such a poor imagination. I mean, I'd like to believe life exists on other planets, but don't you think it's strange all the sightings of alien spaceships and the aliens themselves look just like those in science fiction movies? And that before these movies were made supernatural encounters were always with devils or fairies or vampires? Don't you think if aliens existed they would be unlike anything you could possibly imagine? That they wouldn't walk on two legs and have eyes and think the way we do? They might be the size of bacteria or planets, that they wouldn't reflect light in the visible spectrum, that communication between us would be all but impossible?"

"So if they're invisible they could be here right now . . . We could be teleported into their spacecraft without warning. Strapped to their operating tables."

I gazed at the air above, as if a spaceship hung there like a spider's web, waiting to trap us.

"Why are you so eager to be raped by aliens?" Ben asked.

"Who said anything about rape? I'm all too willing to suffer a few minutes of discomfort if it means advancing galactic science."

"It seems you're also a little too eager to volunteer my services. I've heard they do some pretty invasive procedures."

"Yeah, but they leave no scars."

We walked for a while in silence. It was strange. I was alert and relaxed at the same time, cold and warm inside.

"Maybe we should hold hands to increase our electromagnetic output," Ben said.

I knew what his game was, but it was nice to hold hands, and then to feel his arm around me.

Then he stopped and put his cold hands on my face

and smiled at me, but not critically, like before, but with affection and, who knows, maybe more.

"If I did see an alien tonight, it couldn't be any more marvelous than you!"

I couldn't make any jokes about that!

"Just look at the sky!" he said, tilting my head back. "You're so intent on UFOs you're ignoring the real messages from space, the light from stars, some millions of years old—we see them as they looked before there were men to name them. Many have blown apart or become white dwarfs since sending out the light which now reaches us. What we see are ghosts in far corners of the universe!"

And there was another eclipse as he kissed me again. My head was whirling, from the ghosts of stars and his lips against mine. But, unlike him, I still kept my head. "We're in the middle of the road!"

He led me over to the gravel, beside the car. He pulled my shirt out of my jeans and put his hands around my naked waist.

"Hey, I need more clothes, not less!"

But he was beyond the point of talking. I could hear his breath against my ear.

"Wait! Not here!"

But, truth to tell, by this point I was probably collaborating more than resisting.

And he took me there and then, beneath the invisible gaze of countless aliens of science.

My Baptism of Stainless Steel

Wow. The agony was over. It was ecstasy time. And not the chemical, pseudo ecstasy, but the real thing, pure, uncut, with a capital E. But let me tell you, agony has nothing on ecstasy when it comes to causing insomnia. How could I sleep now? What was I supposed to dream about now that my dreams had come true?

I glowed more than the stars on my ceiling, my heart racing through galaxies of bliss as I gazed at those painted points of light, remembering how the real stars looked on that magical country road—the full moon, Venus and Mars, Capricorn barely peeking over the horizon. And Ben's eyes, like two mysterious stars, gazing into mine.

I wanted to shout and sing, pedal through the sleeping streets until my legs were numb, dive into a pool of cold water. But most of all I wanted to talk, to tell someone—anyone—the story of this night, how I felt, what I was going through, to describe what true happiness was, like someone with perfect vision describing a garden to a blind world. I knew I'd never find the right words, but I had to try.

But who could I tell? Certainly no one at this hour. True, I could get on a chat line, but I needed to talk, not type, and to someone I knew and trusted. After all, this was intimate, confidential information. Miranda, Stacey, Laverne? They certainly couldn't be trusted, and anyway my girlfriends wouldn't take me seriously. Svetlana? I could surely trust her, and she was a good, although expensive, listener. But too clinical for my present needs. My mom? She would take me too seriously. How could I say anything to her? My dad? A great ally, yes, but gushy romance was hardly his forte. He wouldn't care about love until it appointed a board of directors. As I lay awake trying to solve this riddle, like a math problem, I realized in a flash of inspiration that for the stronger sex love is not enough, that a girl needs two things in life—a lover and an audience.

☉ ☉ ☉

I decided to get my hair cut. Short, way short, true to my Capricornian impulsiveness. Yes, I was ready for a change, the summer was heating up, I was tired of the tangles. But these reasons I only thought of later. It was impulse that drove me. Or mostly impulse, because, truth to tell, I did have an ulterior motive—Capricorns can be devious too. You see, Derek, my stylish stylist, sweet Derek with his black silk shirts, polished loafers, and perpetual stubble, was just the man I wanted to see.

I watched him nodding approvingly in the mirror while I showed him the damage to be done—down to the lobes of my ears, to the nape of my neck, a couple bangs in front. In summary, more than six inches of healthy, happy hair—hair which had traveled with me from bleak back alleys to star-filled country roads—destined for the cutting room floor.

"It's going to look fabulous!" Derek said, after an assistant shampooed me, combing out my still-long hair and studying my head like a sculptor looking at a block of marble. "What made you decide to change?"

And I told him about summer and the tangles—but hey, I was here for a heart-to-heart, if I didn't come clean now what kind of example would that set for the rest of the conversation? So I mentioned I had a new boyfriend.

"Ah!" Derek said, testing his scissors like a steak lover waving his knife as the waitress sets down a mammoth sirloin. "And he prefers shorter hair?"

"I don't know." Suddenly I was worried.

"Well I'm sure he'll be pleasantly surprised."

"You think so?" Suddenly I was insecure.

"You want to wait? You want to call him?"

But I was being a coward. "No, snip away. How could he not like it? You're an artist, after all."

"But if you're not doing it for him, why the radical change?"

"Because I need to talk to you, and what I have to say is bound to take more time than a trim." And really, now that I thought about it, this was a more valid reason than the heat of summer.

"In that case I promise to cut slowly," Derek said with a smile.

A long, thin strand fell to the floor like a feather. "It won't be that short, after all," I said. "I mean, I won't be Sinead O'Connor or anything."

"So what's his name, this boyfriend of yours?" Derek asked, like a dentist trying to distract his patient from the drill with idle conversation.

But wasn't that why I was here, to talk? Yes, and to celebrate the change in my life, like a baptism of stainless steel—still another reason for my decision. But I'm not one of those girls whose hair changes with the seasons, like their skirts. I'd had long hair forever—forever! I should have *at least* consulted my horoscope! The fact that I didn't even read it today should tell you all you need to know about the state I was in.

"Ben," I said.

"Wasn't that the name of your old boyfriend, the one who went to jail?"

"Yeah, well I'm dating Benjamins till I get it right. Anyway, the new guy's name is Ben and there the similarity ends."

"I hope so. I just can't imagine you in prison gray."

"But you'd visit me if I was in the slammer, wouldn't you?"

"You'd have the ravest hair of any inmate."

I sighed. "I wish I had more friends like you, Derek. The most magical conjunction of events blesses my life and I have no one to tell!"

"Sounds like you're in—No, you have to say it. Confess, girl!"

"I want to scream it out! No third degree necessary." But I whispered, "I'm in love."

"It's written all over your face!"

"Yeah?" I looked at myself in the mirror.

"You're absolutely glowing today!"

I knew I was glowing! "Derek, I've never been in love like this! I've never been in love at all! It's like all my life I've been playing version 1.0 of Mario Brothers and then, all of a sudden, I'm plugged into the newest update with a million colors and 3-D and dazzling animation!"

"And what separates Ben from all the others?"

"His eyes are like stars! Like two mysterious sapphire stars, deep and unfathon . . . unfathon . . ."

"Unfathomable."

"Yeah. But that's a recent discovery. What I knew from the beginning—from the very first time I saw him in my plastic surgeon's office—which by the way you're sworn to secrecy on and aren't to ask any more questions—what I knew from that day was that his body had exactly the right proportions. I mean exactly! And such a sweet face, and a wise smile—although come to think of it he doesn't smile a lot. And the hair on his arms, manly without being gorillaish—and the way his Levis hug his ass! Although I didn't see that until later. I'm not making you hot, am I?"

"I've been forced to listen to worse."

"Really?" I looked at the long strands falling on my apron and on the floor. I was like a snake shedding its skin. A golden cobra glowing with new scales, packing plenty of poison but charmed to distraction by the music of love.

"He's all that and more, I could go on all day, but I've already used up my year's quota of gushiness. God, I hate when other people talk this way, but it's what I feel—it's so real! Love has to be the most overused word in the language, but when it strikes it's like the only word in the dictionary—how can you say anything else? Have you ever felt its full power, Derek? Have you ever known true love?"

But of course he had. I remembered his boyfriend, killed by AIDS. "I'm sorry," I said. "I wasn't thinking. That's one of the side effects of love. It makes you a raging moron. And don't ask what was my excuse before," I added, as he opened his mouth to reply.

"I was going to ask for all the juicy details. You've told me nothing."

So I described our meeting—although I didn't say anything more about the plastic surgeon—and the wild coincidences that kept bringing us together and the twists of fate that kept us apart, and the disastrous first date with no kiss and no phone number, and so on, and so on. As my head grew lighter with the loss of all that hair so my mind grew lighter as I unburdened myself of the long nights of agony, whose tangled strands had grown much faster than hair and weighed me down like iron chains. There are healers who can take away your pain by laying on their hands, but I believe there are other people just as gifted—and Derek was one—who can take away your pain by listening.

Then finally, as his scissors snipped away, I told him about last night—and everything, every last detail, in hints and winks and whispers, because just as it was crucial to unburden myself of all that built-up agony—which I believed was still inside me like an appendix, useless but hanging around until someone cuts it out—I had to share the ecstasy with someone because, like the direct light of the sun, it was just too bright for the unaided eye. Derek's ears were the Ray Bans that let me look back on last night without being blinded.

"So what do you think?" I then asked, shaking a clump of hair from my shoe.

"I think he's a lucky guy."

"You wouldn't say that if you knew the trouble I've given him. No, I'm the lucky one. Oh, Derek, he's so bright, and stable, and sensible. I've never met anyone like him. He's just what I need in my life. I feel I know him so well. I mean his character, not all the details of his past. I know very little about that. In fact, I think he has a secret."

"Why? Something he said?"

"More like what he hasn't said. I can't put my finger on it. I just know it's there. But it's not something disastrous—like my secrets. No, I'm sure when I find out what it is I'll love him even more."

"And does he know about your secret past?" Derek asked.

"I told him all about Benjamin, if that's what you mean. And everything's cool."

"Promise you'll invite me to the wedding," Derek said, making a couple final cuts.

"Too bad you're not a transvestite, you could be my maid of honor! But I'd like you to be a witness."

"With pleasure."

I couldn't believe I was talking about my wedding! I'd never even thought about marriage before. That's what I liked about Derek, he was always so positive. Anyone else would have been skeptical, would have raised all kinds of questions, would have asked me exactly how long had I known this guy, would have cruelly reminded me of past errors in judgment—as if there were any connection between the mind of a fourteen year old and the mind of a sixteen year old—would have pressed me about Ben's past, would have wondered, with utmost insensitivity, if he tested positive to the allergy to commitment so common in the male population, would have pointed out that the typical traveler lost in the desert—and what is life if not an unmapped desert?—sees a lot of mirages before finally finding water.

But even if Derek thought such things—and he must have—he was too polite to spoil my moment. He wasn't just an expert at cutting hair.

"There, it's not so short," he said, holding a mirror so I could see the back. "What do you think?"

"I love it! You're a genius!" A pair of bangs fell across my forehead, and the sides curled forward into points just below my ears.

"I think it makes you look older, more mature," Derek said.

Older. I had talked this whole time, but I hadn't told him everything. He deserved to know the full story, and I needed his advice.

He unsnapped the apron and brushed some hair from my collar.

"There's just one tiny flaw in this gem of a romance," I confessed. "Hardly worth mentioning, but since you know everything else . . . He thinks I'm eighteen."

"Why would he think that?"

"Because I told him."

"Oh."

It was the first sound of disapproval Derek had made, and I was quick to explain my reasons. "You see, since he's eighteen himself I thought he might not be interested if he knew I was still in high school. I was able to pass myself off because I look and act so mature, and because I have a fake ID good enough to hang in the Art Institute. With the trauma of having to tell him about Benjamin, I thought my age would just be too much. I'll be eighteen soon enough anyway—when he thinks I'm forty it'll be a pleasant surprise to discover I'm only thirty-eight. He won't feel the need to have an affair with a younger woman."

There wasn't even the sound of scissors to soften the blow of Derek's silence. Only background chatter from the other customers. I watched him in the mirror trying not to show his disapproval. "You think I should tell him, don't you? But what if he bolts? Everything is so perfect, how can I risk it all on a technicality? You aren't saying anything. I want the truth."

"I think you just answered the question yourself," Derek said, hiding his scissors in a drawer as if they were evidence of a crime. "If you want the truth, why wouldn't he?"

Venus Gets the Boot

The following Friday Ben came for me like a knight in a black BMW. I was waiting outside and he almost didn't recognize me.

"It's me, Christy, remember?" I said, getting in.

"I don't know. You look different. New earrings?"

"Very funny." I checked the seat adjustments, they hadn't been changed. It was becoming my seat. "Has anyone ridden in this car since me?"

"No. Why?"

"Just wondering."

He leaned over to kiss me at a light. "So?" I asked. "Aren't you going to say anything?"

"About what?"

"You don't like it." I wanted to cry. "I just thought it would be cool for summer."

"Then why don't you just wear an ice pack on your head?"

Now I did begin to cry.

"Hey, I was only kidding! For someone so sarcastic you sure have a thin skin."

"I'm overwrought, OK? It's all your fault."

He played with my bangs for a moment, like I was an infant or something. "It does make you look more mature."

Aha! If this wasn't the perfect opportunity to tell him my real age, I didn't know what was. But I said nothing because I realized in fact this wasn't the best possible moment but the worst. He was disappointed with me for cutting my hair, and if I revealed my age he might order me out of the car and transfer to the Ivy League, where the girls are more predictable.

"I just loved your hair," he said.

"It's still my hair," I reminded him.

"I mean, it's a nice cut. It looks cute. You just should have asked me, Christy."

"Oh right. Like you'd ask me before you cut your hair."

"I would."

Really? Most married couples don't consult each other when it comes to their hair. We were bonded to the core. I took his hand. "From now on my follicles are your follicles."

He parked in an Evanston shopping center. I looked around for a restaurant but he led me into the supermarket. I had no idea what his plans were.

"What do you like to eat?" he asked.

"You're going to cook? You can cook?"

"A little."

"Not even my girlfriends can cook!" I realized I would finally see his apartment and wondered what it was like as we wandered through the aisles.

"So what should we eat?" Ben asked again.

"I'll leave that up to you."

"How about lobster?"

"I can eat lobster."

We went to the seafood counter and picked out two lobsters. Actually Ben picked them out since I can't eat anything I've seen alive—I won't even pick an apple off a tree. Then he got some butter and garlic and corn and zucchini. By this time my stomach was growling and I succumbed to my culinary impulses—more Herman Munster than Julia Child—and began loading the cart: Chips Ahoy, Pringles, Dr. Pepper, and so on. Ben encouraged me, letting me get whatever I wanted, but by the time we stood in line at the register I remembered he'd only invited me for dinner and we had enough groceries to feed the Bears for training camp. Besides, Chips Ahoy wasn't the classiest dessert to eat with lobster, and I knew Ben was trying to impress, so I insisted we take all my stuff back and instead I got Pepperidge Farm Milano cookies—for the snobby name—and Clearly Canadian lemon-flavored water. Yum. I realized my purpose here wasn't to pig out on my favorite foods but to convince Ben I wasn't lower on the evolutionary ladder than the things we were eating. But how could I pass up the *National Enquirer*, which had the headline, "ALIENS ABDUCTED BY RIVAL ALIENS"? At least I bought it with my own money.

Evanston was civilization—laughing children, unleashed dogs, trees without styrofoam cups in their branches, walls without graffiti, windows without bars, parking spaces without cars. Home was a three-story walk-up with a litterless lawn, an unlocked front door, no urine smells on the stairs, and a door that swung open with a turn of a single key. I guess you get used to it.

I was so embarrassed when I saw how clean and organized everything was inside. "You're so neat. I can't believe I let you see *my* room!"

Here was another opportunity to bring up my age. If he knew I was only sixteen he wouldn't hold my messiness against me.

But he said, "I love your room."

"You do?"

"I love any room you're in." And he put his arms around me and we kissed so long I wondered why we bothered going to the supermarket. For my part, I could certainly have waited until breakfast. But he finally let go and turned on the stove.

"Why don't you have a seat in the living room?" he said, filling a pot with water.

"I want to help."

"You can set the table then."

I opened a drawer. Inside were some screw drivers, computer manuals, pens and markers, batteries, and a passport. I was reaching for the passport when he said, "The silverware's over here."

I didn't want to seem to be prying—there would be plenty of time to pry later—so I set the table with loving care and lit two tall white candles. How many guys have candles? Certainly not the ones I've known. Plenty of matches, but not candles.

"Smells good," I said, joining him in the kitchen. The lobsters were in one pot, the corn in another, and Ben was making a salad with his own bare hands. Was this guy perfect?

"What now?" I asked.

"Why don't you wait in the living room. You can put on some music."

I didn't argue, since I hadn't seen the rest of the apartment yet and I wanted to pry. The bedroom door was closed and I wondered if he had Loony Tunes sheets like me. Probably not.

The living room was very uncluttered for a guy's apartment. A glass-topped desk, bookshelves with real books on them, tall CD racks, golf clubs leaning in one corner by the window, my friend the telescope in the other, a stereo, a large-screen TV, blank walls. I glanced at the papers on the desk, careful not to touch anything. But there wasn't anything interesting—an electric bill, some unopened junk mail, a course catalog for Northwestern, and some letters from the admissions office.

I turned my attention to the CDs: Pink Floyd, Smashing Pumpkins, Alice In Chains, Pearl Jam, Cranberries. I looked for something romantic and settled on *Dark Side of the Moon*. Then I went to the bathroom.

I didn't have to go, but I wanted to see the medicine cabinet. Didn't some poet call medicine cabinets the window one to the soul? Maybe not. But they sure did tell you a lot about the body. We'll start with the top shelf, working left to right: Tums, the big bottle—probably bought them after he met me—Alka Seltzer—did he think Tums would be enough?—Tylenol, Coppertone sunscreen. Middle shelf: An empty prescription bottle of something called something mycin from a Dr. Burnami written over a year ago, Visine, Benadryl, cinnamon dental floss, razor blades. Bottom shelf: aftershave, Q-tips, Band-Aids. No herpes medicine, no AZT. Whew.

All this snooping gave me an appetite. By now I was ready to crack open some lobster claws. Ben had everything out on the table and it looked like the best restaurant in town.

He turned off the lights and poured the Clearly Canadian into wine glasses. "To Venus," he said, reaching his glass across the table to mine.

"To Mars," I said back. "To Capricorn and Pisces."

"To the only Christy in my life," he said.

"To the only Ben in mine."

He watched me dig in, as I struggled with the shell—how embarrassing. "Well?" he asked.

"It's delicious!" I said. "I just hope I don't look like Roseanne, I'm suddenly starving."

"Here, let me do it." And he swung his chair over and cracked open my lobster and pulled out the meat with the little lobster fork and dipped it in melted garlic butter and fed me like I really was Venus. I ask you, does it get any better than this?

Maybe it was because everything was so perfect that I felt so guilty. After all, I was enjoying his lavish attention on false pretenses, on—literally—borrowed time.

So I took a swig of lemon water and a deep breath. "Baby," although that was certainly the wrong word to use now, "there's something I have to tell you."

I guess he knew by the robotic tone of my voice that I was referring to serious developments, that I wasn't about to surprise him with a new telescope or something, because his eyes opened all the way and he leaned as far forward as he could, as if I were vanishing. And, actually, two years of my life were about to disappear.

I thought I saw fear in his eyes. I expected disappointment, anger maybe, but not fear. Suddenly my throat was dry. I needed some more water.

"It's him, isn't it?"

Who? I thought. Father time?

"The murderer," Ben said. "I knew he'd come back."

Oh yeah, well maybe there were two things I needed to tell him. Actually, I thought the matter of Benjamin was closed—it had been a week, hadn't it? The uneventful video at the White Hen had been taped over many times. Everyone was still alive. Why make an issue of it?

But if Ben wanted to know—if he wanted to talk about Ben instead of my age—that was fine with me.

"Yeah, he did show up again, but it was over a week ago. I sent him packing."

"I knew it. I knew he'd be trouble!" Ben sat back, crossing his arms.

"He'll always be trouble, but not for us," I said, taking Ben's hand.

"You don't know him."

"And you do? Believe me, he's nothing to be jealous of. I don't care about him. I never really did. Not like I care about you."

"I'm not jealous. I'm worried about your safety."

I laughed. It *was* laughable, wasn't it? "I'm not worth the price of a bullet," I said. "Besides, it would take a whole clip to bring me down, and an elephant gun to finally shut me up, and even in his glory days Benjamin didn't have that kind of firepower."

"It's not funny, Christy," Ben said, waving his lobster fork. Lobster forks aren't very good for driving home points, and I think Ben realized this because he nervously put it down and fumbled with his knife instead. "All the time he's been locked up he's been thinking of you."

"You don't know that."

"He's obviously obsessed. How many letters did he write you?"

"How many letters did I write him? Zero. Zip. Even he isn't that stupid. He knows the score."

"So what did he want last week?"

"Money for cigarettes."

"You can make all the jokes you like, this isn't going to go away."

"What isn't going to go away? Your jealousy? Benjamin is out of my life. I told you, I sent him packing, and he hasn't come back."

But it was obvious Ben wouldn't be satisfied until he heard the full story, so I told him all the insignificant details, leaving out only the part about my having felt just a tiny bit afraid at the time.

"He didn't touch you?" Ben asked, after I was finished.

"No!"

"He didn't threaten you?"

"Of course not. Look, just because he killed a guy, that's no reason to believe he'd ever kill a woman."

Ben thought long and hard about that.

"Don't let this ruin our first lobster dinner," I said. "Look, if he ever comes back I'll break him in half just like this." And I cracked open a lobster leg.

"You have to be careful."

"I've made it to—" And I almost said "sixteen," but I didn't want to tangle up my confessions. So instead I said, "I've made it this far, growing up in the heart of Chicago. I survived the bullet-ridden corridors of Al Capone High. I know how to protect myself. I'm Luke Skywalker with a mace can."

But this didn't seem to reassure Ben, who was gripping his butter knife as if Benjamin was standing behind my chair, pointing a gun at my head. "Promise me if he comes back you'll call the police."

The police? Who ever called the police in this city? Chicagoans expected to settle their differences in a civilized way among themselves and only brought in the police when there were too many bodies piled in the streets for the sanitation crews to cart away. Among my crowd, calling the cops because an old boyfriend was harassing you was like going to a hand surgeon for a hangnail. It just wasn't done. But to ease Ben's death grip on his butter knife, I said I would.

"And promise you'll tell me."

The police *and* you? "How many promises do you want?" I said aloud. "OK," I gave in. "I'll even tell Channel 11 if that will put your mind at rest, but I don't think it'll make the ten o'clock news."

That settled, I felt my stomach growling, and it wasn't from guilt but lust for lobster. My age could wait. One confession per meal was enough, and we were still on the main course.

"So am I going to get fed or what?" I asked, while Ben was still mulling things over.

But he finally traded his butter knife for his lobster fork and we didn't say another word about dangerous liaisons, or anything at all, for the rest of dinner, even through coffee and the Milano cookies, which we shared one by one, from their chocolate tips to the tips of our tongues.

⊙ ⊙ ⊙

I ask you again, does it get any better than this? We were sitting on the edge of the couch, in the glow of candlelight, Fleetwood Mac on the stereo, caressing each other and looking into each other's eyes. If only this moment could be frozen in time, saved like a web page, downloaded at will. If only the inconvenient facts of our lives were unable to interfere with our brief yet eternal contentment.

But someone had to talk eventually. I think human beings could take a lesson from giraffes, who get along quite well without vocal chords. I mean, who ever saw a giraffe at a psychiatrist's office? But destiny plays her cards, and there are jokers as well as kings.

I mean, I wasn't even thinking about my age anymore. It could wait for another day—I didn't want to spoil this night. But then Ben said something that forced my hand. Just when I was feeling royally flushed—and that's as far as I'll go into that kind of descriptiveness—Ben flung a joker into my lap.

"Have you ever been to Blighton Woods?" he asked,

innocently enough. It could have been a purely informational question, like "Have you ever been to Pittsburgh?"

"No."

"Well it's beautiful. There are hills and streams and a lake . . ."

"There's a lake here too." By now I got the buzz of his question and hoped if I stood still it would go away, like a wasp. But I was about to get stung.

"One of my friends has a tent. I thought maybe we could go camping next weekend."

I swallowed hard. "You mean the *whole* weekend?"

"Do you have plans?"

"I have a lot of plans. But maybe we could do a day trip, you know, for the afternoon."

"A day trip?" he said with disgust, like I was proposing a picnic in the city dump. "We can go during the week then. It's not like you have to work."

"Actually, I just got a job at the White Hen. I start Monday."

"Yeah? You didn't tell me. Well what about tomorrow then?"

"Tomorrow?"

"You can stay tonight and we'll swing round Jimmy's and pick up the tent in the morning. And tomorrow night we'll be cooking out our second lobster dinner, surrounded by pine trees and your favorite stars."

He kissed me. Would it be our last kiss? What was I supposed to say, that I wasn't even old enough to crawl into a tent without parental supervision? That my mom wouldn't let me spend a weekend in the woods with the archbishop of Chicago let alone a boyfriend at the exact age of his sexual peak? Yes, my parents adored Ben, there was no question about that, but they had an absolute—and I think overblown—horror of premature grandparenthood.

The kiss ended only when we needed air—and I needed a lot of air. "I haven't been completely honest with you," I mumbled, looking away.

Ben turned on the light, the better to interrogate me with. "What do you mean?" He turned off the stereo. I was on my own.

"I didn't get a job at the White Hen." It was a beginning.

"I didn't think so. But if you don't want to go camping why not just say so? Why lie?"

"To cover up another lie." I slid to the very edge of the couch. Ben was standing in front of the lamp, like a prosecutor. "You see, I'm not eighteen."

Ben stared at me, trying to peel away the years with his eyes.

"My ID's a fake. And I know I'm tall and can pass for eighteen and even older, and I know I'm mature for my age . . ."

"So you're seventeen?"

"I'll be seventeen."

"You're sixteen! You're only sixteen?"

"I've been sixteen for months, I'm almost closer to seventeen. Fifteen is a distant memory."

But I could see Ben wanted to pull the lobster out of my stomach and rewind our whole sordid affair. He was already reading the headlines: ASTRONOMER TURNS TELESCOPE ON TROUBLED TEEN.

But it wasn't that bad, was it?

Apparently it was, because Ben opened the door. "Get out!"

But I clung to him instead, my underage tears staining his shirt.

But it was only more incriminating evidence and he pushed me away. "Go on! Here—here's money for a cab. Now go."

But I couldn't go. I shut the door and stood with my back against it. I knew that if I left I would never see him again, that I had to make him understand now, or everything that had brought us together would explode into unrecognizable pieces. I couldn't give him time to forget me, or to remember me in a different way.

"What was I supposed to do?" I screamed.

"You could have told me the truth."

"I'm telling you now, and see what happens? I knew you'd act this way. But it's not the lie that bothers you, you'd forgive me for that. You probably lie now and then, like most people. I could say I'm sorry and everything would be OK. But I can't do anything about my age."

"You still should have told me Christy."

"And would you have gone out with me?"

Ben wasn't so angry anymore, at least not with me.

The initial shock had passed and he was wrestling with his own feelings. Instead of just me confessing, he was confessing as well.

"Probably not," he admitted.

"See! Can you understand now? I loved you from that first day! I thought about you in the exam office and came back out in my puke-green gown to talk to you some more and when I saw you weren't there I was crushed. I tried to downplay everything, but there's no denying it now. When you walked into the bike shop I could have peed in my pants. And the agonizing sleepless nights I spent when I thought I'd driven you away, when it seemed not meant to be . . ."

"Well it isn't meant to be."

"How can you say that after what we've been through? I've never loved anyone like you, and I never will again."

"You don't know that. You're only sixteen."

"I do know. Besides, women lie about their age all the time," I said, wiping my eyes. "It's like wearing false eyelashes or padded bras."

"But you're not a woman. You're a girl."

"Juliet was only thirteen. And I'm a long way from thirteen."

"You're still a minor."

"So what? You're only eighteen. You can't even buy beer. It's not like you're sixty and I'm fifteen. It isn't fair of you to treat me all of a sudden like I'm a kid when you used to treat me like a woman. I'm sure when you were sixteen you had older girlfriends or wanted older girls. Maybe your first Christy was two years older than *you*."

"I couldn't get college girls when I was sixteen," Ben said, beginning to soften.

"Maybe you should have lied about *your* age! But it's their loss, all those college girls."

I took him firmly by the shoulders and led him back to the couch. I was no longer crying and felt like I still had an ace or two to play. I turned out the light and ran my fingers through his hair.

"Why don't we forget all the shouting and crying and solve this problem like the two mature people we are?" And I kissed him lightly on the lips, and then not so lightly.

"But you're sixteen," he said feebly, like the melting words of the wicked witch. He was mine again—judgment for the defense.

"You're a minor. What about the law?"

"I'm sure it's just a misdemeanor," I said, handcuffing him with my long fingers.

Danger Wears a White Sox Hat

Well that was a close call. But I wasn't out of the woods yet—except for Blighton Woods. Ben didn't bring *that* subject up again. And he didn't ask me to spend the night—no surprise there. But he didn't have to blow out the candles at midnight! I mean, it was Friday night, and I was sixteen, not six. I was hungry again. It would have been nice if he offered me a snack, and we could eat on the floor while watching a horror flick on cable. But he didn't want my mom to worry. As if my mom hadn't made a career out of making *her* mother worry.

Or maybe he was having second thoughts, I thought on the long ride home. I was getting paranoid. Tonight had been so special, the second most wonderful night of my life after our night stargazing, and it was only natural to feel a letdown now that it was coming to a close.

"You don't have to take me home so early," I said, playing with the sunroof.

But it was beginning to drizzle and Ben closed it again. "Your mom said you have a one o'clock curfew."

"I told you she was joking! Besides, that was last week. I'll bring written permission next time," I said, praying there would be a next time. "I hope you're not going to start treating me differently now. I don't want anything to change. I don't have any other secrets. And I've been honest about everything else. I hope you're not worried about the law thing."

"A little," Ben admitted. "I don't want to be your second boyfriend to go to jail. I think I'll call my lawyer Monday."

"You have your own lawyer? I don't know whether to be impressed or worried."

"I mean my father's lawyer. I'll ask him what the consent laws say."

"Well I'm sure they say go for it, have a good time. I mean, in this town they don't even prosecute bicycle thieves. They're not going to come after you."

"I guess not. If your parents objected it would be different. But they seem to like me, and they know I'm eighteen. And I assume they know your correct age?"

"I think they think I'm ten, the way they treat me."

"I think you want all the privileges that come with being older without any of the responsibilities. You really should treat your parents better. You're very lucky."

"I treat them well enough. You don't know what goes on—they were on their best behavior with you. And talk about responsibilities, yeah, maybe it was true a year ago, but I think I've gotten my act together remarkably. I mean, how many girls my age don't smoke cigarettes? I'm the only one I know. I don't even smoke pot. And I haven't cut class since going to the Academy."

"And how many *A*s did you get last year?" Ben asked, turning on the windshield wipers.

"One, in Phys Ed. I have a wicked smash in volleyball. And this year I'm going to play on the basketball team— the Lady Tigers. Why don't they just call us the Tigresses?"

"And how many *F*s did you get?"

"Zero, zip, after the first quarter."

"And how many *Ds?*"

"Did I mention I got an *A* in Phys Ed?"

"That's what I mean," Ben said. "Bright as you are, you should be on the honor roll."

"I was on the honor roll when I was thirteen."

"So what happened?"

What happened was Benjamin, but I wasn't about to

bring that up. "How come we didn't have this conversation when you thought I was eighteen?"

"I don't know, it never really came up. And I thought you had just graduated and just wanted to chill for a while. Like you said, take a year to travel. But now you might not graduate at all, or your grades won't be high enough to get into a good college."

"Well maybe I don't want to go to college," I said defiantly. The rain had stopped again and I opened the sunroof back up. If only I could be a giraffe poking my head through the roof, unable to reply.

"Then what are you going to do?"

"I could be a flavor taster for Wrigley's," I said, opening a stick of gum. "Want a piece?"

"I know what it's like, Christy."

"Sure."

"I didn't apply to Northwestern until the last minute."

"You got in, didn't you?"

"I almost dropped out of high school."

"Right."

"I had to make up classes one summer."

"Yeah? What was that about?"

It started to rain again, but Ben didn't close the sunroof, he was concentrating on the road, or maybe on that summer. I closed the sunroof myself.

"So why did you want to drop out?" I asked. "I can't imagine you getting bad grades."

"It's not important." And he took my hand. "I've never

known anyone like you, sixteen or eighteen or eighty. You're so full of life, I don't want life to let you down."

Gosh! What could I say to that? The argument had ended as suddenly as it had begun. I didn't think for a moment he was kind of talking about himself, in that last statement, as well as me.

Miracle of miracles—he found a parking space across from my house, although he could have let me open the gate and pulled into the driveway or just dropped me off and said goodbye. But Jedi Knight that he was, he had to open my door and escort me safely home.

Which, on this night, was easier said than done. I could have thrown a volleyball from his car to my front porch, but in that short space lurked a whole galaxy of danger. Benjamin Vader himself, wearing a White Sox hat instead of a mask, stood leaning against a lamppost outside my gate, awaiting my arrival.

I saw him first, but my gasp alerted him. What was I going to do anyway, with him standing outside my house like a troll?

Ben was holding my hand and was the last to realize what was going on. Everything developed pretty fast after that. Benjamin rushed over to me, out of the lamplight, staring at me like a madman, as if Ben didn't even exist.

"There you are!" he shouted.

"Get away," I said calmly, stepping back, like I was dealing with a dog that might bite, but might also run away if not provoked.

"I've been waiting all night," he said, stepping closer, too close.

"You have no right to be here! I could call the police."

"I just want to talk to you."

"I have nothing to say."

He grabbed my arm, then Ben grabbed his arm. "You heard what she said!"

For the first time Benjamin looked at Ben. And even though Ben was much taller, and probably just as angry as Benjamin was jealous, Benjamin had the edge when it came to violent altercations. He pushed Ben with both hands and Ben lost his balance and fell.

Without even thinking I reached into my purse and grabbed my mace. At that moment Benjamin looked back at me and I sprayed twice. The first spray was a complete miss, but I think Benjamin was so surprised that I sprayed him that he didn't move, and the second spray got him in the eyes, at least enough to make him scream and spin around.

My hand was shaking so much it would have been difficult to aim a third spray, but fortunately Benjamin stumbled away.

"Are you all right?" I asked Ben, who looked like he wanted to chase Benjamin down.

I dropped the mace back into my purse and put my arms around him.

"We should call the police," he said.

"It's better if you go home," I answered. "I'll take care

of it." I kissed him. "You've given me such a perfect night, not even Benjamin can ruin it."

He waited until I had unlocked the gate and then locked it on the other side. "I love you," I whispered through the wrought iron.

He reached his hand through for a final squeeze.

Inside my house, I waited by the door until I heard the sound of his car driving away. My heart was pounding from the shock of Benjamin's appearance, but I didn't feel frightened for myself. Ben was the one who was probably more in danger—from Benjamin's jealousy, and his own anger. I had never seen Ben enraged like that before. Although he certainly had cause.

"Did you get caught in the rain?" my mom asked, still awake of course. Dad, exhausted from another long day losing other people's money, was snoring on the couch.

"It's only a drizzle," I said, sitting down in the kitchen.

"Do you want some coffee?"

"Sure," I said, looking at the leftovers in the refrigerator.

"Didn't you eat?"

"I've never eaten better," I said.

My mom poured the coffee and gave me one of her "tell me all" looks. And why not—it was a night worth remembering, and I couldn't very well wait until my next haircut, could I?

So I told her everything. Or almost everything. And then I realized I had forgotten to tell her the most important thing. "You'll be so proud of me," I said. "I confessed to my age."

"Oh Christina, I'm so relieved! It was the mature thing to do, he would have found out eventually, and now you can build your relationship on trust. I told you he would understand."

"But he didn't understand. He tried to throw me out!"

"But he changed his mind, didn't he?"

"No, I barred the door!"

And our laughter cast a warm glow over all that had happened that night, except for the unpleasant run-in with Benjamin, which our laughter obliterated.

Bonding With the Big Guy

I was in the middle of a horrible nightmare in which the new school year was beginning and the bell had just rung and I was sitting at my desk without any books or paper while the teacher passed out a pop quiz. Then the bell turned into knocking and I was awakened by my mom's melodious voice. It took me a few seconds to realize it was still only July.

"Christina, Ben is here!"

Ben? Wow. Usually it was the other way around—it was the dream that was wonderful and life that sucked. I looked at my clock—it was only ten. And it was Monday. What was going on?

I got dressed at lightning speed, washed, and ran a brush through my shortened hair. When I reached the living room I thought I must be dreaming. My lounging mom was real enough, but Ben was dressed for success—jacket and tie, loafers, hair in a ponytail, even his earring was gone. He looked great—like he'd stepped out of *GQ*. But I was suspicious.

"Who died?"

"Christina, don't be rude," my mom said. "Ben has come to take you shopping." And she winked at him. I was always the last to know.

"What's in the bag?" I asked, noticing a plastic bag on the couch.

"A pair of stockings and my black high heels," my mom said.

I looked at Ben in confusion. You think you know someone!

"Don't ask questions," he said, taking my hand in one hand and the bag in the other.

"I'm volunteering at the Wellness Fair," my mom said, "so you're on your own for dinner. Have a good day, and good luck," she said, with another wink at Ben.

I didn't like the look of this at all. I should have been happy Ben had come to see me, that he hadn't decided to dump me after the other night. But as I got in his car—the seat was right where I had left it—my paranoid sense won out and I began to panic. What if he was getting his revenge for the other night and I was about to be sacrificed in some unspeakable ritual? A satanic slaughter of under-age girls. He could have told my mom anything. Shopping, right. How well did I know this guy?

"Where are we going?" I demanded. "And why are you dressed like a maitre d'?"

"You'll find out soon enough."

"And what's the deal with my mom's clothes? It looks pretty sick to me."

He didn't confirm or deny. I know it sounds stupid, but I started to really panic. I hadn't even read my horo-scope. I gripped the door handle, and when we stopped at the next light I almost bolted—I mean, the Channel 11 Crimebeat shows more young bodies than a Spice Girls video and most of them are dead. Had I merely traded one jealous homicidal boyfriend for another? I was beginning to think so. He was going to take me to some deserted woods and make me wear my mom's shoes as punishment for trying to pass as an adult. And then he would strangle me with the stockings. But he didn't have to dress up to murder me. And why would he take out his earring?

The light turned green and I realized I was just being paranoid. We weren't going toward Evanston but down-town. "Can we stop for a paper?" I asked.

"A paper?"

"I didn't have a chance to read my horoscope. Some people can't start their day without that first cup of coffee. Well, I have to read my first horoscope."

"A major transformation could be in store for you today, including unforeseen commitments and the strengthening of old relationships."

And I realized that was his game. He wasn't going to take his revenge by killing me—how much pleasure could he get from that?—but by the far more sadistic torture of publicly embarrassing me. Didn't he already have my mom in on the act? She would be all too willing to see me put in my place. He would take me to some fashionable bar, where the dress code required heels and stockings, and the media as well as the cops would be there. And I would be arrested on the spot for my false ID. The thought of being embarrassingly devastated was worse than being murdered.

But he was taking me shopping after all, just like my mom said. And to Saks!

"See anything you like?" he asked, leading me by the hand through racks of skirts and dresses.

"Everything and nothing. I mean, it's all nice, but it's not my style. Besides, it's a little beyond my budget."

"You're not paying."

"Then take me to Rita's Future Shock Boutique. There's a blue vinyl mini I'm dying for."

"Not exactly what I had in mind."

And when the saleswoman came over he said we were looking for a casual business dress for summer.

"We are looking for a blue vinyl mini with black rubber buttons," I corrected.

But they were already deep in the racks, fingering silk and polyester. "I think this salmon dress would look stunning on her," the saleswoman said, as if I weren't there.

"Salmon," Ben said, dangling it in front of me. "It's very Piscean."

"Then you wear it!

"Why don't you try it on?"

"What do I want with a business dress? I'm not in business."

"Not yet. We have a job interview."

"Job interview? We? Don't you know I'm a member of the leisure class?"

"Humor me."

"If I agreed to wear this, I wouldn't wear it to a job interview!" I shouted, ignoring the saleswoman, as she had ignored me.

"I just thought I'd get a summer job, and this would be a way for us to see more of each other."

He started to walk away.

"Well why didn't you say that to begin with?" And I reeled in the salmon dress, with a glance at the price tag. "What kind of job is it?"

"Does it matter?"

"I guess not. But I'll never be able to pay you back. This dress costs more than my bicycle!"

"You don't have to pay me back."

"But it makes no sense. How much money am I going to make with my lack of experience and skills? Certainly not enough to justify my new wardrobe."

"That's not the point," Ben said.

I thought about this, dangling the dress by the hanger, thinking about salmon and Piscean waters. "Couldn't we be lifeguards or something?"

⊙ ⊙ ⊙

Scrutinizing myself in the mirror—heels, stockings, salmon dress, shortened hair—I had to admit whoever was standing there didn't look too bad. It certainly wasn't me. It wasn't like looking into a mirror at all, but through a doorway.

"I'll wear it out," I told the saleswoman, letting her cut the tags while Ben took out his gold card. "I guess I should thank you," I told Ben, giving him a quick kiss on the cheek. "But I don't know how much this is going to cost me."

I thought once we got back in the car he would finally tell me where we were going and what kind of job it was and what I was supposed to say. But he started talking about a completely unrelated subject.

"Did he ever come back?"

"Who?" I was so absorbed with my new identity and the looming loss of my freedom I honestly had no idea what he was talking about.

"Who do you think?" The edge to his voice left no doubt who he meant.

"No, of course not. He's not that stupid. If he didn't know the score before Friday night, I'm positive he knows now."

"What did the police say?"

"They said they only get involved if blood is flowing."

"You didn't call them, did you?"

"No."

"You didn't tell your parents."

"I don't want to worry them."

"You worry them all the time."

"But this is serious."

"I know. That's what I'm trying to tell you."

"You shouldn't have confronted him like that."

"Me? He was grabbing your arm. What did you expect me to do? You're lucky I didn't kill him."

"You couldn't hurt an ant. I had the whole situation under control. Remember, I'm bigger than he is. You're the one who could have gotten hurt. You shouldn't have intervened."

"Yeah, it's all my fault! Blame the victim."

"I'm not blaming you. I'm just saying you have no experience with punks. You come from Evanston, you don't know how to deal with the Benjamins of the world."

"Me? You're the one who panicked, spraying him with mace! What if he had a gun?"

"Well he wouldn't have been able to aim it, would he? Besides he was in too much agony to pull a trigger. Did you see the way he staggered around, trying to wash his eyes with the rain!"

I began to laugh, not so much because it was funny, but because it was easier to think of the scene as comic than as dangerous. And Ben laughed too.

"Did you see the surprise on his face?" he said.

"His maced face! He's probably cursing the day he ever met me. *He* probably called the police!" And I laughed some more.

"Promise me, though, from now on you'll let me fight my own fights," Ben said, serious again.

"I promise. But this wasn't your fight."

⊙ ⊙ ⊙

"What's in the bag?" I asked, when Ben took a slim briefcase from his trunk.

"My resume."

"Can I see it?"

He took it out and I read it while we walked. "Wow! Pretty impressive. Want to see my resume?" And I handed the paper back with the blank side faceup.

He took me to the Hancock Building. The Hancock Building! "The interview's here?" I asked. "Hey, maybe we can stop by my dad's on the way out. I told you he worked here."

But when he pressed the button for the forty-third floor my heart stopped. "Oh, no you don't!"

He had to drag me out of the elevator. "I don't like practical jokes," I said.

He looked at me in the hallway, like I was a horse he had just bet on. "Give me your gum, please."

"But I need my gum!"

He made me spit it in the ashtray. Then he straightened my dress. "You look wonderful."

"I'll be glad to wait out here."

He pulled me inside, through the big room with partitioned desks crowded with brokers busy redistributing the wealth in their favor, into the office with my dad's name on it. Sophie, his secretary, didn't recognize me.

"Christy, I can't believe it's you! You look so different. It's been a long time, what's new with you, where are you going to school? When did you cut your hair?" And so on, and so on.

Ben had made the appointment, but only for himself, as I later found out. So when my dad looked up from his desk and saw me, he wasn't just shocked that I was wearing a dress, he was shocked I was there at all. If he hadn't been on the phone at the time I think he would have screamed. He looked at me like he'd never seen me before, and, well, he'd certainly never seen me like this before.

I hadn't been in his office for months and the first thing I always did was walk behind the desk and gaze out the window at the spectacular view of Lake Michigan. But Ben grabbed my hand and I was forced to sit down beside him.

My dad kept staring at me while he was talking on the phone, as if I didn't feel uncomfortable enough already!

"But I don't know anything about the stock market!" I whispered to Ben.

"Don't worry. Just relax."

"How can I relax? You won't even let me look out the window."

My dad finally got off the phone and stood up to shake Ben's hand. He didn't try to shake my hand, thank God—can you imagine that? It didn't make things any easier to know that he felt as awkward about the whole situation as I did. The only difference was that he was pleasantly surprised, while I was just surprised.

"Can I get you something to drink?"

"No thanks," Ben answered.

"I'll take a vodka martini," I said.

We all sat down, my dad leaning forward, trying to focus on Ben but unable to keep his eyes from straying to me.

"So, I understand you'd like to intern with the firm?" Apparently, this was all Ben had told my father when making the appointment, along with asking him not to say anything to me. Sneaky boy, my Ben, although he probably told my mom everything this morning, which would explain the winks.

"We both would," Ben answered.

"You both?" And my dad turned to me with a look of complete shock, even greater than when my mom had thrown him a surprise fiftieth birthday party and a stripper lassoed him with her feather boa.

"Here's my resume," Ben said, very professionally, like he'd never met my dad before, like he wasn't dating his daughter and had never been to his house and they'd never smoked cigars together. I must admit, I was pretty impressed by the performance. If this was what the business world was like, then there was a lot more room for imagination and acting than I thought. "And here's my high school transcript, and an acceptance letter from Northwestern, and a reference from the planetarium."

"You worked at the planetarium?" my dad asked, looking through all this evidence of Ben's brilliance.

"I volunteered last summer."

My dad handed the papers back, obviously satisfied. I suddenly felt naked. He knew my qualifications all too well. "May I ask why you want to work at a brokerage firm?"

"I've always been interested in the market," Ben said. "And I'd like to have some experience in business, even though my main interest is science. I'm pretty good in math, and I've used word processing and spreadsheet programs. Christy also has some computer experience. And she has her own bike to run errands with. We're both willing to do whatever's needed."

My dad looked at me, not to ask any questions, but I think just to make sure I was still there. I knew Ben wanted me to act professionally, but I couldn't help but smile. My dad was speechless. I even thought I saw a tear in the old boy's eye.

⊙ ⊙ ⊙

We started then and there. The boss found us a couple empty cubicles in the corner with desks and chairs and promised to get us phones and terminals by tomorrow, although I probably wouldn't be trusted with any computer work.

"Can't we get a view of the lake?" I asked.

The boss then showed us around. He could have let Sophie do it, but he gave us a personal tour, a sign, I thought, of Ben's influence with the Big Guy. There were offices I'd never seen before, and new partners. Everyone smiled politely when we were introduced as new interns, and more than necessary when the word "daughter" crept out of their boss's mouth. From then on I was treated with special attention, like a sacred object. Even the partners looked at me in a way that said, "Just knock if you ever need to borrow the key to the executive washroom."

Ben was more or less overlooked in these introductions, except by the young female members of the firm, who were already stealing him away from me with their MBA eyes. Fortunately, there was plenty of work to be done—everyone acted like we were on the verge of nuclear war, yelling orders and running for phones—so there wouldn't be a lot of time for infidelity by the water cooler.

The Big Guy promised to put us on the payroll, although Ben—a better astronomer than negotiator—said we'd be happy to volunteer our services. "Speak for yourself," I told him. "I want a package that includes stock options."

"I'll be glad to give you options when you know what they are," the Big Guy said, calling my bluff. "Now you'll work a forty-hour week, but we're not going to keep you on a time clock. You get an hour for lunch, and when I don't have a lunch meeting you're welcome to dine in style with me at the hotdog vendors in the park. You'll get your assignments from either me or my partners, and you'll be doing mostly clerical work until we can train you for anything else."

"I need to be trained for clerical work," I pointed out, popping a stick of gum in my mouth.

"And Ben," the Big Guy said, putting a fatherly hand on his shoulder, "my door is always open to you."

"What about me?"

"By the way, Miss Marlowe, I should remind you this is a gum-free building."

What a character, the Big Guy! Someone might think we were related.

⊙ ⊙ ⊙

I lost my labor virginity in the filing room, sorting piles of paid bills, which I learned in the business world are called invoices. It wasn't long before I remembered why I hadn't joined the labor force before. I had been lucky to have liberal parents who believed I should develop at my own speed, which happened to be SP with frequent pauses. Yesterday I would have laughed if anyone had suggested I would willingly be filing invoices in my dad's office, which, of course, was why Ben had kept his bold plan secret. It was unthinkable that I would be trading my precious summer freedom, sleep time and cycle time, to do drudge work for a few pitiful dollars. But, truth to tell, I was as happy as a clerical clam because Ben was nearby, or within view, or even beside me. At the end of my first day as a breadwinner, as Ben and I rode the elevator back down to civilian life, I squeezed his hand like we had just left the movies.

⊙ ⊙ ⊙

No one was home when Ben dropped me off, which was just as well, because I was beat. Filing takes a lot out of you, and I had been awakened earlier than normal. So I took a nap until my mom woke me up, brimming with excitement. She had to hear everything immediately, and it wasn't enough to show her the dress. I had to put it back on. At the end of my story she hugged me and cried.

"Ma, my dress!" I said, backing away. "I only filed a few papers, it's not like I graduated med school!"

And then my father came home after a late meeting and she had to hear it all again from his point of view, which he told in as few words as possible. But he was grinning the whole time, and close to tears himself. I never thought a girl's first day in the office could be so dramatic, but I guess it's like someone in a wheelchair taking a step.

"That Ben is something else," my dad said in conclusion.

"And what's he doing with me, right?"

But my dad gave me a surprise compliment. "You were very professional today," he said.

Now tears were welling in my own eyes. There were good-night kisses all round. "I don't know where all this functionality will lead," I warned.

⊙ ⊙ ⊙

The next day—my first full day on the brokerage payroll—the Big Guy took us to lunch. We sat at a concrete table in Lincoln Park, in the shadow of the Hancock Building, dining on chili dogs and sodas with straws. "Is this where you take all your important clients?" I asked.

"Only when I particularly want to impress someone," my dad answered, loosening his tie. "Who needs table cloths and wine lists when you can watch the sailboats on the lake and let the cool breeze blow through what's left of your hair?"

And you wonder where I get it from?

"And we've had so few clear days this summer. It's a shame not to take advantage of it." He wiped some mustard from his chin. "How do you like the firm so far?" he asked.

"Everyone's been very nice," I said. "But the work's kind of boring. How about installing a sound system?"

"She's worked here one day and she's ready for management," my dad said to Ben.

"And I could really improve on the decorating. The main office doesn't have any interesting pictures on the walls. And all the business mags on the tables. I know it's a brokerage company, but a *Rolling Stone* or two wouldn't devastate you."

My dad smiled. "Anything else?"

"Well, everyone seems stressed to the limit. You might want to consider a couple meditation periods."

Ben laughed. But my dad said, in a serious voice, "You know, some companies actually do that."

"She'll be on the CEO track any day!" Ben said.

"Cool. I'll be expecting a raise."

"No raises for relatives."

"By the way, I was wondering, what should I call you?"

"What do you usually call me?"

"No, Dad just won't do. I mean, we're all professionals here. Do you have a nickname, like JM or Chief? How about Big Guy?"

"Sir will be fine," my dad said, throwing the rest of his bun to the seagulls.

☉ ☉ ☉

I never did get a computer and phone for my desk, and my assignments rarely came from my dad or the other partners but from the overworked secretaries who were glad for some extra water cooler time. By the end of the first week I knew every shelf in the office, and every unlocked drawer at the secretaries' stations, which I pried through when I covered the phones.

Ben was given a computer and spent most of the day in his corner doing God knows what. When he tried to explain it to me I just got a headache, but he found it interesting and, after all, that's what was important.

What was more important was that he was always within kissing distance. Throughout the day I'd blow him kisses through glass doors or sneak up on him when he was staring at rows of numbers. Once I even groped him in a crowded elevator after work. It's true what they say about secretaries. Spinning in their chairs all day, all that pent up passion.

Overall, though, I behaved with utter professionalism—not too loud, no bubble blowing, sir and ma'am, no cursing on the phone. I couldn't wear the salmon dress every day, of course, and with my first paycheck bought my own black heels, corporate skirts, slacks, and blouses at Field's. I tried not to embarrass my dad, or Ben for that matter, and restrained myself at the water cooler during clerical gossip sessions, where, by the way, I would have learned all I needed to know about male treachery if I didn't know it already.

I knew I would enjoy spending the whole day near Ben—after all, that was why I'd agreed to his scheme in the first place. But an unforeseen advantage of working for my father was the thrill of seeing him in action—the lion in his den. I was proud of him, truth to tell, watching the way he calmly gave orders, all the people who called him sir, the rich-looking old clients in dark suits who patted his shoulder like he was their nephew. He flew through the place like a bat, with a cell phone, or a stack of papers, or a staff member trying to keep pace—a far cry from the couch potato I knew and loved. After a few days watching him like this I realized it would now be hard to keep treating him like my personal servant at home. Not impossible, just hard.

⊙ ⊙ ⊙

The best days were when I got to run errands. I'd ride my bike downtown and speed through traffic delivering critical letters to wheelers and dealers. I was free, outdoors, and had an urgent purpose at the same time. Important people were depending on me not to scatter their portfolios to the wind. And Ben was always there when I got back.

And on the days I didn't run errands I'd gulp down an espresso and skim my horoscope as I heard the most wonderful horn in the world—my horn—and Ben would be waiting outside, engine running, seat always where I'd left it the night before. Always. And after a magical day filing kisses and I love yous and looking into each other's eyes over hotdogs or pizza, we'd spend most of the night together, eating at his house, or mine, going to movies or concerts, renting videos, talking for hours about nothing at all. I never got tired of him. He never got tired of me.

It was too good to be true. But it was true to the core.

And everyone lived happily ever after.

Finito Benito.

End of story.

part two

Ominous Skies

It was another cloudy day. Storms were in the forecast and my horoscope said, "Today you'll be murdered—wear black." But why should I pay attention to these warning signs when everything was going so well and I was so happy? I mean, I was getting up in the morning without having to push the snooze button once! And at night I lay awake in something like a trance state—perfectly contented, but too wired to sleep because I couldn't wait for tomorrow, when Ben's horn would call me and we'd ride into the city for another perfect day.

I should have known things were turning ominous when I found mousy Miranda sniffing around my doorstep. It was Saturday. My dad and Ben—those inseparable office buddies—had gone to play golf, and I had just come back from working out at Bally's with my mom. I gave Miranda a big hug, and why not? After all, she was my best friend.

"Where have you been girl?" I asked.

"Me? You're the one who's gone AWOL. You're never here when I call."

"I've been working. I'm climbing the corporate ladder."

"So your mom says. And what about after work? And weekends? You're spending every minute with your crush," she said, lighting a cigarette. "I hope you'll at least invite me to the wedding."

"If I ever get married you can be my maid of honor. And I'll make you buy the ugliest dress in Chicago!"

"I like your hair," she said, as if she only just noticed. "You've changed a lot."

"There's a lot that needed changing."

"Think I should cut my hair?"

"Sure, and you could use a nose job too."

"I only asked about my hair! It's nice to know some things haven't changed. Well, are you going to invite me in, or is your fiancé hiding under the covers?"

I crushed out her cigarette and led her into the inner sanctum.

"So what's new with you?" I asked, closing the door.

"Is this him?" Miranda asked, picking up a framed photo of Ben from my night table. "He's cute! So when am I going to meet him?"

"I don't know. He doesn't like to hang out with sixteen year olds."

"What about you? Or doesn't he know your age?"

"Of course he knows. I wouldn't build a relationship on lies."

"What are his friends like? Any major prospects?"

"I don't really know his friends, we don't like to crowd the scene, if you know what I mean." I took the picture out of her hands and set it back on the table. She was holding onto it the way she had been holding onto her cigarette outside and I didn't want her to form a new addiction.

"Besides," I said, "you're not in the hunt."

"Yes I am. Mike and I broke up last night." She slumped down on the bed and took out another cigarette, just for something to hang on to.

"Oh yeah?" I sat down next to her, we were two females, after all. And no matter how much I loved Ben, it was a point of honor among all women of the world never to forget that the battle of the sexes—although there may be a truce in your own camp—was still a battle, and the walking had to carry the wounded.

"So what happened?"

"I was the one who ended it," Miranda admitted. "For one thing, he was doing too many drugs."

Everyone has standards, I thought.

And for the next two hours it was the Miranda Calipano show, with brief appearances by your host to offer comfort and consolation, and tissues for her tears. Actually, Mike hardly deserved tears and a two-hour monologue. It scared me to think of the state she'd be in if *he* had dumped *her!* In any case, I'm sure he wasn't talking about it all afternoon with *his* pals. But girls are fragile creatures, and anyway, what's worse, to bawl for two hours or to keep it all inside and one day take a rifle to a shopping center?

Still, I could have given her a better shoulder to cry on. Not that I think she noticed, but I kept squirming around and even put my hand on the doorknob a couple times—a hint she didn't even see. I just couldn't pay attention. My mind kept drifting to more interesting things because, truth to tell, after being with Ben it was hard to be around people who weren't as mature and sophisticated. Ben might talk for two hours but he had interesting things to say—he didn't make the same obvious points over and over again, like Miranda. He wasn't self-absorbed.

Of course, this was a traumatic time for Miranda. But there's trauma and there's *trauma*. It's not like they were in love or anything. It's not like they were on the same planet as me and Ben. How many boyfriends had Miranda had? At least four since I first met her when I transferred. Not even a whole year! Did it have to be a soap opera every time?

Still, I guess I was a little self-absorbed too. I mean, when you're miserable yourself or just slogging through life it's nice to have friends like Miranda. But when you're as happy as I was—when you're breathing in bliss every moment so it's just another invisible particle in the air, like dust mites, other people's suffering is like smog and you just want to blow it away. It's like if I went to a smoke-filled club I wouldn't even notice the haze, but if Miranda lit up in my room I'd immediately open the window and turn on the fan. I tried to sympathize, but it was sympathy at a distance, like the light from a star. Because it's hard to feel another person's loneliness when you're no longer alone yourself.

But, thankfully, Miranda didn't notice. She began scooping up unsmoked flakes of tobacco that had spilled on the bed. "You're a true friend," she said, as if I didn't feel bad enough. "You want to go dancing tonight?"

"I'm supposed to see Ben."

"Oh. And three's a crowd."

She looked so pathetic. What would it hurt to bring her along? But some urges are meant to be suppressed and I kept my silence.

Miranda was looking at the photo. "I'm glad you're in love again."

"Again!"

"Oh yeah, that reminds me. With all that's been going on I completely forgot. Benjamin stopped by the other day."

Now it was my turn for comfort and consolation. "Benjamin! He stopped by where?"

"My house. He came to my house."

"Your house? But he doesn't even know you!"

"You had him send his letters from jail to my address, remember?"

"Oh shit!" Well I sure was paying attention now, standing over her as she continued to finger the photo of Ben. "Why didn't you tell me?"

"You're never home! Besides, it was just a couple days ago. You could have told me he was out."

"You didn't say anything to my mom?"

"Doesn't she know either? He sure doesn't look like a murderer."

"What did you expect, fangs? How do murderers look?"

"Well, he was so shy, and he seemed nice enough. And not bad looking. Though you've definitely stepped up in the world," she said, staring at the photograph of the law-abiding Ben.

I waited while Miranda stared. "So! What did he want? Did he threaten you?"

"No, I told you he was nice. He said you wouldn't talk to him, so he wanted me to give you a message. He said he forgives you for what happened."

"*He* forgives *me!* What nerve!"

"Why? What happened?"

"I beat him arm wrestling. How embarrassing!"

"Well, he says his feelings haven't changed. And that he's moved uptown, and has a job."

"Everyone's getting jobs! It's an employment epidemic!"

Miranda was looking at me closely now, as if trying

to look through me. "He said his name was tattooed over your heart," she whispered.

"He told you!" I screamed. "I'll kill him! *I'll* kill *him*!"

"Then it's true?'

"Of course it's not true! Are you stupid? Do you think I'd ever sink so low to get an illiterate punk's name tattooed for eternity on my breast? The same breast that one day might feed an innocent baby?"

"I . . . I didn't know."

I could see she was still uncertain, so I angrily pulled up my halter. Here! Look for yourself if you don't believe me!" I'd had my second treatment and the ink was only visible on close inspection under bright light. The letters themselves were gone, and Dr. Dobrowski promised me in a few weeks even these last traces of my youthful folly would vanish.

I quickly lowered my top.

"I didn't say I didn't believe you," Miranda said. "What do I do if he comes back?"

"Ask him out. You have my blessings."

"Right. Then I'd really never see you again!"

⊙ ⊙ ⊙

It was raining by the time the boys came home but they weren't very wet. "We were lucky," Ben said, giving me a quick kiss. "The rain didn't come until the seventeenth hole."

"Who won?"

"Fortunately I don't gamble on the weekends," my dad said. "Where's your mother?"

"She's dining with the homeless tonight. I hope you don't mind if we leave you alone? After all, you've had him to yourself all afternoon."

"Don't stay out too late," my dad said, just for form's sake.

"Too bad we won't be able to ride tonight," I said to Ben when we were outside. We had planned to go to his place and then ride our bikes though the picturesque streets of Evanston.

"Why not? It's only a little rain."

"It's supposed to storm."

"It will probably be over by the time we've finished dinner. The air will be cooler. It'll be a great time to ride."

So we put my bike on his car and drove to Evanston. I should have known the day was going from bad to worse when the Chinese place we picked up from gave me vegetable chow mein instead of lo mein and my fortune cookie read, "You're about to get run over by the Wheel of Life."

It was dark when we started our ride—outfitted in rain gear—and still drizzling. But the air was clean and the street lamps glowed like in a horror movie. I followed Ben without asking any questions, not knowing how far we were going or if he had a plan.

We hadn't been riding long when we came to a golf course. We parked our bikes and walked across a soggy fairway to a gazebo on a small hill.

"Haven't you had enough golf courses for one day?" I asked.

"This is my favorite spot," Ben said, taking me by the hand. It was raining harder now and the drops made a soothing sound as they hit the roof, like one of those nature CDs at Sharper Image. "During the day you can see the whole course from here and at night it's like being in the middle of nowhere. No lights, no people. Listen."

We were quiet for a minute. I could only hear the rain against the roof. "I have a surprise," I said. "Close your eyes and hold out your hand."

"I don't like surprises."

"I promise it's not poisonous. I mean, at least you won't die right away."

I placed a cigar in his palm and kept another for myself.

"What's this for?"

"I stole them from my dad's desk. Borrowed them, really, because I plan to replace them tomorrow."

"I didn't know you smoked cigars."

"I don't. But I wanted to try it. Besides, I'm jealous because you do it with my dad."

"You want to learn how to play golf too?"

"One thing at a time." I took out some matches and tried to light mine.

Ben laughed. "Wait, you have to cut it first!"

"What do you mean? You can't just puff away?"

"Through what?"

I looked at my cigar. I'd never really looked at a cigar before. "Jeez Louise! Do you have a knife?"

"No. You'll have to bite it off."

I could already smell the thing and it wasn't even lit. I was liking this cigar business less and less every moment.

"Go on!" And Ben expertly bit the small end off his while I waited like a claustrophobic at the hatch of a submarine. "You were a lot more adventurous when I met you!"

"I was older then."

"You want me to do it?"

But I wasn't going to give him the satisfaction. I took a deep breath and a deeper bite and the next thing I knew enough tobacco to fill one of Miranda's cigarettes was sticking to my tongue. I gagged and spit out several times, while Ben laughed, greatly entertained.

"You're already choking and you haven't even lit up!" he said, striking a match. "You better stick to bubble gum."

Bubble gum! I quickly unwrapped a piece and popped it in my mouth to take the bitter taste away. "OK, I'm ready now."

"You can't smoke a cigar while chewing gum."

"I didn't know there were rules!" I put my gum back in the wrapper—I might need it again—and leaned over as Ben lit another match. The cigar caught fire and I took in a deep breath to catch the full aroma, but that only made me retch and start coughing like crazy.

Ben was laughing hysterically, unable to smoke his own cigar because he was laughing so hard. "It's not a joint!" he said. "You're not supposed to inhale!"

"Why didn't you tell me that before?" I wheezed.

"Everyone knows you don't inhale cigars."

"Then what's the point?"

"You're just supposed to enjoy the flavor."

"That's the dumbest thing I ever heard. You might as well drink wine and spit it out!"

"That's just what wine tasters do!"

"Right! And spaghetti grows on trees!"

I gathered my courage and took another puff, this time a micro puff, with hardly any smoke coming out. "It tastes like shit."

"So put it out," Ben said sensibly, enjoying his own cigar like it was made of chocolate.

"No, this is a bonding thing, a special moment for us, so I might as well do it to the core, especially since I'm not going to do it again." There was a clap of thunder in the distance. "Maybe we should go."

"We just got here."

"Couldn't it be dangerous to be stuck here when the storm comes?"

"If you're afraid . . ."

"Of course I'm not afraid. I'd just hate for anything to happen to you. I'm not sure I know my way home."

He put his arm around me. "The gazebo has a concrete floor, it should be pretty safe. Unless the roof falls from a direct hit, in which case I'll protect you with my body. Would you like to do a practice drill?"

"I don't know. With our burning cigars it might be more dangerous than the lightning. But I'll settle for a practice kiss."

He kissed me, and then we smoked with our arms entwined, taking turns on each other's cigars.

"I bet you don't do *this* with my dad!"

"There are a lot of things I don't do with your dad."

"But I bet you guys talk a lot. What kind of things do you talk about? What did you talk about today?"

"I don't know. Woods."

"What woods?"

"You know, metal woods versus wood woods, club lofts, golf stuff."

"You didn't talk about me?"

"Why would we talk about you?"

I leaned my arms on the ledge and gazed out at the rain. "Men and women sure are different," I realized. "Miranda spills her guts to me all day about her ex, her hormones, her period, her family, what she ate for breakfast. And in the meantime the two most important men in my life are talking about lofts!"

"I didn't know you wanted me to talk about you."

"Which reminds me, if you ever meet Miranda—and I'm sure you will—you're not even allowed to shake her hand! She's got a major infatuation!"

"But I've never even seen her."

"She's seen you—your picture in my bedroom. And she's on the rebound. So be warned." I cleared my throat from the cigar smoke. "Speaking of friends, how come you don't have more friends?"

"How many should I have?"

"I mean, you've mentioned some names, but we never do anything with them."

"We never do anything with your friends."

"Yeah, well you wouldn't like my friends. But you should be more popular."

"You want me to run for president?"

"It's just that you're such a private person. We spend every day together and yet in some ways I feel I don't really know you. You're very mysterious."

He laughed. "Does your father think I'm mysterious?"

"My dad only cares about your golf score and rap sheet. But I want more."

I had smoked over half my cigar and decided that was good enough. I ground it out on the ledge and threw it into the grass.

"Hey, what are you doing?" And Ben ran out into the rain to find it and put it in a trash can. He threw away his own as well.

"What's the big deal? It's biodegradable."

"It's not going to degrade by morning when the first foursomes roll through. There are certain things you just don't do on a golf course."

"Oh yeah? Show me what else you're not supposed to do. I see a sand trap with our name on it."

"Before you were afraid of the rain and now you want to get muddy."

"Who says *I'll* get muddy?"

Just then lightning flashed and I jumped. Ben pulled me into his arms.

"I'm ready for protection," I said.

But he only protected my lips. "*You're* the mysterious one," he said.

"Not anymore. You know all my secrets."

"All?"

Well, there was still the tattoo. Did that count?

"You haven't been contacted by any criminals?"

"No, I swear it." And *I* hadn't been contacted, had I?

"You haven't sprayed anyone with mace lately?"

"I'll spray you if you don't keep kissing me."

There was a great clap of thunder, a thunderous clap of thunder, and I screamed. "What happens if lightning strikes one of us while we're touching? Will we both get zapped?"

"We're not going to be hit by lightning."

"But what if?"

"Yeah. Probably."

"Then don't let go. I'd rather get fried together than watch you fry alone!"

A flash of lightning lit up Ben's smiling face, followed closely by another tremendous clap of thunder.

"Don't worry. We're not in danger."

"The storm's on top of us!" I shouted, genuinely afraid.

"What do you think it's like when it storms during the day, when the course is filled with golfers?"

"People get fried! Golfers get struck by lightning all the time."

"Well we're not carrying any big metal things, so I wouldn't worry."

"Besides, this is night. There are all these negative ions in the air."

We kissed some more, but I just couldn't concentrate on romance with the clouds of our destruction rolling overhead. "So how did you get your money?" I asked.

"My money for what?" Ben said, surprised by the question.

"You know, your money. For the BMW, the apartment, school, everything."

"I have a trust from my father. He left all his money to me. Why are you asking now?"

"I've been dying to ask for a long time, but you know how polite I am."

"You were afraid it came from some criminal activity."

"No, that wouldn't bother me. Unless you were destroying the environment, dumping toxic waste, or smuggling endangered species."

"You have such an active imagination."

"I know you wouldn't do anything like that. I mean, I do know you, even though there's so much I *don't* know. I just thought I should fill in some of the blanks before we get incinerated."

The thunder came so hard and fast I couldn't talk for a while. "How did your father die?" I finally asked in a pause between thunderclaps.

"He killed himself."

I shuddered. Ben and I were no longer holding each other. And he wasn't joking. The lightning lit up the pain in his face. I was dying to ask how, when, all the morbid details. But even I have some tact.

"Oh," was all I could say for a while. And Ben didn't volunteer anything more.

Then suddenly I remembered our first walk in Lincoln Park. How he gazed at the lightning—and suddenly I understood it was a lover's gaze. It confused me at the time, his calmness, his strange words. But I understood it all now. And yet he wasn't paying any attention to the storm tonight.

"Have you ever tried to kill yourself?" I asked nervously.

"Why do you ask that?" he said in an angry voice, a defensive voice.

But there weren't any scars on his wrists or downers in his medicine cabinet. He didn't seem like the kind of person who killed himself.

But as I looked into his face in the strobe light of lightning strikes, I realized he wasn't telling me everything. And suddenly I felt I was about to lose him—that any second he would fling himself out into the rain and give up his life to a force he loved and longed for even more than me.

I locked him in my arms, determined not to let go until the storm had passed.

Crop Circles R Us

I was pedaling to nowhere at Bally's the following Saturday with my mom. I hadn't spent much time with dear old mother since joining the rat race, so it was nice to sweat out the morning together. I also needed to talk, and what better expert could I find on the subject of self-destruction than the crazy woman who brought me into this crazy world?

"Oh Mom . . ."

"Yes?"

"Did you . . . did you ever try to kill yourself?" I said, jumping right in.

"What a question! Why do you ask?"

"Why does everybody ask me why I ask? Just tell me."

"I once had a minor overdose, but it was an accident."

"A *minor* overdose!"

"Christina . . ." My mom was looking at me with that worried look now and had stopped pedaling.

"But you had friends who killed themselves? And you once volunteered on a suicide hotline, until the numbers went way up."

"Christina, have you been depressed?"

"Depressed? Why should I be depressed? I've never been happier." I continued to ride at full speed. I didn't want this to be a heavy conversation.

"Then why . . . ?"

"I'm just curious about some things, that's all. Who's asking the questions here?" But I could see my mom was already wondering what size she should order for the straitjacket. "I swear I don't want to die. I'm concerned about a friend," I said, to throw her off the scent.

"Which friend?"

"You want me to betray confidentiality?"

"This is a serious subject, Christina. If someone's considering suicide they need help, maybe intervention."

She still thought it was me, the cynical woman. "Miranda just broke up with her boyfriend," I said, to throw her completely off, and because I knew she'd believe Miranda capable of anything. "But this goes no further."

"Of course," my mom said, looking sympathetic but I think very much relieved. "And she told you she's contemplating suicide?"

"No, not at all. That's just it, you see. She talks around the subject."

"How do you mean?"

"Like she asks what it would be like to be struck by lightning."

"I see."

"And her father killed himself."

"Oh." The wheels were no longer spinning on my mom's bike, but they were spinning in her head. "I didn't know."

"Is that important, her father I mean?" I asked. "Is suicide genetic?"

"Depression can be genetic. But apart from that, a parent's suicide has a lifelong impact on the child and sends the message that suicide is an acceptable method for dealing with trauma. In some families suicide is as common as cancer is in others."

I slowed down. This wasn't what I wanted to hear. "But what if the child is very well-adjusted and stable, and has a charmed life?"

"Any child whose father killed himself doesn't have a charmed life," my mom pointed out. "It's very easy to view the parent's suicide as personal rejection and to be more sensitive to other rejections than most people. As in the case of Miranda and her boyfriend."

"Miranda? Oh yeah. But what if there isn't any rejection? I mean, she dumped him. How do I know if she's serious? What are the warning signs?"

"The main warning sign is literally a warning, or a threat, since many people attempt suicide as a means of retaliation, or a plea for attention. Beyond that, you should look for sudden changes in behavior, especially withdrawal and risk taking. Such a person needs special support in times of crisis, like your friend. Most attempts are impulsive, and if someone is there to lend comfort—a friend or even a counselor's voice on a hotline . . ."

"But what if someone's obsessed with the idea?"

"I thought you said Miranda hasn't mentioned suicide?"

"Right, but let's say she keeps talking around it, saying weird things long after she gets over her ex."

"Well, she could still be depressed."

"But she's not depressed. Let's say she's in love again, full of energy, preparing for college or a career. When she says these weird things it's like she's talking about an experiment, like something scientific."

"A lot of artists—writers and philosophers—are fascinated with suicide in this way."

"But they just think about it, right? They don't do it?"

"Actually a lot of artistic types do."

I stopped pedaling. "What about scientific types?

What if he—I mean she—has never tried to kill herself, falls in love again, only talks about suicide now and then in a roundabout way, and doesn't even have any pills in her medicine cabinet to OD on?"

"You should talk to Miranda about it. Get her to open up, and tell her how much she means to you."

"That's impossible."

"Nothing's impossible when it comes to saving a life."

"But let's say at the end of the day there's still no heart-to-heart, and her intentions are as much a mystery as before?"

"I'd say she's probably not at risk, until she faces another crisis. Remember, most people who try to kill themselves don't really want to die. If someone is there for them in their moment of crisis . . ."

I started pedaling again. "And what about the people who want to die?"

My mom shook her head. "Those are usually the most difficult ones to spot. Those are the ones who often give no signs at all of the danger they pose to themselves, and their attempts tend to be much more successful."

I stopped pedaling.

⊙ ⊙ ⊙

When Ben picked me up that night I looked at him like he was a member of an unknown species and it was up to me to figure out how to keep him from becoming extinct.

I'd intentionally stayed out of the water after Benjamin because I didn't want to get involved with another dangerous guy, especially a killer. And now that I thought it was finally safe to dive back into the dating ocean, now that I'd fallen in love, I realized I had another homicidal boyfriend on my hands, only this one's gun was pointed at his own head.

"Is something wrong?"

"No, why?"

"You're staring at me."

But if he wanted to die I certainly wasn't going to find any signs with my eyes. Maybe it was just my active imagination being too active. Besides, it was Saturday night.

"So where are we going?"

"It's a beautiful sky," he said, as we stepped outside.

"For once! How about miniature golf?"

"Miniature golf? I thought we'd solve the mystery of crop circles."

Crop circles were perfect circles of flattened corn or wheat that appeared mysteriously in the middle of a farmer's field. It was thought they were made by aliens. Ben had seen me buy a *National Enquirer* the other day with a story about crop circles and we'd had an argument about their origins. I was convinced they were made by aliens—after all, people don't go around making perfect circles. Ben insisted they were hoaxes. I ask you, is that a far-fetched idea or what, as if a few teenage pranksters could pull off such a sophisticated feat of engineering. In the end I admitted some of the less-than-perfect circles might be copycats trying to duplicate the genuine alien circles.

So now we were once again traveling into the countryside in search of alien adventure. But this time it was Ben who had the plan, and while I admit I was excited by the idea, I was also suspicious. I mean, how were we supposed to see crop circles in the dead of night? Even in daylight, they weren't visible from the roadway, and were best viewed from the air. And if Ben didn't believe in them, what was the point? Was he hoping to catch some pranksters in the act?

He didn't answer any of my questions, so I turned up the radio, opened the sunroof, and communed with the stars.

When we finally stopped we were on a two-lane road as dark and quiet as the road where we had first looked at the stars together. "I hope you brought your telescope."

"Not tonight," Ben said, measuring himself against the wheat stalks. They were slightly taller than he was. Then he hurried back to the car and opened his trunk. It looked like the Home and Garden channel inside.

"What's the idea?" I said, as he unloaded bricks, two-by-fours, metal poles, rope, and string. "Are you going to build a patio?"

"No, a crop circle. Keep an eye out." And he carried the bricks and boards into the field.

"This is crazy! We can't do this!"

"Keep your voice down," he said, returning for more bricks.

"This is trespassing. We could get arrested."

"All of a sudden you're a straight arrow."

"I just don't see the point," I said, leaning against the

car. "We could be watching the stars. We could be doing a lot of things!"

"Take your shoes off."

I complained, of course, but I finally did as he asked and followed him into the field. There was some barbed wire, but it was easy enough to get through. As far as the wheat, it was pretty close together, but it bent easily and we could walk through it without breaking any stalks.

Just a few feet into the field, far enough to be hidden from the highway, Ben had assembled his crop circle machine. It was pretty low tech, considering that the real crop circles were made by state-of-the-art alien spacecraft. A couple two-by-fours tied together with three rows of bricks tied on top of them, and a rope attached at each end for Ben to pull. To finish the job he tied a second, much longer rope to the tops of two long metal poles, like the poles on halogen floor lamps. One of the poles he then screwed into the two-by-four. The other he handed to me.

"Walk out as far as you can, keeping the pole vertical, and the rope above the stalks. Be very careful not to break any. When the line's absolutely taut, plant the pole in the ground as far as you can without the rope touching the wheat. Then hold onto it tightly while I make the circle."

Aha! Now I saw his game. But it certainly wasn't going to fool anyone, and in the mean time I'd be wasting a magical night in the countryside holding a stupid metal pole in some farmer's wheat field. But Ben had that determined look on his face, so I marched.

When there was no more slack in the rope I stopped and stuck the pole in the soil, like the obedient accomplice that I was. "OK, now what?"

"Don't shout. Are you holding the pole?"

"We're like one, me and the pole."

"Make sure it's absolutely straight. If it starts to lean let me know."

"You'll be the first. What are you doing?"

He didn't answer, but the rope began to move ever so slightly. The pressure on the pole was pretty strong, though, so I leaned my body against it for support. I started to sing, but he told me to be quiet. "What are you doing? Can't we at least talk?"

I couldn't see anything with the wheat surrounding me, a few inches over my head. It was spooky. I began to feel claustrophobic and looked up at the sky for a sense of open space.

"I'm getting tired!"

"Already? It won't be long."

But I could see the rope hadn't moved very far— maybe from twelve o'clock to ten o'clock—he was going counterclockwise.

"I need to rest!"

"I'm the one pulling the bricks!"

But he must have been tired too because he stopped for about a minute. "How far away are you?" I asked when I felt a tug and the rope began moving again.

Ben's soft voice sounded miles away. "Sixty feet, six inches."

"I mean exactly!"

I tried to find a comfortable position. I put my right hand on top, then my left, I wrapped my arms around it like a thin metal Ben. The wind blew the wheat stalks into my face and I could smell them. I didn't know wheat had a smell.

"I have a sudden craving for a bowl of cereal!"

He stopped again at about six o'clock. I looked up at the stars but they gave me no comfort now.

"I'm frightened."

The rope began moving again.

"No one can see us. If you keep quiet no one can hear us either."

"I'm not frightened of humans. I mean, what if crop circles are signs of destruction, like the yellow rings the city paints around dead trees before it cuts them down? We could be vaporized the instant you finish!"

The stars seemed angry, like we were committing blasphemy—two urban pranksters playing with the dark secrets of the universe. This wasn't like cutting class.

But Ben and I were bonded to the core, and right now we really were tied together, weren't we, connected by a rope sixty feet, six inches long. Well, I wasn't going to be the one to let go. If Cosmic forces were displeased, let them zap me, their disloyal disciple, and spare innocent Ben, who, after all, was not a true believer.

I forgot where twelve o'clock was. "How much longer?" I asked.

"How should I know? Aren't you watching the rope?"

"I lost track at six o'clock. I sure hope you're close."

"*You* hope!"

I could hear him panting. I could also hear the wind rustling the tops of the wheat stalks, blowing in clouds, blocking out the starlight.

"I hope it doesn't rain."

"I hope it does. It'll wash out any traces of our footprints."

"You're taking this whole thing much too seriously. I think my dad needs to give you more work—you obviously have too much free time on your hands. But the one thing you haven't thought of is that whoever owns this land probably won't come out here for months, and by then the wheat will have grown back."

"Maybe. But someone's bound to see it from the air. And if not I'll just have to tip off Channel 11 myself."

The rope stopped moving. "Can I rest now?"

"We're finished! It worked! I've reached the beginning and it's perfect! When you take the pole out fill in the hole and smooth it over carefully. And erase your footprints as you come back.

I followed the rope back out to him, holding the pole straight up as I walked. Ben was so proud of his circle, like a little boy with a Spirograph. But I couldn't see much with the clouds rolling in.

I helped him carry the bricks back to the car. He was tired and sweaty but smiled at me triumphantly. Perfectionist that he was, he had to go back to examine everything one last time, and probably make sure I hadn't spat out any terrestrial bubble gum at the center. In the car I told him once again it was all a waste of time, we could have been holding hands and munching popcorn while semis plummeted from overpasses in *Seismic Summer*, we could have been drinking vanilla malts at a midnight picnic under the stars. But when he told me what a good job I had done I couldn't help but smile back, and be glad to have assisted my crop circle mate in his misguided experiment.

⊙ ⊙ ⊙

Of course, there was no news the next day, or the next. Ben watched all the channels, read all the papers. I wasn't much help. I didn't expect there to be any coverage, and was just glad we had gotten away with it. Even Ben's anonymous calls to Channel 11 came to nothing. As far as I was concerned, our crop circle forgery was history.

At first I gloated. Then I simply teased him. Then I actually felt sorry for the guy and offered to make a crop circle in Wrigley Field where there was a better chance it would get noticed. Finally I forgot about it altogether.

I was in the shower, recovering from another long day filling the suggestion box at work, when my mom pounded on the door. "Ben is on the phone. He says your crop circle is on Channel 7!"

Channel 7! Who would have thought? I raced out, dripping wet, while my mom nervously fumbled with the remote. "That's Channel 5!" I shouted. "Give me the control!"

I took it by force, but it was already a commercial. I grabbed the phone and demanded all the details. Ben had just caught the end, but he was sure they would repeat it tonight.

So at ten o'clock we all sat anxiously—my parents, Ben, and I—around the TV, like we were in a movie and our scene was about to come up. My mom, always ready with a dramatic touch, even made low-fat popcorn.

And there it was, right after the local scandals and pile ups, our magnificent crop circles, as seen from the air in broad daylight by the Channel 7 weather copter! And magnificent it was. At first I thought it must be a mistake, that they weren't reporting our crop circle but a real crop circle made by real aliens. Only when they named the road and county did I realize it was ours. The radius was the same too—which happened to have some relationship to the distance from the earth to the sun. Ben was especially pleased Channel 7 caught on to that one. It was so beautiful I didn't even hear the interview with the farmer. You would think a circle's a circle. I had no idea while we were making it that it would look so big and impressive and—well, circular. Trying to keep the pole straight in the starlight it was hard to imagine. I couldn't believe I had helped create something so perfect.

"No footprints, no holes, no tool marks," Sven Nordquist, Channel 7 reporter said. "Could this be the work of beings from above? A message or a landing site? It's hard to know. What does seem certain is that this crop circle could not have been made without sophisticated equipment and the scientific knowledge of an advanced race."

Gosh! For a flash I felt like a god. If you're ever feeling low self-esteem go out and make a crop circle and listen to yourself being referred to as an advanced race just for holding a stupid pole! I was supposed to go back to the filing room after this?

Ben was rolling with laughter. I'd never seen him laugh so much. My mom was excited and proud. She seemed to overlook the fraud part and the trespassing part and kept saying it was a marvelous example of organic art, whatever that meant. My dad just shook his head.

It seemed I was the only one with a tinge of conscience. After my initial euphoria passed, my astonishment and godlike feelings, I realized we had just conned an entire metropolis.

"This was wrong," I said. "Now thousands of people will think our crop circle made in a couple hours with bricks and poles is evidence of alien contact!"

"Yes!" Ben said with a triumphant sneer. "Now do you understand how gullible people are when it comes to aliens and paranormal claims."

I ran to the phone. "I have to tell them!" But when information answered I hung up. Channel 7 probably had caller ID. We could be arrested for trespassing, destroying wheat, impersonating aliens. "I'll leave an anonymous message tomorrow from a pay phone."

"You'll be wasting your time," Ben said. "They'll never run a retraction. Besides, think of Sven, he could lose his job if the truth got out. Demoted to the Animal Abuse Squad."

"But now the whole city's been fooled because of us."

"I'd fool the whole world if it meant enlightening you."

"Enlightening me!"

"Don't you feel smarter now? Glad to have solved a mystery?"

"No! I believe as much as always—more than ever!" I said defiantly. "In crop circles and aliens and astrologers and Ouiji Boards. What would I be if I didn't believe?"

"You'd be like me," Ben said, no longer smiling.

Lusting after lightning, I thought cruelly.

Bombs Away

We were gazing at the sky again, but this time it was daylight and we were far from alone, sitting on beach towels in Lincoln Park with half a million of our closest friends for the annual Air and Water Show. It was a nice day for once—puffy clouds and hot enough for shorts, shades, and a bikini top. Ben and I could have watched the whole spectacle from the air-conditioned comfort of my dad's office but I wanted to feel the excitement of the crowds, to hear the roar of the planes and, most of all, to lie on my back as they zoomed overhead.

We had come just after dawn to stake out our territory—my usual spot, on the southern edge of the park near the Hancock, with a couple beach towels, a cooler filled with sodas and sandwiches, a radio, sun lotion and, for Ben, a thick book about dead scientists.

Now it was afternoon and the sky was filled with daredevils and Blue Angels, biplanes and B52s. The announcer was explaining it all on the loudspeaker but I wasn't paying much attention. Besides, it was more fun asking Ben, who began to get irritated and told me to listen to the announcer. War planes weren't one of his strong points, which, I guess, was a good thing.

There was a lot of action on the lake too—packed with pleasure boats and navel vessels—everything but an aircraft carrier.

"I wonder if this is what an invasion is like," I said, as some jet fighters in formation swept along the shore. I opened the cooler and looked through the sandwiches. I'd made them myself—avocado and mint jelly—and they were awful. I thought of the gourmet pizza and shrimp cocktail being served up in my dad's office.

"I hope you don't mind sitting out with the masses," I said. "After all, we could be partying with the wheelers and dealers on the forty-third floor."

"But we couldn't work on our tans."

"Exactly!" But this made me sad, to think how few

sunny days we'd have left to lie out together. It was the end of August and tomorrow I'd be slithering through the dark hallways of the Academy. Tomorrow!

"I'm sure the food's better in my dad's office," I said.

"I don't know. This looks OK," he said, eying a sandwich. "What is it?"

"Avocado and mint jelly. Take a bite."

He obeyed, and tried not to make a face.

"See, it's horrible!" I said.

"It's OK."

"You're just being polite. You don't want to hurt my feelings because you know it took me hours to make them. But I don't care if you want to go to the Hancock and grab some gourmet pizza. I'll guard the towels."

But he didn't take the hint. Instead he simply put the sandwiches back in the cooler and lay down with his hands behind his head while some parasailers drifted to targets on the lake.

"I can't believe summer's over," I said, lying next to him, watching the trails of smoke dissolving in the sky. "It seems like we just met in Dr. Dobrowski's office."

"It seems like ages to me."

"Thanks!"

"I don't mean it that way. I mean that we've been through a lot. And we've changed so much."

"You mean *I've* changed."

"I've changed too."

"How?"

But he didn't answer. Instead he talked about school.

"You're lucky," I said. "You don't have to start for weeks."

"I wish I could start tomorrow."

"I'm already having nightmares about school."

"Like dreaming it's the day of a test and you haven't studied?"

"That's no dream. No, my nightmares are about you picking me up after class."

"What's so terrible about that?"

"Well I can't find my way out. I open a door, but it's just another class. And when I finally do get outside there's another girl in your car, sitting in my seat, playing with the adjustments."

Ben laughed. "I didn't know you were so insecure."

"Only in my nightmares."

"Who's the girl?"

It was Miranda, but I couldn't tell him that, could I? So I said, "No one I know." And I couldn't tell him about a worse nightmare I had—where I was trying to hit a golf ball out of a huge sand trap so deep I couldn't see over the top and it began to storm but I couldn't get out until I hit the ball and it kept rolling back and lightning was striking right on the green and I called out to Ben but there was no answer.

"At least the internship's over," he said.

I hadn't had any nightmares about work—only pleasant dreams. "I'll miss it," I admitted.

"You'll miss filing and answering phones?"

"There are worse ways to spend a summer."

"It was fun working together, wasn't it?"

I'd hardly call it working together, since he was usually wrapped up on the computer and I was cubicles away. But it was our being in the same office, going to work together and having lunch and going home together—knowing he was always just a few yards away if I needed a hug or a kiss, that made the hours pass like minutes. "I wish we could go to school together," I said.

"Maybe I could lie my way back into high school."

"Wouldn't that be great? It would be just like it is now. You could drive me to school and we could have lunch together and I could cheat off your exam papers."

"No you couldn't. But I'd help you study."

"And now you'll be so busy with college. We won't have any time together."

A U2 spy plane flew high overhead, its long wings ominous like a bird of prey. "You know air shows are very dangerous," I said, thinking this might be a way to draw him out. "Planes crash all the time, and people on the ground get killed."

"Are you scared?"

"I wasn't a moment ago." A stealth bomber roared lower in the sky, flying right over us, blocking out the sun. "What would you do if we were in a war," I asked, "and the stealth was bombing us?"

"No other countries have stealth bombers."

"So we're in a foreign country then. And a US stealth

is flying as close as it is now, raining down bombs. What would you do?"

"I'd probably cover you with my body."

"You'd sacrifice yourself to save me?"

"I really don't think you'd be saved. I think it would be pretty pointless."

"And what if the plane was shot down and heading right toward us?"

"I don't think a stealth bomber would get shot down."

"It's just a question! Say it's plummeting right toward us and there's no time to get away. Would you be afraid? Or would you stare at it like a lover?"

"Why are you talking about bombs and crashes? Did your horoscope mention a war?"

"You brought it up, about air shows being dangerous."

"No, you brought it up."

"Well, whatever." The mysterious stealth flew away without bombing us or crashing on our heads, and without getting Ben to talk about death. Maybe *I* was the one with the morbid imagination.

"Speaking of danger," I said, opening the cooler, "how about an avocado and jelly sandwich? I made six." But Ben was looking enviously at our neighbors' picnics. "I have an idea! Why don't you run up to the office and grab some real food? I'm sure there's plenty left. I'll keep our spot."

"But you can't get in the Hancock without a pass."

"I have passes." And I dug one out of my pocket. Ben seemed pretty happy. I guess he was getting hungry.

"I won't be long," he promised. "What do you want?"

"Just fill a trash bag."

I kissed him goodbye and lay back down as a huge Hercules transport circled over the lake. I closed my eyes. A moment later an ominous shadow hovered above me. But it didn't have wings.

"Hey," it said.

I looked up. Benjamin!

"So I see you've kept our old spot."

"It's *my* spot!" I shouted above the roar of the planes, standing up to protect my turf. But it was stupid to have come here—the one place he could find me out of half a million people. But, truth to tell, Benjamin hadn't crossed my mind lately. He hadn't stalked me or talked to Miranda again. I thought he'd finally gotten the message.

But he acted just like he had on day one. He even sat down on Ben's towel.

"Hey! Get off! You have no right here!"

He opened the cooler. Maybe I could poison him with the sandwiches. But not even Benjamin was dumb enough to fall for my cooking. "Where is he?" he asked, closing the cooler and looking around, ready for a fight.

"Get out of here now!"

But he made himself comfortable on Ben's towel. "I'll wait."

I thought of Ben coming back and finding Benjamin sitting on his towel, and it seemed half a million people weren't enough to protect us. I had to get him away from there, so I pulled on his arm, and when that didn't work I walked off to find a cop.

Benjamin ran after me, but at least now we were mixed in the crowd. If Ben came back he would just think I had gone to the bathroom. I walked as far away as I could, until Benjamin blocked my way and grabbed my arm.

"I'll scream," I said, although there was so much noise from the planes and the crowd I doubt anyone would have noticed.

"Why are you afraid of me? What have I ever done to you?"

But his eyes were full of criminal intentions and I looked away. Despite the crowd I felt completely helpless. I had left my purse at home, thinking it might be stolen, so I didn't have the mace.

"What do you want? Why don't you leave me alone?"

"Just tell me what we had was nothing." He took his shirt off and pointed to his heart, with my name on it in all-too-clear blue ink. "Tell me I mean nothing to you."

I stared at him as jets roared overhead. His eyes tried to burn through me, but then he looked down and his mouth fell open.

"Where is it?" he said, hardly loud enough to hear. He reached out to me but I backed away. "Where's the tattoo?"

Shit! Why did I have to wear a bikini top? Why did I have to pick my regular spot? Destiny was conspiring to make this day an ordeal.

"You had it removed!"

I thought for a moment about denying it, but the evidence—or lack of evidence—was as obvious as his jealousy. So I stood my ground. "So! So what if I did?" But the rage in his eyes scared me and I added, "My parents made me!"

I didn't know if he heard this. I didn't know if it mattered. The only thing I knew for certain was that I was being strangled, right there in broad daylight in the midst of half a million people, and all the bombers in the air force couldn't save me.

"I'll kill you!" he said. "I'll kill you."

And then he let go and ran away into the crowd.

I stood there gasping for a moment, not really hurt, but in shock, too shocked to cry, feeling helpless and angry. He'd never threatened me like that before, even when we fought. He'd never tried to choke me.

I rubbed my neck, as if marks from his fingers were imprinted on my flesh, visible to everyone. All these fellow creatures and not one pat on the shoulder, not one sympathetic smile. No one knew I was suffering. They were all too busy having a good time.

I wiped my eyes and took some yoga breaths. At least Ben hadn't seen. And then I went into survival mode. If he were to find out what happened there would be more than a few seconds of choking to contend with, and we might all be lying in the morgue before day's end. So I put on a brave face and went back to our spot.

Fortunately, Ben wasn't there, but neither was the cooler and the radio. Some thief was going to be very sick before morning. I guess the matching Road Runner and Wile E. Coyote beach towels were beneath him.

I tried to concentrate on the planes, a squadron of navy fighters. I was looking at the sky when Ben returned with a feast. The gourmet pizza cheered me up, and I felt less helpless with Ben beside me, even though before I had always worried about *him*.

"Where's the cooler?"

"I gave it to the homeless."

"And the radio?"

"They can't live on avocado and jelly sandwiches alone. I had to go to the bathroom."

"And you left everything here?"

"Relax. It's just a radio."

I began to feed him grapes. After all, why should I let a homicidal ex get me down on such a picture-postcard day at the Chicago Air and Water Show?

I was living moment to moment in classic Capricornian fashion. My planet was in the House of Denial.

Starcrossed

○──○

Like I said, my planet was in the House of Denial. You might think I would have been overwrought, that Ben would've noticed my anxiety, that I could've come up with some excuse for rolling up our beach towels and moving on. After all, Benjamin could've come back any minute with firepower. And wouldn't it have been stupid—wouldn't it have been the stupidest thing

I could've possibly done, to still be in the place where he'd found me—a sitting target?

You might think I was comforted by the crowd, but the crowd hadn't stopped him from grabbing my throat, had it? No, I knew he was capable of anything. Anything. It was denial pure and simple that kept me acting so cool. And it wasn't even acting. I mean, after the initial shock I wasn't even nervous anymore. If I stopped to think about the situation it would have occurred to me that he might have come back. That he might have returned with a weapon. That Ben was in as much danger as I was. But I didn't think about it. Not at all. I ate my gourmet pizza, asked Ben to spread some lotion on my back, and watched the smoke trails dissolving in the sky.

When I was in love—that was another story. In the beginning with Ben, for example, I couldn't think about him enough, I couldn't get him out of my mind. I couldn't sleep, and he filled my dreams. But when it came to people I hated or feared—unpleasant people—it was like wars and famines on the news, like the car wrecks I passed when cycling—I simply put them out of my mind.

So there was nothing to tip Ben off. We had a great day. And that night I slept the sleep of deep denial—no insomnia, no staring at my painted stars, no nightmares.

And it wasn't like I had oodles of time on my hands to think about people like Benjamin. There were enough clear and present dangers to keep my mind abuzz. For the next day my glorious freedom ended, and I rode the El to the Academy.

New teachers, old friends, the chilling echoes of lockers opening in the main hallway. Miranda wanted to sit in the back row in homeroom but I steadied myself like someone about to bungee jump off a bridge and sat up front. Miranda followed me and took the desk to my left.

"It's harder to cheat in the front row," she said.

"What's life without a challenge?" I shot back. "Anyway, who am I going to cheat off, you?"

"I didn't know you were in the running for teacher's pet," Miranda said, sneering at Mr. Crump, our homeroom teacher, who looked kind of like a rhinoceros without the horn. "I think being this close we'll be in for some serious B.O."

"Well I don't plan to spend the rest of my teenage years in high school. I'm on track for the honor roll. So you're welcome to come with me or wallow in the mud."

"You're doing it for him, I know it."

"Hey, I'm my own person. I don't need anyone to set my agenda."

"Right."

I let her believe what she wanted because, truth to tell, I had made a kind of promise to Ben. What else could account for this exceptional transformation? I'd cut my hair, dressed for success, cashed paychecks, stopped swearing at my mom—Thursdays and weekends—why shouldn't I sit in Mr. Crump's front row? Besides, Ben promised if I made the honor roll I could drive his car!

So there wouldn't have been much time to think about Benjamin that week even if I wanted to. It took all my concentration just to make sure I got to class on time and kept my notebooks in order. It had been years since I'd been organized and it felt like the first week of kindergarten without the nap time.

Still, I couldn't forget the incident at the Air Show completely, and every now and then I had a spare moment to think about it. But I not only downplayed the danger, I convinced myself it was a blessing in disguise. First, I argued that you couldn't really call it a *violent* incident. Yes, he'd grabbed my throat, but he let go, didn't he? And of his own free will, not because I maced him or someone intervened. That counted for something, didn't it? When I examined my neck in the mirror that night there weren't any marks or bruises, so he couldn't have been *trying* to choke me, right? I mean, he was thrown for a loop. What would I have done if I still cared for him and I saw that he'd erased my name from his chest? Probably the same thing, I realized. Only I wouldn't have let go so fast.

Second, the part about killing me was just a reaction, and I'd be stupid to take it literally. Hadn't he said that a million times when we were together? "If you're late I'll kill you!" "I'll kill you if you get me menthol's again!" People threatened to kill each other every day, in traffic, in bars, in offices behind partitions. At Wrigley Field hardly an inning went by without coaches, pitchers, and base runners being threatened with death by their loyal fans.

Third, I told myself this was not only not a bad thing—it was, in fact, the very best thing that could have happened. After all, what had I been trying to do all this time if not convince Benjamin I was no longer interested in him? Didn't he keep pursuing me because he didn't believe me? Hadn't he said as much? What good were words to such a person? But now he knew for certain where he stood—that he was literally out of the picture. If I had any brains I would have shown him the evidence right off the bat.

Fourth—he hadn't come back, had he?

So I convinced myself that Benjamin not only posed no danger to me, but that he was in fact out of my life— finally—forever. Denial by numbers.

⊙ ⊙ ⊙

It was Friday and I was getting dressed to go over to Ben's. I'd just come home from school and was going to grab a quick snack before catching the El to Evanston. I hadn't seen Ben all week and was dying with yearning. We'd talked each night on the phone, but this was the longest I'd gone without seeing him since that historic morning he took me to Saks.

But before I could step out the door my dad came home. "How was school?" he asked.

"I'm not on detention." I kissed him on the cheek. "Mom's at the shelter and I'm on my way to Evanston."

But he held my arm. "Christina, I want to talk to you."

That tone, that phrase! I hadn't heard him say those words to me in all the weeks I worked in his firm. It almost made me shudder. He used to say that to me all the time—with a Clint Eastwood mumble and angry or worried eyes. After I'd broken the law or the dishes or screamed at my mom. Those words usually meant an embarrassing lecture immediately followed by cruel and usual punishment.

"I hope you're not going to ground me," I said, retreating to my room. I sat on my bed, racking my brain for the crime I'd committed. But I couldn't think of anything. I was a model citizen.

My dad remained standing and closed the door, even though we were alone in the house. He looked at me closely, like he was looking for guilt. But I was as innocent as my stuffed animals.

Or was I?

"I spoke to the prosecutor today," he said. "He informed me Benjamin was released over two months ago."

There wasn't any emotion in his voice, which made it sound more ominous than if he had screamed the news, like my mom would have. I tried not to show any emotion in response, and waited for the obvious question.

"They promised to notify me before he got out . . . Christina, has he tried to contact you? Have you seen him at all?"

I couldn't stand the way he was looking at me, but I kept my eyes on his like all good liars do and told him I had not seen Benjamin.

"He hasn't phoned?"

"He wouldn't call here. And you'd know if he did."

"But you'd tell me, wouldn't you, if you saw him?"

"Of course, why wouldn't I?"

My dad sighed, and all—or most—of the tension went out of his face. He opened the door. I was a free woman.

"I want you to promise to tell me if he ever comes around."

"I have no secrets from the Big Guy!" I said, giving him a sympathetic hug. "If Benjamin has any sense he'll be light years away from Chicago, with those gang punks after him."

"I hope you're right," my dad said, running his fingers through my hair.

The man had an uncanny knack for guessing the mysterious ways of international commodities, but his only daughter fooled him every time.

⊙ ⊙ ⊙

Ben was beat after a long day doing whatever college freshmen do to prepare for university life—so we decided to eat in. He put some pasta on the stove while I looked over his textbooks—*Introduction to Physics, English Composition, A Short History of the French Revolution, A Cultural Anthropology Reader.*

"Aren't you going to take astronomy?" I asked.

"Not the first semester."

"What a drag. I bet they don't even have a class on astrology."

"No, but there's a great course on Nostradamus. Everyone gets the answers first."

"Well, if I go to college I'm going where I can study the subjects I'm interested in. Besides, I bet I'd make a lot more money as an astrologer than you'll ever make in a planetarium," I said, leafing through the complicated pages of *Introduction to Physics*.

Ben came out into the living room and wrapped his arms around me. "I won't be working at a planetarium. I'll be working at a remote observatory in Arizona or Hawaii or even Australia, if I have my way. And if I have my way you'll be with me. Think how romantic it would be, living on top of the world on Mauna Kea in Hawaii, the mountain practically to ourselves."

"Mmm," I sighed. "And I'll bring you coffee at night and you'll let me look through the telescope."

"Astronomers don't look through telescopes anymore," Ben said. "Everything's computerized."

"Well then I'll bring you coffee and you'll let me look at your monitor."

"Agreed," Ben said, and we walked as one back into the kitchen.

I was looking in the drawer for a can opener to open the spaghetti sauce when I noticed the passport. I had forgotten about it after that first dinner together, but now

I took it out and flipped through the pages. There were stamps for England, France, Italy, Japan, Australia.

"Wow! You've been to Japan—and Australia! You never told me. You're a world traveler! I had no idea. When did you see all these places? I've only been to Canada. Did you climb Ayers Rock? Did you feel its mystic power? And what about Mt. Fuji? How were you able to go to all these countries? With your parents?"

I turned to the front to look at his picture and was amazed to see the face of a child, no more than five years old. Short blond hair, baby fat, he was completely adorable. I'd never seen a picture of Ben that young. In fact, he'd never shown me any photo albums from childhood. But then, I hadn't shown him my pictures either. It just never came up.

"Why don't you have a more recent photo?" I asked.

"What? Oh, well passports are good for ten years, I think. I haven't used it in a long time."

"Since your parents died?"

I looked at the date of expiration and, true enough, it expired three years ago. "Wouldn't it be great to go to Europe together?"

"Yeah, we'll go next week."

"Well why not? I can get a passport and you can get yours renewed and we'll take a cheap flight to London for a weekend and go clubbing!"

"If only you hadn't spent all your money on magazines and clothes!"

"I'll get an advance from my dad against next sum-

mer. I'll work Christmas break. We'll make a pilgrimage to
Stonehenge!"

"Sounds great. But before we go to Stonehenge can
you heat up the sauce?"

I was about to put the passport back, my mind swimming with images of sacred Druid ceremonies. But just
before I closed it another date caught my attention—you
could say strangled my attention. The date of birth.

"Christy . . ."

"Look at this . . ." I was in a kind of shock, a kind of
denial. I almost said, "Look, honey, they got your birth
date wrong!" But not even I could deny this terrible truth.
I mean, passport officials are pretty good with little facts
like birth dates. The year was as it should be, the day too.
But the month was wrong. I stared, my mind reeling, not
knowing what to think. All I knew was he wasn't a Pisces.

"I'll do it myself then," Ben said, reaching for the can
opener.

I grabbed his arm. "You said you were born in February."

"Huh?" He glanced at the passport and took it from
my hands. He put it back in the drawer.

"You were born in November. You're not a Pisces."

"Oh yeah, I'm a Sagittarius," he said with a smile. "But
I'm sure we're just as compatible."

"Why did you lie to me?" I screamed.

"You know what I think of astrology. I can't stand it
when people ask your sign and when you tell them you're
a Sagittarius or a Cancer or a Gemini they say, 'Of course,

I knew it.' I was just playing with you. I didn't think I'd wind up going to Svetlana! And by that time I was hooked. I was going to tell you, but I don't dwell on these things the way you do and eventually I just forgot."

"You forgot!"

He put his hands on my shoulders. "I'm sorry I lied to you."

"I don't care that you lied to me!" I shouted, pushing him away. "I care that you're not a Pisces!"

I started to cry.

He tried to hold me. "I'm sorry, really. I should have told you long ago. It was a thoughtless thing to do, but it was only a joke."

"Don't touch me!"" I yelled, throwing him off.

"Hey!" he said in a louder voice. "I'm not the only one who lied about my birth date!"

"But this is different! This is your sign! Damn it, don't you see what this means?"

"That you'll have to buy me a present in November instead of February?"

"Here's your present," I said, and threw a wine glass against the wall. I wanted to take the pot of boiling spaghetti and throw it at him, but I didn't have the strength.

He came forward and took my arms and shook me. "Don't you believe what we have is more real than what you read in your horoscopes? If you really loved me you wouldn't care about my sign!"

I tore free of him, still crying, and ran out the door.

He ran after me, and stopped me on the lawn, but I broke free again and ran down the street. By the time I looked back he wasn't there.

⊙ ⊙ ⊙

I burst through my front door and hurried straight to my room without a word to my parents and slammed the door and collapsed on my bed without turning on the light and cried for real.

My mom knocked softly. "Christina? Christina? Are you all right?"

I hadn't thought to lock the door and she peeked in and turned on the light. "Honey, what's the matter?"

I tried to wipe away the tears. "Go away."

But instead she sat down on the bed next to me and took my hand. "What happened dear?"

"I don't want to talk about it."

"Did you and Ben have a fight?"

"I said I don't want to talk about it!"

"Come on," she said in her most cheerful voice. "It can't be all that bad."

"It's the worst possible thing!"

"He's seeing someone else?"

"Is that all you can think of? He's a Sagittarius!" I shouted.

My mom didn't say anything for a moment. "What's wrong with Sagittarius? Your father's a Sagittarius."

"He said he was a Pisces! This ruins everything."

My mom laughed, convinced I was overreacting. She believed in astrology, but basically just listened to the good parts and ignored the doom and gloom stuff. "I'm sure you can love a Sagittarius just as much as a Pisces."

"You don't understand!" I screamed. "Sagittarius is the worst possible sign for me! I thought we were meant for each other, but in fact we're starcrossed!"

I began crying again, on my mom's shoulder.

"But think of Ben, dear, he's still the same person. If he told you he was a Pisces I'm sure he meant no harm. Now stop crying, I'll make you some tea. Do you want chamomile or valerian?"

"Chamomile," I whispered.

She came back with a pot and tray. "Tomorrow you'll call Svetlana and she'll tell you everything's all right."

"I don't have to call her. I already know."

"Nonsense!"

"She told me to avoid Sagittarians! Benjamin was a Sagittarian!" And the tears flowed.

My mom said these were special circumstances. She urged me to call him. Then the phone rang and it was Ben. I refused to talk to him. I could hear my mom reassuring him, but she didn't understand. This went to the core.

My mom came back to provide comfort, to make sure I didn't do anything drastic. "Get some rest sweetheart," she said when she was too tired to continue her suicide watch. "I'm sure everything will work out."

When she was gone I turned on my computer and

booted Tamarind Ellerbee's *The Complete Capricorn*. I clicked on Compatibility Charts and then on Sagittarius, and there—like I feared, like I knew—was this warning:

"Not good for the long haul."

I lit a hyacinth candle and sadly took Ben's photo from its frame, like he was already dead. I tore it into a thousand pieces and fed them to the flame one by one. And then I snuffed out the candle with my tear-stained thumb.

The constellations on my ceiling glowed like burning souls. I lay awake all night, lying deathly still on my back, and contemplated my mispainted stars, my mispainted love, my mispainted life.

Hard Rock Therapy

My parents were both gone by the time I finally woke up, sometime after noon, and I didn't even have the energy to open the refrigerator. I lay in bed feeling sorry for myself, angry at Ben, angry at the universe. I decided I needed to kick in some endorphins to help me cope with the pain, so I forced myself into some ragged clothes and cycled through the dismal streets, pedaling furiously. But the endorphins kept their distance and the sound of my spinning wheels only reminded me of that magical day when Ben and I met for what I thought was good at O'Shannon's Cyclery.

At dinner my mom tried to draw me out, but I gave her the silent treatment. She wanted my dad to talk some reason into me, but with all the aggressive colors in my aura, it was a stretch for him just to ask me to pass the parmesan cheese.

I refused to answer the phone for fear it might be Ben, and when it finally was I heard my mom say, "Give her a few days," before I slammed my door and turned on the radio. How wrong she was, I thought. This wasn't some little wound time would heal, but fate at its cruelest.

If it were up to me I never would have gone back to school—what's the point? But mom was home to make sure I got out the door Monday, pointed in the right direction. I guess I wasn't hiding my feelings well because the first thing Miranda said when she saw me was how awful I looked.

"I've been sick," I told her.

"Are you pregnant?"

"Is that all you can think about?"

"You split up, didn't you?"

A better detective than friend, my Miranda. But I didn't feel like talking and glared at her like the guiltiest of criminals. In homeroom I moved my desk to the back row in protest against all the false optimism that had crept into my being. My star had collapsed into a black hole and the laws of the universe no longer applied.

⊙ ⊙ ⊙

Ben and I were dancing circles in a wheat field, bound together by the silver cord that connects you to your astral body and—who knows—maybe to your soulmate too. Then we were at Stonehenge playing hide-and-seek, and then on an endless beach, lying next to each other, melted by the sun, melting into each other as seagulls and stealth bombers circled overhead. I woke in the darkness with a serene smile. But the contentment I felt was just another illusion. The best dreams are worse than any nightmare. The images that had been so real a moment ago faded and I stared at the place on my nightstand where his picture had stood, how could I hold back the tears?

⊙ ⊙ ⊙

It was family group-therapy night at the Hard Rock Cafe. Another bad idea from my mom, who figured if I had a cheeseburger and chocolate shake in my hand the stars would fall from my eyes and I would drift back into impending disaster. But my dad hardly said a word, obviously wishing he were on the driving range. He didn't like the food, he didn't like Simple Minds blaring on the megabucks sound system, and what little conversation there was made him reach for the ketchup.

"Christina, you're being unreasonable," my mom said, I think.

"What?" I shouted.

"I said, you're taking the whole issue of natal signs too literally. Surely there are other factors."

"What? I can't hear you."

She leaned across the table, but I only heard guitars and drums. Thank God for Simple Minds. I kept beat with my straw, watching her lips move.

". . . reconsider," came through as the song faded out.

"So how was your day?" I shouted to my dad, ignoring her.

"Lawrence, tell her what you think," my mom said.

"How can I even know what I think with all this racket?" my dad complained. "We might as well be eating in Christina's room!"

"Are you going to let astrology rule every decision in your life?" my mom asked, turning back to me. "In spite of everything your head and your heart tell you?"

Yes, that's exactly what I'm going to do, I thought.

"Is it your destiny to be depressed?" she argued.

"I'm not depressed!" I shouted, trying to show a brave face. But then the Jaundiced Eyes came on and it was all I could do to keep my own eyes dry.

⊙ ⊙ ⊙

Friday night and I was voluntarily grounded, a prisoner of destiny, sentenced to a miserable life of internal exile. Maybe I'd go to India like Mother Teresa and care for slum children. Maybe I'd volunteer at a leper colony—there still were leper colonies, weren't there? Maybe I'd join the Moonies and get married to a brainwashed stranger with ten thousand other zombies at Shea Stadium. But my horoscope said there was a plane crash with my name on it, so I stayed in my room.

Miranda wandered by. She had a Firebird in need of a muffler coughing in the driveway, filled beyond the fire marshal's limit with happy-go-lucky youth—did I want to join in the fun?

But I was in mourning and locked my door. Alone, I didn't have to pretend and could grieve to my heart's content. This was the first weekend since Ben and I had started going out that we hadn't spent together. Watching the minutes pass was harder than an algebra exam. My mom kept trying to bring me food, as if that's what I needed. But I just wanted to starve away, to vanish.

When I got too lonely I logged onto a chat line, but my cyberspace was filled with morons. What color is your hair? Do you like to snowboard? Do you wear a bikini or a one-piece?

Please. Please!

Saturday afternoon I went to the hardware store and bought some black paint. I covered over all the stars on my ceiling, my friends no more. Mine was a dark, empty sky.

⊙ ⊙ ⊙

Just when things could get no worse, they got worse. I was in social studies when the principal announced on the intercom, "Miss Marlowe, please come to the office. There are three gang members to see you."

OK, so it happened on the lawn after class. But I couldn't have been more shocked had their arrival been announced by the principal. I mean, this was Academy turf. It cost megabucks a term just to sit on the grass! These boys were a long way from home.

"You Benny's chick?" one of them asked.

It was clear they weren't afraid of fried foods, but they still failed to fill out their elephant-plus size jeans. I avoided eye contact and kept walking, like they were harmless homeless people who just wanted a quarter and not wannabe gangsters who have seen too many Charles Bronson flicks.

"I asked you a question girl!"

"I'm not here to answer questions!" I said, holding my books tightly to my chest, imagining the headlines: "Senior's life saved when knife blade snaps on *Classics of English Literature*."

But they surrounded me and I really got scared. Mace was out of the question. I tried to look beyond them for a knight in any kind of armor. Where was Miranda? All last week I couldn't get rid of her and now that I needed another pair of lungs to help me scream she was nowhere to be seen.

"I'm no one's chick," I snarled, trying to move on.

But they closed in further. I could smell the smoke from their cigarettes. "You aren't going nowhere till you tell us where he is!"

"If Mrs. Williams hears you using bad grammar I can't answer for what might happen."

But Capone and Company were evolutionary ladder rungs beneath my subtle wit, so I decided to come clean. "I don't know where he is. I dumped him several felonies ago."

I must have sounded convincing, they must have

heard the contempt in my voice, because they shuffled uneasily for a moment before their leader said, "Well, if you see him tell him we're looking for him!"

"And if *you* see him give him a bullet for me!" I said, trying to sound tough. "You *do* have bullets this time, don't you?"

⊙ ⊙ ⊙

I may have appeared tough and composed, but I was jelly on the inside, and as soon as they left I collapsed on the front steps and shook like a traffic light in a tornado.

"What's with you?" Miranda said, looming over me.

"Where have you been?" I asked angrily.

"Is something wrong?"

"PMS," I answered in a language she could understand.

"Who were those guys?" she asked, trying to look into my eyes.

"I don't know," I answered, and I realized I didn't know. I couldn't describe them at all, except for being white and young and ugly. I could probably guess the brand of cigarettes they smoked, but I couldn't tell you what they looked like. At first I had avoided eye contact completely. Then I had been so scared, and everything happened so fast, I didn't pay any attention to their faces. I wouldn't have been able to identify them in a police lineup.

⊙ ⊙ ⊙

But how did they track me down? I didn't know them; I'm sure they didn't know me. I figured they must have been hanging around my old school, asking questions, and a former friend or enemy gave me away. But after the initial shock I really wasn't afraid of them. I didn't think they'd come back. But if they could track me down at the Academy, so could the object of their affection.

So it was that I was frightened but not surprised when Miranda ran up to me at the end of the week as I was coming out from class and yelled, "Benjamin is here!"

I turned back to the door but it was too late. Kids were stampeding out, blocking my retreat, and Miranda was glued to my arm.

And then I saw him, walking over. But it was the wrong Benjamin. Or rather at this point they were all the wrong Benjamins. Miranda must have recognized him from the photo, because they'd never met.

He stopped a few yards away and smiled at me nervously. I felt my heart sink. I hadn't seen him since that fateful night. I hadn't looked at him since feeding his picture to the flames. And now here he was.

"I thought you might want a ride home," he said, flashing a smile.

"I have a ride."

He stepped closer, and when he took my arm I thought of the other Benjamin taking my arm. But I didn't flinch. For a moment I looked into his eyes, but only a moment. God this was hard! It was the hardest thing I'd ever done, not to squeeze him and cover him with kisses! Not good for the long haul, I chanted to myself like a mantra. Not good for the long haul.

"I didn't think you were the type to hold a grudge," he said.

"It's not a grudge. It's destiny."

"I thought you cared about me!"

"Don't do this," I said, walking away. I could barely get the words out. I felt completely weak. Where was Miranda?

When he grabbed my arm again I felt his nails biting into my flesh. "Look in my eyes and tell me you don't love me."

Liar extraordinaire that I was, I thought I could pull it off. But I couldn't. I just couldn't. All I could say was, "You're hurting my arm."

"I'm not letting you go," he said, letting go of my arm. "I'll be back." And he walked to his car without turning around.

"Is it OK if he takes *me* home?" Miranda asked, coming into view.

I couldn't let her see me cry, not mousy Miranda. But I was beyond repair and the damn burst.

"I was only teasing," she said, as if it were her fault. And she led me to the now-empty stairs to regroup.

Two Benjamins in and out of my life, I thought. One who wanted to kill me, one who wanted to kill himself. I was in the middle of a long tunnel and trains were coming from both directions. Would any of us survive the wreckage?

My Vesuvius

But I had to go on, didn't I? In four days it would be Friday again—another long lonely weekend in store. And if I got through that, well, in another five days I'd have to suffer through it all over again. What was I supposed to do? Steal my dad's nine-iron and offer myself to the first bolt of lightning that came along? But I wasn't the one with a death wish. Much as I sometimes regretted.

Life was my obsession. Unjust, cruel, miserable life. Survival was my destiny—unfortunate as that now seemed.

So it was that when Miranda wanted to fix me up with a basketball player in her history class I only said a timid no and not my usual emphatic, end-of-the-world no that had always been my answer to Miranda's meddling attempts to fix me up.

And when she described him to me after school—"A cinch to start at center, a bod to die for, long hair like your ex . . ." My ex! "But dark. Not the prettiest face in the world, but seen from the rear he's enough to stop traffic! And speaking of traffic, he drives a Camaro . . ." When she said these things I didn't glare at her and reply, "So what? Who cares? Big deal! You're wasting my time. If I want a date on Friday night I'll put myself in the path of some Romeo and wait for sparks to fly!"

No, I didn't glare. I didn't say those things at all. I just kind of looked away and mumbled, "Mmm . . ."

And when Miranda pointed him out in the hall the next day—he didn't see us, he was walking away, I was privileged to see his "good" side—and she said, "Isn't he gorgeous? A hundred percent hunk!" I didn't say, "I'd blow him away like a dandelion! He's about as graceful as a mastodon! His hair isn't anything like . . ." No, I didn't say any of those things. I just stared absently down the hall like a shell-shocked vet and mumbled, "He's OK."

And when she jabbed her straw like a dagger into my shoulder in the cafeteria and said, "Melissa and Jason and

Wayne and me are going to *Brain Dead* Friday night, why don't you and Bradford come along? Wayne's already spoken to Brad and it's cool with him, so what do you say?"

When she asked this did I scream back, "What! Are you crazy? Who gave you permission?" and so on, and so on. Did I tear her straw into shreds and storm out like a friend betrayed? Or did I let my fork sink into my mashed potatoes and grumble in a beaten voice, "Why not?"

Well, why not?

⊙ ⊙ ⊙

I regretted my decision immediately. I mean immediately! But the card had been played and Miranda was not the kind of friend to let me fold. I only hoped the stakes weren't higher than one night of excruciating embarrassment, that I wouldn't be paying for this moment of weakness all my life.

I regretted my decision even more the night in question, searching for something passable to wear—not moronic but not too sexy. And nothing I'd ever worn with Ben. But I regretted my decision the most when I opened the back door of Jason's Buick and saw Bradford's bent body squeezed next to Miranda and Wayne. Well, he may have been hot stuff from behind the basket, but seen from the scorer's table he was just another guy named Bradford.

And *Brain Dead!* I mean, you'd think with twenty-two movies playing at the super-duper plex the odds against picking the absolute worst flick would be pretty low. I mean, was this supposed to be funny or scary? I certainly didn't think it was either. And what was worse was that Bradford was enthralled! And he laughed at all the parts that were supposed to be scary and jumped at all the parts that were meant to be funny. And on top of all that—stale popcorn.

I didn't just want my money back—I wanted my youth back. When he put his arm around me after the first corpse appeared I felt like a corpse myself, entombed in the arms of a center I could never love or cheer for. But I let him keep it there. Well, why not?

⊙ ⊙ ⊙

I prayed for an early night, I pled migraine and curfew, but they weren't my wheels and the majority was thirsty. So there we sat in a booth for six beneath the cold fluorescent glare at Denny's, drinking milkshakes and coffee. I hadn't looked very closely at Bradford until now. Like with those unoriginal gangsters, I wanted to observe as little as possible. But sitting next to each other beneath the bright lights he was kind of hard to miss. And, truth to tell, he wasn't ugly or anything. He had a straight nose and clear skin and OK hair. I mean, for guys named Bradford he probably ranked near the top.

But that just wasn't good enough for me.

Besides, those were his physical qualities. When it came to charm, personality, and intelligence he probably ranked near the bottom, even among Bradfords. You'd think someone who stuffed point guards for a living wouldn't be intimidated by a girl out of uniform, but he seemed pretty nervous to me, quiet as a giraffe, squirming in his chair, avoiding eye contact.

"Christy's an expert on astrology," Miranda said, playing matchmaker. "Why don't you tell her your sign and she'll tell you how many points you're going to score?"

None with me, I thought.

"I don't know my sign."

"What's your birth date?" Miranda pressed on.

"July fifteenth."

"Then you're a Cancer. Tell him about Cancers, Christy. That's good, isn't it?"

"Sure, it's wonderful," I mumbled. "You'll have a long life."

"What's so good about cancer?" he asked, and the frightening part is he wasn't joking. Ben didn't know much about astrology, but he hated astrology. Bradford, on the other hand, was just ignorant.

Our astrological conversation bit the dust right there and then. I couldn't bear the tense silence, everyone looking to me for direction. So I decided to give him the Marlowe SAT.

"Do you believe in karma?"

"What's that?"

Minus two. "What about reincarnation?"

"You mean where you were an ant in a past life?"

I wasn't an ant, but you might have been, I thought. "What about crystals?"

"Sure, *they're* real enough." And he laughed like I was the loony one.

"I mean crystal power. But you obviously don't believe." We weren't getting very far on the mysticism test, so I moved on to traditional science. "What do you think of the theory of black holes?"

Blank stare. Time's up.

"What's the second largest planet?"

"Neptune!" Miranda shouted.

"I'm not asking you! Besides, it's not Neptune."

"Mars?"

Mars! Mars!

So much for science, on to career choice. "So what do you want to do with your life if NASA turns you down?"

"Well, if I can't get a basketball scholarship I'd like to sell cars."

Sell cars! No offense, members of that noble profession, but I always thought selling cars was what people did after they failed the polygraph for the third time.

The boys then started talking about torque and horsepower and the conversation drifted away from me. Bradford didn't even have the sense to feel insulted. Obviously he was only thinking of one thing when it came to me. If he was thinking at all.

⊙ ⊙ ⊙

I breathed a deep, deep sigh of relief when I finally got home, knowing I'd never have to see Bradford again, except maybe at a basketball game with referees between us. And then in the candlelight of my room I cried. Dead tired as I was I couldn't go to sleep, a thousand memories pounding my brain. Ben's picture was ashes but I'd never seen him as clearly as he appeared before me now. It seemed every word he'd ever said to me, every moment we'd ever spent together, was preserved in my mind, to be played over and over like a video of Atlantis before it crumbled into the sea.

I spent Saturday in the confines of my room, venturing out only to cycle a couple laps around the block. When Miranda called to find out if I had a good time last night I was as blunt as a basketball. After all, I was in no mood for diplomacy, and my usual gentle way with words went by the wayside.

"You're still in love with Ben," she said. "You never should have split up."

You too? I thought. Is everyone against me on this? Am I the only one who thinks I made the right decision?

Apparently so, because after I got home from school Monday, Svetlana called. She wasn't naming sources, but she wanted to know if I could come over now. Now!

I backed my mom into the corner of the kitchen. "It's not enough you're all against me!" I yelled. "It's not enough my parents and my friends think I did the wrong thing! You have to bring in my astrologer!"

"Christy, I don't know what you're talking about."

I almost didn't go. I thought Svetlana was unbribable,

but by this time nothing surprised me about human nature. Or maybe my mom had threatened to sue her for endangering the health of a minor and Svetlana was forced to redraw the skies to stay out of court.

But I went just the same, partly because I was curious what she would say, partly to get my mom off my back, partly because it was my fate to go.

But when plump Svetlana pulled open her door I glimpsed a familiar figure sitting confidently in the wicker chair, a teacup in his hand.

"Oh no, you don't!"

But Svetlana grabbed my arm as I struggled to leave. It seemed the whole world was grabbing my arm these days. And the Russian lady's grip was as powerful as any. But then she had the gravity of the stars pulling behind her.

"Have a seat, Amushka," she said with a smile, using the affectionate name, but in a firm voice, like she was commanding an infant. "Sit in that chair."

I obeyed without further protest. Ben didn't say anything, and he wasn't smiling. But he kept his eyes on me. I still felt them on me when I looked away, like drills gouging out my heart.

"Would you like some tea, darling?"

"No thanks."

But she poured me a cup anyway. Ben's new chart was spread out on the table, but I intentionally looked away.

"I don't want to be here. Say what you have to say and let me go."

I thought this would draw her fire, but my anger had the opposite effect. She came over and smothered me in her arms. "My poor Amushka! My poor, foolish girl!"

She returned to her chair, sat back like she had no other appointments today, and stared at me with her heavily painted blue eyes. "Why didn't you come to me at once?"

"I knew the score."

"Not even doctors diagnose themselves."

"I wasn't following my diagnosis. I was following yours."

"But situations change, darling. The stars don't stand still."

I stole a glance at Ben. He was wearing chinos and a denim shirt, and his long blond hair shimmered. I wondered if he had a date last night.

"I took the time to redraw Ben's chart," Svetlana said.

"It's no use," I argued. "He's still a Sagittarian."

"Yes, darling, but even Sagittarius for you is not a death sentence. There are positive values in all natal combinations. And with Mercury in the second House and Saturn in the fifth, I see hopeful possibilities."

"Benjamin was a Sagittarian."

"I remember."

"And Tamarind Ellerbee says about Capricorn and Sagittarius, 'Not good for the long haul.'"

"Yes, yes."

"And you told me yourself in this same room to stay away from Sagittarians!"

Svetlana sighed.

"Are you telling me you can interpret the stars to mean anything you want? Because if that's the case I don't see the point . . ."

"No, darling. I'm saying astrology is a complicated art. And for all your knowledge you're still an amateur."

"But I was listening to you! And you specifically told me to stay away from Sagittarians!"

"Sure, sure. But do you remember that I also told you reading the stars is like predicting the weather? In the same way I would warn you not to walk beneath black clouds without an umbrella, I would advise you to shield yourself against Sagittarians. But sometimes it's better to get wet. And some days you take an umbrella and it never rains."

I felt my stomach turning. I wanted to believe, of course. But everything I knew warned me to be on guard. Ben had probably come to her, pleading, and she was just being kind and generous.

"But it can't work in the long run," I said.

"Why not?"

"You know why not. Look what happened with Benjamin. You're the one who told me not to date Sagittarians."

"No, I never speak in absolutes. Like a meteorologist, I only describe tendencies. Yes, I would prefer Ben were a Pisces. I think your road would be easier. But since he's a Sagittarian that doesn't mean a successful relationship is impossible. True, I wouldn't advise you to go looking for a Sagittarian any more than I would advise you to live under a volcano. But millions of people live under volcanoes without ever seeing an eruption. If you fell in love with someone who happened to be Sagittarian, I would never tell you it can't work, but only advise you of the perils. You have your own role to play in your life, after all. Now look at the chart."

And against my will I leaned over the table while Svetlana went through all the planets and their houses at the time of Ben's birth—his real birth—along with the aspects of the sun and moon, and patiently explained what it all meant for our future. It certainly wasn't the rosiest of pictures, and I could see she wasn't just handing me a line, but it wasn't a death sentence either. There were real signs of promise.

Throughout my rediscovery of Ben's astrological nature, the accused himself sat comfortably in his chair, sipping tea. For a complete skeptic, he sure had a lot of faith in Svetlana.

When it was all over I sat back myself and finally picked up my own cup of lukewarm Russian tea, the planetary symbols flashing like neon signs in my brain. I was one confused girl.

"Do you have any questions?" Svetlana asked.

I was torn. Of course, I still loved Ben. That was never an issue. Of course I wanted to believe. But I'd been so wrong before with Benjamin. I didn't think I could survive another massive mistake.

"You're saying there are no guarantees . . ."

"There are never guarantees," Svetlana said, looking at me very seriously. "That's a fate all of us share."

"But what should I do?"

Her face relaxed into a huge smile. "He's a good boy. I should keep him if I could."

I grinned, secretly bursting with happiness inside, like a volcano of relief. "Is that the stars talking or cash under the table?"

Svetlana pretended not to hear. As she led us to the door she gave Ben as big a hug as she gave me, and kisses on both cheeks. My body was tingling with nervous energy as I ran down the stairs, ahead of him. I didn't want any tearful reconciliation. I didn't want to push fate too far.

But Ben caught up with me outside. "Can I give you a ride home?"

It was the first time he had spoken, the first words I'd heard from his lips since he said he wouldn't let me go. Well he hadn't, had he?

"That's OK."

"Did you ride your bike?"

"I took the El."

"Then come on." And when he took my hand it was like I wasn't even touching another person but another part of myself, my renegade twin. Still, I had my doubts.

"Another hundred and fifty dollars down the drain," I said.

"Don't you think it was worth it? Anyway, she wouldn't take money."

"She wouldn't? Wow."

He kissed me—our first kiss in eons, and yet it all felt so familiar. But I didn't put energy of my own into it.

"What's the matter?"

"It's just that we're so different," I said. "While Svetlana's explaining your chart you're scoffing at the whole idea. It's just something you did to get me back. It's bad enough we're starcrossed, without believing in different things. Or I should say without you believing in anything."

He turned to me and put his hands on my shoulders, like he was going to shake me, and vowed, "The first star I discover I'll name 'Amushka!'"

Alas, Romeo

Friday night—my favorite night!—and I had another nine o'clock movie date. But Bradford was history—had he ever been anything else?—and I wasn't seeing Brain Dead at the super-duper plex but a four-star French import at the closet-sized Roxy in Evanston.

The stars were back on my ceiling, freshly painted and in the right direction this time. Progress always comes from what seems at first glance to be total disaster. My mom no longer brought carbohydrates to my door and my dad stopped looking at me like I was a Cubs' ace who can't find the strike zone.

I took the El to Evanston. The season was beginning to get cool, but it was still warm enough for short skirts and open windows.

"Hi sweetie," I said, kissing Ben inside the apartment. He pulled me so close there wasn't any space between us, like we were custom-made to fit together. "How was your first week of college?"

"Busy, but exciting."

"You'll have to tell me all about it!"

"And what about your week?"

"I'm back in the front row!"

"To stay, I hope."

"My desk's bolted to the floor. So what's this flick *Genevieve* about?"

"Not Jen-e-veve! Zhon-vee-ev."

"I've had my limit of psycho killers. I hope it's a love story."

"All French films are love stories. Did you bring money?" he teased.

"For popcorn."

I asked Ben about the plot and read the poster at the theater, but once the film began, I didn't even read the subtitles. Because, truth to tell, there was too much contentment in my bloodstream to concentrate on anything for long. I just watched Zhon-vee-ev drift between the arms of her two lovers while I sat comfortably wrapped in the arms of my own and let the violins massage my ears.

⊙ ⊙ ⊙

Stopping for coffee afterwards, Ben quizzed me on the plot and it came out that I hadn't read the subtitles.

"I can't believe you," he said. "You complain about these awful movies you go to, but when I take you to a first-rate film you don't even read the subtitles!"

"I got the gist. Besides, how could I concentrate on anything with you breathing next to me?"

"What happened to your sarcasm?"

"It's in remission. I'm too happy to be cruel! God, that guy I went out with last week was such a moron! I mean, he's probably OK, but he's not in your league. I missed you so much! If you had a date last week don't tell me. I don't want to know."

"No, I stayed home."

I smiled. "Really? Did you rent a video?"

"No. I had a lot to do to prepare for school. It was nice not to have any distractions."

I elbowed him in the ribs. "You don't mean that?"

"No," he admitted, smiling back. "It was a rotten weekend."

⊙ ⊙ ⊙

My house was a scene of celebration. Ben was welcomed like a son returning from war. My mom insisted on serving him carrot cake—I didn't even know we had carrot cake. My dad went for the cigars. After a while jealousy got the best of me and I dragged Ben back to my room for some serious kissing.

"Look, I repainted my stars!" I pointed out proudly.

"Now everything's where it's supposed to be," he said. "I'm surprised in your anger you didn't paint them over."

"Yeah, well . . ."

"Where's my picture?" he asked, looking at the night-stand.

Damn. Damn! "It was an accident, I swear!"

"You shouldn't have put it so close to the candle," he said with a grin.

"Exactly! I promise it won't happen again."

We said goodbye outside, holding each other at the front gate, at the threshold, so to speak.

"Let's get married!" I said, without thinking. But I was glad I said it, and I looked closely into his eyes for a clue to his feelings.

He laughed, but all guys laugh at first, don't they? Laugh first, cry later.

"I thought the man was supposed to ask that question?"

"Well I'm a new age woman. If I want to smoke a cigar, I light up. If I want to propose, I pop the question."

"You're a new age *girl*. And a wild girl. Too wild for matrimony."

"No, Marlowes mate for life—or until a murder conviction. I'll never want anyone else."

"You're only . . . How old are you again?"

"You're just saying that because you want to play the field. I'm fine for a fling, but a guy like you would never marry a girl like me."

"I didn't say that. You don't know what I think," he said mysteriously, but with a hint of promise.

"Tell me!"

"No."

"Well, how am I supposed to know?"

"What's your hurry?"

"I don't mean for now. I mean in the future. When I'm freezing my ass on some remote snow-capped observatory, will I be wearing a ring under my mittens?"

"Why don't you ask Svetlana?"

⊙ ⊙ ⊙

I began to understand our twisted lives in a new light thanks to Mrs. Williams having assigned us *Romeo and Juliet* in English class. I knew the story—everyone knows the story. I mean, I'd seen the music video. But now I was reading the actual play, and there were the words, right up front in the prologue:

"From forth the fatal loins of these two foes
A pair of starcrossed lovers take their life."

Of course it wasn't an exact match. We weren't Italians with feuding parents. But Benjamin filled the part of Paris pretty well—the jerk pledged to Juliet. And "take their life," well there was Ben's lust for lightning. And "star-crossed—" definitely.

I read the play straight through Sunday night, and even the notes and introduction. It was ominous to the max, but also strangely beautiful.

Ben found me rereading it on the front steps when he came to pick me up from school on Monday.

"Have you ever read *Romeo and Juliet*?" I asked.

He sat down beside me and looked at the cover. "Sure."

"Isn't it ominous? Isn't it our story too?"

"What do you mean?"

"Well, there are all these similarities."

"Like our families fighting for generations?"

"Forget about that. But the play starts with a brawl that brings in the authorities. Well that could be Benjamin's fight that got him sent to the slammer. Then Romeo's in love with this girl named Rosalina. That could be your first Christy. Then he meets Juliet at a masked ball. Well, we met at a plastic surgeon's office, which is a place of disguise. Then Tybalt vows revenge against Romeo. That could be Benjamin too—he covers all the villains in our version. Then there's the nurse, who advises and helps Juliet. That could be Svetlana. Then Romeo and

Juliet, having already fallen in love, discover their identities and that they're starcrossed. Isn't it phenomenal?"

But Ben seemed unimpressed. "Don't they get secretly married?"

"By the friar. I'm willing if you are."

"And I seem to remember a double suicide."

"Yes, suicide's a major theme, although they're driven to it by circumstance, not like . . ." I almost said "you," but held my tongue.

"What does that have to do with us?"

"Well we don't have to follow the story in every detail. But don't you think it's remarkable?"

"I think you could find as many similarities in *Hamlet* or the *Wizard of Oz*. It's like astrology. You can always find patterns if you look hard enough."

I was disappointed by his skepticism. He was wrong, pure and simple. There was no other story that so clearly explained our own love. And it was written hundreds of years ago.

"I don't care what you say. Shakespeare's our Nostradamus. Only we'll change the ending. Just tell me, would you kill Paris?"

"I don't remember that part."

"Paris was Juliet's betrothed. When Romeo thinks she's dead he goes to the crypt to drink poison beside her body. But Paris is there and won't let him in. So they draw swords."

"Couldn't Romeo just come back later? If she's supposed to be dead I don't understand his hurry."

"You're so damn practical, I hate that. OK, so you wouldn't kill Paris. Would you kill yourself if you thought I was dead?"

"No."

"No!"

Ben laughed. "You sound disappointed."

"Well I am, I mean kind of." I wanted to shout out, "You're the suicidal one. If you'd do it just to do it, why wouldn't you do it for me?" But maybe it had just been a phase. Maybe I'd blown the whole thing out of proportion.

"You wouldn't kill yourself for me," Ben said.

"Sure I would! 'Dagger, find thy sheath.' I think that's beautiful."

"It's sick. It's terrible."

"Well how would you live without me?"

"The same way I lived without you last week. I'd be miserable for a while and then eventually, hopefully, find someone else."

"Someone else!" I was already a ghost, jealous of Christy number three.

"So would you."

"No I wouldn't! We're destined for each other. We're soulmates."

"Do you really think among six billion people you couldn't find someone else to be happy with?"

"It's only three billion, because half are women. Then if you take away China and all the countries I'll never visit, and all the people too young or too old or too sick or already happily married, there aren't that many guys left to choose from. I'd never find anyone like you."

"How do you know? You're only sixteen. Anyway, you shouldn't have to kill yourself."

"Well I think it's beautiful."

"You wouldn't think it was beautiful if Juliet were your daughter, or your sister, or your friend. Remember, she was a child."

"I know. Thirteen. And you were worried I was under-age! But what would you have them do? I mean, Romeo's been banished and if the friar hadn't come up with his dangerous plan to fake Juliet's death, she would have had to marry Paris. Except she wouldn't. Because she vowed to kill herself if it came to that."

"Why couldn't she just run away after the marriage?"

"Her family would kill her. It's not like today, she didn't have a car, she couldn't hop on a plane. Besides, if Paris found out she wasn't a virgin *he'd* kill her."

"But why trade the risk of death for the certainty of death? I don't think it would have been the end of the world. They could have waited. They could have found some way to be together. But then who's to say they wouldn't have been better off apart? How long had they known each other? How many Romeos turn into Casanovas and how many Juliets into Jezebels after a few years? What if Romeo wanted a large family and Juliet wanted a career? What if Romeo got trans-ferred to England and Juliet wanted to stay in Italy? What if

Romeo gambled all their savings away? Or Juliet, lonely and frustrated, drank all the wine in their cellar?"

"But it's true love!"

"True lovers don't destroy each other. They save each other."

"OK, OK, maybe you're right," I gave in. "But it's beautiful for a play."

Wasn't it strange that after worrying all summer that Ben was suicidal and might try to take his life in the next storm—and after trying without success to draw him out, to have a heart-to-heart, that when the subject of suicide finally came up, *I* was the idiot arguing in favor of self-destruction, and Ben against?

What was I thinking?

I opened the book at random and read:

"Give me my Romeo, and when I shall die
Take him and cut him out in little stars,
And he will make the face of heaven so fine
That all the world will be in love with night . . ."

Then Ben took the book and searched for a minute before replying, as if to rub my idiocy in:

"Come death, and welcome! Juliet wills it so."

An Arsenal of Words

Academy turf was the school itself—a modern one-story number with graffittiless walls, no metal detectors, and that special feature not found at Al Capone High—worth paying the big bucks for—running water in the bathroom. In the back there were four tennis courts, with nets, and a baseball diamond, with grass. In front was the sacred Academy lawn—no crabgrass here—with carefully trimmed bushes lining the semicircle drive. And it all looked out onto an upper-class suburban street with old-money homes owned by the kind of white-collar criminals that made my dad famous, with swimming pools, gardeners, and designer dogs.

I was waiting on the front steps for Ben when Miranda walked over.

"Wanna come to my house?"

"I would, but Ben is picking me up."

"Really? You didn't tell me you got back together!"

"Yeah, well everything happened suddenly."

"I thought you were crazy to break up, even if he was the wrong sign. With all he has going for him, how many guys like that do you see around?"

"I've seen only one."

"So what happened? Our triple date from hell open your eyes?"

"It gave me a push. What really did it was my astrologer. Seems I was overreacting."

"So you're compatible after all?"

"I didn't say that. But it's my destiny, you know."

"Poor Christy. What sacrifices you make for destiny. Oh look, there's his BMW now. When am I going to get to know your mystery crush?"

"After the honeymoon."

"Why don't we all go out Friday night?"

I didn't say yes, I didn't say no. I left Miranda fumbling for a cigarette and trotted to Ben's car.

But danger intervened. Another car, the likes of which

had probably never been seen in the Academy semicircle drive—a rusting Pontiac with front-end damage and a trash bag where one of the windows should have been screeched to a halt behind us. The driver was wearing a White Sox hat.

"Hey, I want to talk to you!"

"Too bad!" I shouted, hurrying to open the door.

But before I could get in, Ben stepped out, and Benjamin was fast approaching. "Not you," he said. "Him!"

"What are you doing here?" I shouted. "Aren't you getting hives, being so close to a school?"

"What do you have to say?" Ben asked in a calm voice, swallowing the bait, probably thinking the best thing was not to challenge him. Which probably was the best thing. But I was angry.

"Beat it before I call security!"

I wasn't afraid at all. I mean, we were in a public place in broad daylight swarming with teenagers, what could Benjamin do?

Well, he'd tried to strangle me at the air show, hadn't he? In broad daylight in view of all of Chicago. But that frightful example was forgotten in the stress of the moment, and only Ben's hostage-negotiator cool prevented a general massacre.

"Let him talk, Christy."

"Not in front of *her*." And the way Benjamin said "her" without even looking at me, drove my non-violent nature completely underground. "Let's take a walk."

"Oh no, you don't!" I said, restraining Ben, who had taken a step. "There won't be any fighting!"

"Don't worry," Benjamin said. "He's bigger than I am."

"Yeah, but fists were never your weapon of choice."

"Frisk me then."

"You should get out of here," I warned. "Some gang kids were looking for you the other day."

I expected Benjamin to ask questions, look worried, or accuse me of making the whole thing up. But he just stared like I was speaking Japanese. Obviously I wasn't the only one in denial.

"It's all right," Ben said. "Wait in the car."

"No!"

"I'll be back in ten minutes. Wait in the car."

The look in Ben's eyes told me there was nothing I could do. This was a guy thing, a stupid guy thing. "Promise no fighting," I said to Ben. "Remember that kid you almost killed in karate class."

Ben tossed me the keys and they walked out of view without coming to blows. I turned on the radio but the music only made me more nervous.

Miranda peeked in. "What's going on? I just saw the two Benjamins walking to the ball field."

I jumped out of the car. "Get some people, there may be a fight!"

I left her and ran around back to the baseball diamond. I stopped when I saw them in the outfield talking, or rather Benjamin was talking and Ben was standing by the fence, his back turned away. His back turned! What was he thinking? Didn't he care that he could be strangled, stabbed, hit on the back of the head with a rock? What were they talking about that he didn't even think of protecting himself?

I didn't have time to guess the answer myself because Miranda ran over with half our class. I think they were hoping for a fight by the looks of disappointment on their faces. When Benjamin saw all of us standing there he took the hint and made off behind the fence. The disappointed crowd left, Miranda threatened to call me later, and Ben slowly walked back alone.

"So?" I asked nervously when he didn't say anything, or even look at me.

"So nothing," he said. And that was all he said until we reached the car.

"Get out," he said, when I got in.

"No!"

He pulled out of the semicircle drive, but instead of turning toward Evanston he headed for the city.

"You're not going to fight," I told him.

"Who says anything about fighting?" He wasn't looking at me.

"So what happened?"

"Nothing."

"What did he say? Did he threaten you?"

"No." But Ben couldn't face me.

"I don't believe you. You agreed on a time and place to settle the score."

"Don't be stupid!"

"Well then, promise me."

"You don't want me to fight for you, is that what you want me to say?"

"Why are you yelling at me? It's not my fault."

"It's all your fault!"

Well, I guess it was, after all.

I noticed he was driving to my place. He was dropping me off.

"You can at least pull into the driveway," I said after he stopped on the street in front of my house, traffic piling up behind, cars starting to honk. I stayed put and Ben turned into the driveway. But he kept the engine running. And he wasn't saying goodbye, let alone leaning over for a kiss. Talk about men going to battle, putting on their game face!

"Come in for a minute," I said, easing the car door open.

"I have to go."

"Where?" As if I didn't know.

"I'm going home."

"Then why don't you take me with you?"

Finally he looked at me, but it wasn't war paint that made his face so red but anger, jealousy, blood-boiling resentment. "I want to be alone," he said.

Suddenly I realized it wasn't Benjamin he wanted to take his vengeance out on, but me.

"Fine!" I shouted, getting out. I slammed the door. I'd

never slammed his door before. What a complicated species we are! I mean, a micro-second ago I was worried for Ben's life, but now I wanted to wring it out of him with my own bare hands! And if I couldn't do that, I would take it out on his car.

I climbed on the rear bumper before he could back out and sat on the roof, my legs dangling over the rear windshield and in his rearview mirror. I admit it was a rough thing to do to a BMW, but I couldn't let him just drive away, could I?

He turned off the engine and jumped out. "What are you doing?"

I climbed down and confronted him, just like Benjamin had confronted him on the ball field. "You can't drive away without explaining what crime I've committed to make you hate me!"

He could have said he didn't hate me, he could have said his anger had nothing to do with me. Instead he walked around the car, maybe thinking what he should say, or if he should say anything, or maybe just trying to cool down. I'd never seen him so overwrought.

Finally, after circling the car, he faced me and said quietly, like a prosecutor, "You told me you didn't write any letters to prison."

I was completely unprepared for this. I had been so worried they were going to fight, the thought had never entered my brain that Benjamin had come not to fight with fists or knives or guns, but with another kind of weapon—an arsenal of words. That he had come as he said, to talk. To talk about me.

Ben pulled out a copy of the letter from his pocket—it must have been a copy because Benjamin would never part with the original of such a damaging piece of evidence.

"'My poor baby,'" he read without emotion, which somehow gave the words all the feeling in the world. "'I can't imagine how lonely it must be for you, locked in a dark cell with hardened criminals. I'm deathly afraid for your safety—I worry those guys have connections on the inside . . . but I can't even think about it. All I think about is coming to visit my precious darling and pressing my lips to the glass . . .'"

There was more, but Ben had made his point. I was guilty as charged. But we were all guilty, weren't we?

"So? What's the big deal? I'm sure you wrote plenty of love letters before you met me."

"No."

"OK, e-mail then, notes passed under the desk in school. I'm sure Christy number one poured Giorgio on *her* letters!"

"She never wrote any letters," Ben said bitterly. "You told me it was over before the trial."

"It was, it was! I only wrote him that once, I swear! I never visited him, you can ask my parents, Miranda, you can check the reformatory records. I never read his letters."

"You told me you never really loved him. But you did love him. Even afterwards."

"No! I was confused! I felt guilty myself, it was all just dramatic excess. Anyway, that's history, and I don't see why you're even bringing it up. Do you think I don't love you?"

"I thought you didn't love him."

"I don't, I don't," I said, wiping my eyes.

"But you did." And he dropped the letter between us, like a broken treaty.

"No! Never! Not like I love you!"

He paced around the car again.

"Why am I the one on trial here? How do I know you don't still love that other Christy?"

Ben looked at me with enraged eyes. "I never loved her!" he said, and he said it so forcefully I couldn't help but believe him.

"You've had other girlfriends, I'm sure. I don't know anything about them."

He backed me against the car. "Why didn't you tell me about the tattoo?"

I swallowed hard. I thought he'd never have to know. Damn Benjamin! If I ever saw him again I'd tear him to pieces.

I walked to the gate and leaned against it for support. It hadn't been that long ago I'd brought up the subject of marriage on this very spot, this threshhold between home and the cruel, faceless world beyond. And now we were breaking apart.

"We've both kept secrets from each other," Ben said in

a wounded voice. "We've both lied. But I thought our love was real."

"I was a child!"

"Is that what you'll tell your next boyfriend? That you were still a child with me?"

"I'm not the only one with a tattoo."

"I know. But I ask myself, how much does a girl have to love someone to get his name tattooed not on her arm or shoulder, but over her heart? And I can't bear to think of the answer."

"Oh Christ!" I cursed, getting up. "You're more jealous than he is!"

"So what if I am? I think I have reason!"

"What do you want me to do? Tattoo your name over his? Tattoo your name on both breasts? Tell me! What do I have to do to prove I love only you?"

He looked away. He didn't have an answer. "I believed in you, that's all."

"Well, you can go to hell," I said. "You can go back to that other Christy!"

And I stormed into my house, suddenly wanting to be alone as well.

Total Eclipse

I didn't have a chance to sort through yesterday's events the next morning at school because *Romeo and Juliet* was up for discussion in English class and I found it all pretty fascinating, so for the rest of the day I was awash on the blood-stained streets of fair Verona.

It wasn't until sixth bell rang that I descended back into the bowels of gangland Chicago. From the relative security of the front steps I looked for my pals from the hood, but all the tough-looking guys were wearing polo shirts. No sign of Benjamin either. Thank God. He was the one I was really worried about.

My parents had pretty well reassured me last night. When the story came out at dinner and I told them how angry I was, how Ben had mistreated me, how the whole thing was so unfair, etc., etc., they wholeheartedly stood up for him, which made it easier for me to forget my anger and sympathize for the poor fool too. I mean, I may be good looking, and clever once school lets out, and loyal if not 100 percent truthful, and galaxies of fun, but I never claimed to be uncomplicated. My parents both thought a little jealousy on Ben's part was natural and expected, considering my rocky past. And that was without telling them about Benjamin's stalking me, about his appearance at school, about the letter to prison, about my tattoo. Come to think of it, what *did* I tell them?

The bottom line was they liked Ben too much to let me let him go. And as long as he didn't commit a federal crime, as long as his only flaws were a slight suicidal tendency and a little jealousy—or a lot of jealousy—I should keep my mouth shut and count my blessings.

"Call him," my mom had said. "Don't go to sleep angry at each other."

But he wasn't home, or he wasn't answering his phone. So I left a sweet message, and then another before I went to sleep, with an apology to his car, promising to pay for damages.

⊙ ⊙ ⊙

After school I waited a few minutes for a black BMW with scuff marks to roll by, but I was betting on a dead horse—or I should say a jealous horse. I guess I should have been angry myself that he was taking it this way, but we had been through so much already I didn't want to let the imperfect past destroy our perfect future. Besides, I was so touched that he went back to Svetlana—the sight of him sitting confidently in the wicker chair, well, that counted for something.

So seeing how I was the more rational partner at the moment—how long would that last?—I decided to go up to Evanston and surprise him. Reassure him that he was my only Romeo. And maybe snoop around a little.

He didn't answer the door. I didn't expect him to. He was probably still at class. He had given me a key for times like this. Would he be glad to find me here?

Not if I was looking through his bedroom drawers. So I decided to take care of that business first. I already knew all there was to know about the living room, kitchen, and bathroom, but I had never opened his dresser drawers or peeked in his closet. What was I looking for? Clues to his past, anything that would make him less mysterious. But most of all I was looking for Christy. I figured maybe something happened between them to explain his jealousy, something he was too sensitive to talk about.

My soulmate's bedroom—an unmade bed, two dressers, his bike leaning against the wall, a laundry basket, a night table, a closed closet. What stories was it waiting to tell me?

I started with the dressers, but there were just clothes, except for a couple pornographic magazines. But nothing gay, S&M, or with children or animals. That was always good news.

Maybe they were engaged, I thought, feeling under the matress, looking under the bed. Basketballs of dust. I made a mental note to sign him up with a cleaning service.

Nightstand drawer—his checkbook. But after working for my father all summer and learning respect for sensitive financial transactions I decided not to peek. Besides, what could it tell me? Well, he could have bought her a ring, an multi-carat ring, never returned. I gave the checkbook a real quick glance, my eyes open for jewelers. I didn't look at the balance.

Finally the closet. It creaked open. Tons of clothes, the famous Northwestern jersey on its hanger, skis, boots, old books, a Stone Age computer, and four boxes on the top shelf. The first box was pretty big and didn't have a lid. I pulled it down but there was just junk inside—tools, old cassettes and CDs, loose golf balls and tees.

The other three boxes were smaller and had lids. The first was filled with bills, but nothing very interesting. I went through it quickly because Ben might be home soon.

The second box was documents. I sorted through it on the bed. Insurance policies, his parents' divorce decree, papers that had belonged to his father, that he had inherited, that meant nothing now, but which he couldn't throw away. It wasn't organized at all, and like the other boxes was kept on the top shelf. It didn't seem like he ever looked at this stuff, but had just stored it away, out of the way.

And the third box? Photos. Not in albums, not organized in any way but just piled in the box. I sat down on the bed and went through them carefully.

They were all out of order, so after looking at a prom picture of Ben with some dark-haired beauty—was this her?—I picked up a team photo from little league baseball, then an older picture camping with his father. I looked closely at his father for signs of depression, but saw none. He didn't look much like Ben, except for the piercing blue eyes. He was smiling in the photo, like he would live forever.

There were more pictures of Ben with his father. On the baseball diamond, on the ski slopes, squinting at the Statue of Liberty. But where was his mother? He told me she died when he was a baby, but why didn't he have her picture?

And then I picked up a photograph that chilled me like a snowstorm, that blinded me and opened my eyes completely. It made no sense at all, and yet it made perfect sense. It explained everything, but I stared and stared and couldn't bring myself to grasp it.

He must have been eight or nine. Older than the passport photo, but with the same cute cheeks and boyish haircut. But there was nothing boyish about the tattoo on his arm. He sat on a woman's lap, a young woman, blond, pretty, his arm entwined with hers, and each engraved with the other's name.

I stared for a long time. I no longer thought about Ben coming through the door, I no longer thought about my Ben at all, but about *her* Ben, the child in the photo, trying to imagine what she must have done to him to make him deny her existence.

I stared for a long time, silently sobbing. Except for this photograph, he had erased her from his life, more completely than I had tried to erase Benjamin from mine. Why?

I looked again at the birth certificate. I hadn't noticed his mother's name before, but I memorized it now: Christy Shire. Place of residence: Newport Beach, California.

I replaced the boxes, except for the photo, which I kept, and hurried out. I didn't want Ben to find me here. I was in too much turmoil. There had been so many lies flying through the air I didn't know what to believe. I had to try to make sense of everything myself.

On the ride home I thought of calling Svetlana. I needed a horoscope desperately. But when I locked my bedroom door it wasn't Svetlana I called but Newport information. There was a C. Shire. It might not be her. She might not live here after all these years. But I had to try.

My heart froze when a woman's voice answered the phone. "Hi," I said in my best corporate voice. "I'm an old friend of Christy Shire's from high school and I was trying to locate her."

"Well she's not in," the voice answered.

My heart jumped. "Then this is her house?"

"I'm a neighbor, just stopped by to feed her cats," the woman said.

"Is she out of town then? It's important I speak to her," I added when I didn't get an answer.

"Well . . ."

"It's nothing bad," I assured her.

"In that case . . . I'm sure she could use cheering up. I guess I can tell you, being an old friend. She's at the Sorenson Rehabilitation Center."

"A rehabilitation center!"

"She seems really serious about giving up the booze this time, after the breakdown. Why don't you give her a call?"

I didn't have a chance to absorb this latest shock, because as soon as I hung up the phone rang.

"How was my Juliet's day?" Ben asked in a bright voice.

I took a deep breath. "Fine."

"I'm sorry about yesterday. I let my jealousy get the best of me."

"That's OK . . ."

"Is there a bad connection? I can barely hear you."

I could barely speak. I held the photo in both hands, staring. "I'm just wiped."

"Oh. I thought I might swing by, take you for ice cream."

"I'm sorry."

"That's all right. I'm pretty beat myself. I'll call you tomorrow. I love you."

"I'm so sorry . . ." And the tears rolled onto the photo.

I sat on my bed and glared at Ms. Shire, the former Mrs. Penrose, as if I might understand everything—all the cruelty and treachery in people's souls—if only I looked into her empty blue eyes long enough.

$\odot \odot \odot$

My dreams were filled with alcoholic mothers screaming in rehab centers and gang fights in Verona. I got a *D* on a pop quiz in History class—how could I concentrate on stuff that happened hundreds of years ago?—and when my day was done I thought I saw those gang punks drive by in a pickup. But I could have been mistaken. I kept my eyes peeled for signs of danger, but then Ben pulled up and I forgot all about *those* troubles.

I tried not to cry when he kissed me or console him like an orphan. I tried to show a brave face, and I guess I did, because he smiled at me like I had never opened that last box.

"So you want to go back to my place?" he asked.

"I feel like walking. Why don't we go to Northwestern? You promised to show me around."

So we went to the university, and Ben pointed out the buildings where he had classes. It was a beautiful campus, with old buildings, open spaces and a lot of trees, but all I could think about was Ben's past. We went into the Student

Union building for a bite to eat, but this was not the place to talk.

"Why don't we get away from all these people," I suggested.

We walked to the football stadium, which was as quiet as a church. Ben followed me through the empty rows. It was a sunny day, for once, and I could see his long shadow blending in and out of mine as we walked.

"Forget what I said the other day. You were right. I'm as jealous as Benjamin."

"Don't talk about him."

"I'm talking about me. I've always been jealous. The tattoo just pushed me over the edge."

"I shouldn't have lied to you about the letter. I should have told you about the tattoo."

"It wouldn't have made any difference. I would have reacted just the same."

"Then let's not talk about it. It's in the past."

"But it's a flaw in my character. The jealousy, I mean."

"That's OK. You're allowed one flaw."

He kicked me from behind as we continued to walk around the stadium. "You're very forgiving today."

"I'm very understanding," I corrected. But I wanted to understand more. I should have used this opportunity to ask what I wanted to ask. But I didn't say anything.

We walked in silence for a while and then, near the open end of the stadium, I climbed up, all the way to row ZZ, and sat down.

"How do you like the campus?" Ben asked. The field was empty, as were the stands. We were completely alone, and it was perfectly quiet, the kind of silence you never hear in the city.

"It's beautiful," I said, putting an arm around him.

"Think you might want to come here?"

"I might. But then there's that minor stumbling block called grades."

"You'll make the grades. And I'll help you study for the SAT."

"I don't know if I can bring myself to root for the Wildcats," I said, gazing at the white letters painted across the end zone.

"I'm sure you'll manage."

"I don't know. I've always been a Michigan fan."

We both laughed, and I felt so content in that moment, sitting together in the empty stadium, dreaming about our future, that I forgot about the picture in my purse.

But only for a moment.

"What did your father do?" I asked, trying not to sound too interested.

"He was a teacher."

"Oh really? Where?"

"Here."

"Here in Chicago?"

"Here at Northwestern."

"Was he an astronomer?"

"No. He taught English Literature."

"Well I'm sure he would have been very proud of you. Is that why you came here?"

Ben didn't say anything.

"Did he teach *Romeo and Juliet?*"

"I don't know."

"I guess he was an expert on tragedy." I didn't know what to say, and Ben was making this impossible with his one-word answers. So I finally came right out with it. "Why did your father kill himself?"

He looked at me. "I don't know."

What now? This was so hard. I lifted up the sleeve of his T-shirt and looked at his tattoo. Christy, in corpse blue capital letters. It made me shudder.

"So tell me about her," I said.

"I already have."

"Was she pretty?"

"Not really."

"Did you love her?"

"No."

"Where did you meet?"

Ben fidgited on the bench. "At a party."

"What attracted you to her, if she wasn't so pretty? You must have liked her a little bit, if you got the tattoo."

"What if I told you she drugged me, and when I woke up the tattoo was on my arm?"

"And what about her? Did she get your name tattooed on *her* body?"

"No."

I took a deep breath, trying to smile. "Why not?"

"I told you," he said, trying to keep the irritation out of his voice. "We meant nothing to each other."

What was I doing? After all, I understood so much now. His father's suicide, Ben's own suicidal thoughts, why he'd turned his sights to the stars. If Ben had gone to such lengths to keep his mother's existence a secret, why couldn't I let him? What more did I need to know?

The answer was everything. Pure and simple, for better or worse, for his sake and mine. Everything.

"I'm sorry about all the lies I've told you," I said, taking his hand. "It's really not such a good idea for a relationship as deep as ours to have so many untruths flying around. You may not know it, but I'm really a big fan of honesty. Yep, when that curtain is pulled at the polling booth of Life, I vote for truth every time!"

Ben stared at me with a worried expression. "What is it now?"

Well I'd really dug myself into a hole with that line, hadn't I? Here I was trying to get him to come clean and I made him think *I* was the one holding back.

"It's not me, honey, it's you," I said with a forced smile.

He let go of my hand. "You think Benjamin and I made plans to fight? Is that it?"

I looked at him. He really didn't know. He was going to force me to go all the way.

"I swear he didn't threaten me. He didn't want to fight, or if he did he didn't say or do anything. I'd tell you if he did."

We weren't holding hands anymore, there was no reason I couldn't reach into my purse. There wasn't anything keeping me from taking a certain photograph and bringing it out into the light of Ryan Field.

And presenting it for analysis, like a natal chart.

"Don't tell me that's not you," I said in a weak voice, placing the decade-old photo on his lap. "Don't tell me you got the tattoo because of some sixteen-year-old sweetheart with implants."

I tried to look into his eyes but he wouldn't let me. He got up without even touching the photograph and walked down the stairs.

I caught up with him a few rows down and grabbed his shirt from behind. "Did you think I wouldn't understand?"

He turned to me and looked up at me with wounded eyes. "How could you understand?" he said.

"I'm sure she loves you, Ben."

"That's what I mean!"

And he continued to walk down, until I ran past and blocked his path. Now he was on a higher step and I was looking up at him. But I only saw that little boy in the photograph.

"Think of her Ben! She needs you now. Have you even tried to call her? You have to call her, Ben!"

He pushed past me but didn't walk all the way to the gate. Instead he sat down a few rows lower and gazed at the empty field.

"You're right," I said, sitting beside him, hoping he

wouldn't walk away again. "I don't understand. I don't understand how any mother couldn't love a son like you. But she must have been a good mother once. She took you to all those countries. My parents never took me to—"

"Don't compare her to your parents!" Ben shouted. "She wasn't a parent at all! Never! She forgot to pick me up from school, she left me with strangers, she left me alone. When I was five she went to visit her mother in Florida and my father flew me out to spend a week with her. She never came to the airport. To this day I don't know what happened. They put me on the next plane home. At my seventh birthday party she got mad over something I can't even remember and threw my cake in the pool. When I was nine she gave me cocaine. When I was ten, after the divorce, after my father got custody, she told me I wasn't her son and those were the last words she ever spoke to me."

Tears were falling down my cheeks.

"Don't cry!"

"I'm sorry." I tried to put an arm around him but he wouldn't let me. "Tell me about the tattoo."

"My father didn't know about it. It was one of her drunken impulses. Just another way to prove how close we were."

"To herself?"

"Maybe. But I think she was mostly trying to prove it to me. You know how perceptive kids can be—much more perceptive than adults. She knew I saw through her. She hated me for it."

"I'm sure she didn't hate you."

"She hated me! She erased me from her arm. After the divorce she erased my name from her arm!"

"I didn't know your parents—"

"Not my parents—her. My father was a wonderful man, a wonderful father."

"How could he be a wonderful father if he killed himself?" I asked. "Don't you feel abandoned by him?" I didn't know why I was asking this; I didn't want to make him feel worse. But I guess I thought the answer would tell me something about Ben himself, and maybe even something about us.

"I know a lot of children of suicides feel that way. But I didn't feel abandoned by my father, and I didn't feel guilty. He was very depressed, but he always kept that separate from his relationship with me. Sure, I resented him for a while after he died, but not long. Even after he killed himself I felt his presence more strongly than I'd ever felt hers when she and I were together. She always wanted me to call her 'Christy.' Not 'mother.' She thought by being best friends she would be a better parent. In the end she was neither."

"Why are you harder on her than on your father ?"

"Because she was harder on me. My father left me, but he didn't forget me. He made sure I was provided for. He probably would have killed himself years before if he hadn't felt responsible for me. He didn't say, 'You are no longer my son.'"

I laid my head on Ben's shoulder and cried on his shirt. "What can I do?"

"It's in the past," Ben replied, moving away.

"The past is ruining our lives, destroying our love!" I cried. "You're in denial that your parents are still a force in your life, just like I've been in denial that Benjamin is still a force in my life. Both of us have to come to terms with our past."

"I don't want to talk about it."

"We can sort it out," I said hopefully. "Your mother needs you. If you call—"

"No! I'll never call her."

"Ben . . ."

"Even if I did she wouldn't talk to me. She hates me."

"You were ten years old. How could she hate you?"

"She hated my father and she hates me. She destroyed him, and as far as I'm concerned she's dead as well."

"You don't mean that!"

"I've never meant anything more. She destroyed my father. He liked order, like me, and she was a tornado who turned everything she touched upside down. He got a position at Northwestern after they separated and brought me. It was all very draining for my father. I think it would have been easier for him to let her have custody, but he couldn't do it for my sake. Besides, she didn't put up much of a fight. She abandoned us both."

I took him in my arms, and this time he didn't resist. He closed his eyes, and I could see tears forming under his lashes.

"I don't believe she doesn't love you," I said, stroking his hair. "Didn't she ever say she loved you, when you were little?"

"She said it all the time. She said it so much it meant less than nothing. Christy, she hasn't talked to me in eight years!" Ben said, wiping his eyes and looking forcefully into mine. "She's forgotten eight birthdays, my father's funeral, my graduation. For all she knows I could be a father myself—she could have a grandchild. Or I could be paralyzed from an accident or need a liver transplant. I could be dead. In those eight years she might have re-married, raised other children, and never thought once of her own son."

"You don't know that."

"How old do you think I was when my father died? Old enough to live by myself?"

"She didn't fight for custody?"

"What fight? There wouldn't have been a fight. My father was dead. She was still my legal mother. She only had to come get me. She only had to send me a ticket."

"Maybe she was . . . sick. Maybe she didn't know."

"Christy, she didn't want me. And that was fine with me, because I wouldn't have wanted to live with her again. I went to live with my uncle."

"Well, I still don't think she really hates you, or that you really hate her," I said, trying to hang on to this little scrap of hope. "If you really hate her, why did you keep the tattoo?"

"I kept it for you."

"I mean before that. Why did you wait so long?"

Ben looked down at the field. "I was going to have it taken off after my father's funeral. She killed him and she didn't even come to the funeral. She didn't even send a card. But I didn't have it removed. I don't know why. Then when I was accepted to Northwestern, I decided I had to do it. I couldn't go to my father's school with her name on my arm."

"Ben, look at me!" I took his face in my hands and forced him to lock his eyes on mine. "I've found her, Ben. I haven't talked to her, but I know where she is. She's had a breakdown, she's in a rehab center sobering up!"

Tears started streaming down Ben's cheeks, but I didn't let him wipe them away. "Tell me you don't feel anything! Tell me you aren't thinking about her every day?"

"OK, OK!" he screamed, pushing my hands away. "Of course I think about her, how could I not think about her?"

"Look me in the eye, Ben, and tell me you hate your mother."

He tried, but he just couldn't, and his tears got the best of him. "All right, I love her, is that what you want to hear? I love her, I love her!" he cried, and fell against my shoulder. "I love her . . ."

I thought it was good that he was crying, and I cried too, in sympathy, sadness, and relief, foolishly thinking this was the beginning of a reconciliation, as if life were ever that simple.

Going Retrograde

The first thing I did the next morning—I say the next morning because I was too overwhelmed to do anything last night—was call information for the Sorenson Rehab Center. I wrote the number on a slip of paper and put it under my crystals to gather strength.

Then I went out to lunch with my mom. That was the price I had to pay for staying home from school. She knew I wasn't sick, and could tell something was bothering me.

So after assuring her at 7:00 a.m. that Ben and I hadn't broken up and that it had nothing to do with his suicidal nature—although it did have something to do with it— the good woman left me alone until noon.

And, truth to tell, I needed to talk. I was dying to tell someone, and who could I tell? Certainly not Miranda. And my dad? "What's this have to do with the price of soybeans?" he would say.

Of course, Ben had sworn me to secrecy. But in my book that means you limit yourself to telling one person. And you have to make that person swear in turn.

So there we were, Mom and yours truly, dipping tortillas in the green salsa at Don Pablo's.

My mom was shocked and saddened as I told the tale, which almost didn't get told because she kept interrupting. But I managed to slog through it—the little I knew—only filling in a few gaps myself with pure conjecture. My mom kept saying she couldn't believe it, she just couldn't believe it.

She took out some tissues from her purse after I showed her the fatal photo. "It's such a tragedy! His poor father."

"Poor Ben!" I added. "Neglected, forgotten, abandoned." I started to cry myself and reached for the water to clear my throat.

"How could that woman be so cruel?" my mom asked. "And when so many children abuse drugs or join gangs, do you know how many parents would give their right arm to have a son like Ben?"

"I know it's *your* fantasy."

"I don't believe it. I just don't believe it."

"You know how you're always saying opportunity comes out of tragedy? Well I have an idea. I see Ben's tragedy as my opportunity to save him. I mean, to save his relationship with his mother."

"Christina, he has no relationship with his mother."

"I can't believe you're being so negative."

"What do you plan to do? Bring them together on *Oprah*?"

"I thought I'd bring him to her."

"Christina . . ."

"Think about it. She's strapped down in a detox clinic, a sitting target. I break the ice with a phone call, and then Ben and I fly out to sunny California for the tearful reunion. She needs him now, after all, in her battle with the bottle. And Ben needs a mother. He's always needed a mother, hasn't he? I'm so worried about him. He's an orphan, really, when you think about it."

"Darling, *you're* the one I'm worried about. Ben has dealt with this his entire life. But it's caught you unprepared, and in trying to make something positive out of a mother's neglect you've blinded yourself to the truth."

"There's your negativity again! I might as well have told Dad."

"I'm not saying good can't come out of this. You certainly have a better understanding of Ben's depression now. I think you can save him, in little ways, in other ways. I think talking about his past will bring you closer together. But it won't bring his mother back."

◉ ◉ ◉

It won't bring his mother back. Those words echoed in my ears all afternoon as I waited for Ben. Mrs. Natalie Marlowe, prophetess of doom. But I didn't believe her. I just didn't.

When Ben finally stopped by he showed no signs of the emotional wear and tear I expected. He was calm, rested, his shirt tucked in, his hair combed. But my suspicious side told me he was smiling *too* much.

He wanted to go out but I had other plans. I made him promise to stay put on the bed and took the slip of paper from under the crystals.

"Who are you calling?" he asked, as I dialed.

"Yes, I'd like Christy Shire's room please," I said in my corporate voice.

"Oh no you don't!"

He lunged for the phone but, like one of the musketeers, I was expecting this move and lunged back with greater force, pinning him on the bed, keeping the connection.

"I won't talk to her," he said, trying to get up.

"You will!" I insisted, jabbing him with an elbow. I was using a lot of force, to be sure, but I didn't think a reconciliation could be achieved without some pain.

"Christy Shire," I said when someone came back on the line. "Tell her it's her son."

Ben moved away. "Fine. They won't let you through."

"I'll get through!"

"She won't talk to me."

"Hello, is this Ms. Shire? . . . Her nurse? . . . I'm calling for her son. He'd like to speak to her."

Ben looked at me long enough to frown before turning back away. "I never should have given you a key to my apartment," he said. "I should have known, after you looked through my passport, that you would snoop around."

"I found the girlie mags too!" I teased him.

I heard footsteps on the phone. My heart was pounding. I was bringing a family together. I had never done anything so noble and good before. Once I had helped my mom at the shelter when they were understaffed, but my heart hadn't been in it.

I waited eons, honestly believing I was about to hear his mother's voice. But it was only the nurse again.

"I'm sorry," she said. "Ms. Shire can't come to the phone right now."

"What do you mean? This is urgent. Her son—"

"She's indisposed."

I knew the witch was lying. "Then please tell me when I should call back. An hour? Two hours?"

"I'm sorry, but Ms. Shire doesn't want to speak to her son."

Just like that. Ms. Shire doesn't want to speak to her son. How could anyone be so heartless? What's wrong with you? I wanted to say. Don't you have a mother? But Ben was sitting right there, so I forced a smile and politely hung up.

"I told you," he said.

"She was sleeping. We'll try later."

I tried to keep from crying but I didn't have Ben's will-power. I couldn't be calm, keep my shirt tucked in, and my hair combed. I was a Capricorn, after all.

So, instead of jetting off to palm trees and Rolls Royces we were stranded in my sad little room, where a formerly hopeful girl had to be consoled by the boy she'd planned to save.

⊙ ⊙ ⊙

I shouldn't have gone back to school the next day. What was I thinking? Wasn't Mars going retrograde? Didn't my horoscope say, "Tread carefully, conflicts will clutter your path like fallen leaves"? But I thought that was referring to Ben's conflict with his mother and my conflict with Ben about engineering a reconciliation. I could have prevented a lot of misery if I'd just played dead for twenty-four more hours. But, at the core, nothing would have changed.

I was helpless to change the Big Picture. And if you'd asked me that morning, as I slogged from Algebra to English to History, exactly what the Big Picture was, I would have answered, "Christy Shire."

Christy Shire, Christy Shire, that's all I thought about now. She seemed to be the key to everything; not only Ben's past, but the door to his future as well. And my future too. I was torn. I mean, it was so tragic, so utterly sad. But it also made me dream. And between dreaming and weeping there wasn't much time to find the value of *x*. But I was wasting my energy. My mom and Ben were right. Christy's nurse was right. Not meant to be. Anyway, Christy Shire wasn't even part of the Big Picture. She was like a burned-out star long gone from our universe, which we only think still exists because we see its ghostly light. No, the Big Picture was filled with other—not so heavenly—objects, and they were heading for a collision.

It was a long day and I was exhausted by the end of it. I hoped Ben would be able to pick me up, I didn't have the energy for the long El ride to Evanston.

Miranda stopped by my locker after sixth bell to invite us to a party Saturday night. I told her sure and spent a few minutes cleaning up my stuff.

The halls were empty when I walked out. I remember feeling relief at the sight of Ben's car. He was leaning on the hood, talking to Miranda. When he saw me he waved and started to walk over.

And then I saw Benjamin. I don't know where he came from, I didn't see his car. But he had spotted me and was walking toward me from the entrance of the semicircle drive, cutting across the lawn. He was at least fifty yards behind Ben, his hands swinging at his side, empty. Ben kept walking toward me, not knowing he was there. I remember thinking Benjamin had come for me this time, because if he wanted to confront Ben he could have done so while

Ben was waiting in plain view. But why he came—whether to plead with me or threaten me for the millionth time, or whether he came to kill me, I'll never know.

And then I saw a shape running up to Benjamin. You know how in the movies the violent scenes are always in slow motion? Well this was like watching a scene in fast forward. I didn't see a man, I didn't see a Bulls jacket, I didn't see the gang punk who'd asked me about Benjamin—although it was the same guy, because the police later arrested him—no, I only saw a shape, a blur. And then I heard two shots.

People started screaming, and running in all directions. Some pushed past me heading for the safety of the school. I saw a car speed away. Or maybe I just heard it. Or maybe I didn't see or hear anything.

The next thing I knew I was kneeling on the lawn, holding Benjamin's body in my arms. I don't remember how I got there, whether I ran or walked, whether I was screaming or in mute shock. He was dead, and I knew he was dead. His eyes were closed, and blood from his heart had already poured out, staining the sacred grass. But I cradled him in my arms as if it weren't too late to protect him, as if my only role in life were to protect him. As if I couldn't live without him. As if he'd never stalked or threatened me.

My clothes were covered with blood, but I didn't even notice it at the time. I stared at the ragged White Sox hat, lying upright on the lawn several yards away, like a tombstone.

And then I saw Ben. He wasn't at my side. He hadn't gathered around the body with the morbidly curious students and faculty. I saw him through a gap in the spectators and he was very far away. Very far away. He was staring at me, with his arms crossed, frowning. At the time I thought he was frowning because of the shock of it all, because of the danger, because his rival lay dead, because he felt relieved, and glad, and triumphant.

But I later realized it was just the opposite, it was a frown of despair. That he wasn't frowning at Benjamin at all, but at me. That in my going to him, in my holding his dead body, Ben saw not the impulsive, emotional reaction of a girl who knew the victim—no, he saw himself in divorce court all those years ago, rejected and abandoned. He knew that I'd once loved Benjamin. And now, by my blood-stained jeans, he believed he could never completely replace Benjamin in my thoughts, that I loved him still, that I would love him always. His frown, as I would only later realize, when it was almost too late, was a sign of defeat, a frown that said there was only one way to compete with the dead.

The Clouds of Our Destruction

The wind was beating against my window. A branch from the elm tree scraped against the glass like a fingernail against a blackboard. I sat up in the darkness, wide, wide awake.

I'd just had a nightmare that Benjamin had risen from his grave, climbed out with dust and Academy turf clinging to his skeleton, his White Sox hat covering his skull.

"Christy," he was saying. "I'll never rest until I hold you. Christy . . ."

It had been a full week now since Benjamin's funeral and I'd had this nightmare every night. Each time I saw him crawling out of the earth. God knows what I was doing at the cemetery to begin with. He was always wearing the White Sox hat. Being a skeleton, he couldn't move very fast, and he never caught me. I always ran alone through the cemetery, calling for Ben. But Ben was never there.

Maybe I was having this dream because I felt guilty for not going to the funeral. I had been torn. Part of me felt I should go, it was the right thing to do. It would put everything to rest. But my parents, who never learned the full story of Benjamin's stalking me—thank God—were against it. As was Ben, although he didn't say it. But his silence had grown stronger since the shooting, and told me everything.

It had been a gray week. Storms were in the forecast. As the wind blew and the branch screeched back and forth across my bedroom window, I prayed. I prayed that I would survive this terrible night. I prayed that it really was the elm tree scratching the window and not Benjamin's skeletal hand. I was praying a lot these days, for a thousand different things. For sleep, for peaceful dreams, for a day of sunshine, for Ben to get over his jealousy. I even prayed for Benjamin's soul, which I figured must be somewhere now. I prayed it was somewhere far away.

If you told me two weeks ago that Benjamin would

be dead I would have been relieved. What better solution to our problems? I would never have to worry about him stalking me again. He could never pose a danger to Ben, or try to come between us.

How wrong I was! If a genie came out of my cereal box tomorrow and granted me one wish, I would bring him back to life. Time would have eased his jealousy. He would have found someone else and moved to another town. But now he was a ghost, and I couldn't even hide behind the walls of my room. He could haunt me the rest of my life. And he would haunt Ben, who could only hide behind his silence, which grew longer every day.

As I lay back down and closed my eyes I thought how poorly we understand life. We think we've got it down, know exactly where it's going, get confident and plot its course for the next twenty years, and then—boom—it goes retrograde, like a planet, and streaks backwards in the sky.

⊙ ⊙ ⊙

It was raining when I woke, steadily, hard. The wind had died down, the branches on my elm were still as the fingers on a corpse. It was almost noon, my parents had gone out to brunch with friends, the Sunday *Trib* lay in sections on the table and chairs. I poured myself a bowl of Coco Puffs and grabbed the "Arts and Entertainment" section. It was so quiet I could hear the rain beating against the roof, so I turned on the stereo in the living room and changed the tuner from my mom's rock classics station to alternative. Then I peeked at my horoscope:

"This day could be your last."

All right, it wasn't that specific, but it was bleak enough. I called Ben, but he wasn't home. Where was he in this rain? I left a message for him to phone me the second he got in. I missed him terribly, even though I'd seen him less than twelve hours ago. We'd gone to a movie last night, but it seemed all twenty-two screens at the super-duper plex were showing flicks about mothers. Even the alien film, *Rendezvous With Antares*, featured an alien mother. We didn't talk much afterwards, and he dropped me off early.

I put my empty bowl in the dishwasher, turned off the stereo and looked for a sitcom or football game to take my mind off the weather. The Bears were playing the Vikings at Soldier Field. Wide receivers were slipping on the wet turf. Both quarterbacks were having a hard time gripping the ball. Fumbles came fast and furious. And in the stands our loyal fans sat wrapped in ponchos, miserable.

At halftime Happy Sanderson of the Channel 11 Sun Squad showed us the big picture on the radar screen. Red all around, and more on the way. "This low pressure front will stay throughout the afternoon," Happy was saying with a stupid grin. "I'm afraid we'll continue to see rain in the second half, with gusting winds and a chance of a thunderstorm. And this evening we may have heavy thunderstorms as another low pressure system moves into our area."

Why did I feel a chill run up my spine? It wasn't cold,

just raining. I stared out the window, waiting for Ben to call, wondering where he was. For a while I thought about taking the El to his place. He hadn't taken back his key. I guess he figured I'd already found everything worth hiding. But I didn't want to walk to the station in this rain.

In the fourth quarter, the game got close and kind of took my mind off things. But only kind of. When it was over I went online and checked out another horoscope. It was as bad as the first. I called Ben again, I left another message. I called Miranda, but not even she was home.

By the time my parents got back I was climbing the walls. "Drive me to Evanston. Please!" I begged my dear, dear father.

But he just shook the water off his hat and asked me the Bears' score.

"Ma? What do you say?"

"In this rain? Why doesn't Ben pick you up?"

"His car's in the shop," I lied.

"It's pouring, Christina. There are severe thunderstorm warnings."

"We have plans!"

"Do you have to see him every day?"

This from the woman who not long ago thought my astrological breakup with Ben was the biggest disaster in American history since Reagan's landslide. "Yes!" I shouted. "Every day!"

They went off to the bedroom to change out of their wet clothes, leaving me alone by the door. I looked at the rain bouncing off the driveway, the front gate shaking in the wind. I was shaking myself, from a fear I didn't want to admit.

I put on my Bears poncho and made sure I had tokens for the El in my purse.

"You're not going out in this weather," my mom said, as I headed for the door.

"It's either this or you drive me."

"Lawrence, tell her she shouldn't go."

"You shouldn't go," my dad said, tuning in to the late game.

It was warm outside, even with the wind. Tornado weather, unseasonal. But it wasn't the wind that frightened me. As the El crawled uptown I tried to think about anything but the weather. Surely Ben would be home when I got there. He wasn't really depressed about me and Benjamin, not that depressed. It was clear he hadn't lost me. Was there anything I wouldn't do to prove my love?

The sky was dark purple as I ran from the station. I would have called it beautiful any other night, but today it was truly ominous. At the sound of thunder I nearly jumped through my poncho.

Ben's car was parked in its usual spot, which was a good sign—or was it? I ran up the stairs and banged on the door. No answer. I took out my key. The lights in the hall and kitchen were on. Was that unusual? I couldn't remember.

It was ominously quiet, but then shouldn't it be quiet if he wasn't home? I wondered if he had taken his bike, but

I was too scared to look in the bedroom. I was too scared to do anything but stand in the doorway, shivering.

And then I noticed his golf clubs, or rather I noticed his gold clubs weren't there, in their usual spot in the corner. I ran across the room. The golf bag was lying on the floor. I knelt down and desperately counted the clubs. I was in such a panic even a simple thing like counting the numbers on golf clubs seemed impossible. The nine iron was missing.

Now that I knew Ben wasn't in the apartment I rushed into the bedroom, grabbed the bike, and dragged it downstairs. I started pedaling without even thinking where I was going. I had only been to the golf course that one time, but I remembered how to get there—or did I? It wasn't far, a mile, a mile and a half. But how could I be sure that's where Ben had gone? Why hadn't he taken his car, or his bike? But why shouldn't he walk, what was his hurry, why should he care about getting wet?

I thought about what he had said, that true lovers don't destroy each other, they save each other. He had certainly turned my life around, put me in the labor force, got me back in the good graces of my parents and the front row at school. I hoped I'd given him something in return, something for his random-loving logical soul to believe in. It had been a long time since he had made one of his ominous comments about death that so worried me when we first met. He was happy, and I think some of that happiness was because of me.

But now he was out in the storm because of me, wanting to die because of me, because he thought he'd lost me, and more than me, that whole world of family he so desperately needed, my parents, who were fast becoming his new father and mother. The possibility of losing all this was too much for him to bear, had pushed him out into the storm.

And I was in the storm too, wasn't I? In trying to save him, would I only destroy myself as well? It seemed strange that we kept swinging from one extreme to the other—from saving each other to putting each other at risk. I had been so convinced it was Benjamin who was dangerous to me, to us. But I had the wrong Benjamin. It was my Benjamin who posed the greatest danger to our love and our lives.

Oh God, I was lost! Lost! In all my thinking about things I hadn't been paying much attention to the road. And I heard rumbling in the distance. I stopped at the next corner to get my bearings. I tore off the hood of my poncho to get some air, my tears mingling with the rain. I tried to remember that night we had ridden here together. I remembered brick houses along tree-lined streets, but what were their names? I had no idea. I remembered turning right at a gas station. But there weren't any in view.

I saw a lightning flash. Oh God, every minute could mean life and death. Why hadn't I come sooner? I'd wasted the whole day, and now he might die because I didn't know whether to go straight or turn.

I went straight, pedaling furiously. I would have asked someone for directions, but there was no one to ask. There weren't even any cars on the street. It was like the day after the end of the world.

Two blocks later and there it was—a Shell station. Was it the right one? I didn't know, but I had no choice. I turned onto a small winding street that sloped up. My legs were killing me, but I raced on. Then I saw a white fence, with a golf course on the other side!

I was so panicked I didn't even follow the entrance in but ditched the bike right there, hopped the fence, and started running. The sky was black now, and the rain beat into the lake. Despite the poncho, I was soaked, so soaked I couldn't get any wetter.

Where was that damned gazebo? It took all my will-power not to scream Ben's name. But I knew if I did he might run away. This whole thing was about running away, wasn't it?

What hole was this? Where was the tee? I finally saw a marker—sixteen. I wanted eighteen. I ran on. It was hard to see, struggling against the wind, the rain stinging my eyes like a million pins. But then a bolt of lightning lit up the gazebo on the hill. I couldn't tell if it was empty.

I reached it with my last breath and collapsed inside. He wasn't here. But why should he be? I leaned against the railing, panting. The rain was so loud hitting the roof I couldn't even hear myself gasp.

And then I saw him. Standing near the lake on the eighteenth hole, standing deathly still holding the club in the air, like a sacrifice.

"Ben!"

I couldn't help it, I couldn't keep from screaming his name as I ran over. He didn't move at first but turned to me slowly as if awaking from a trance. A flash of lightning behind me lit up his face, ominously confident and calm. He wasn't wearing a jacket—but then why should he?—and his saturated hair clung to his cheeks.

I threw myself on him, so forcefully we almost fell over. I was sobbing uncontrollably.

"What are you doing here?" he yelled.

"What are *you* doing here?" I shouted back.

I gathered myself together. I didn't have time to be a basket case. I had to get that club out of his hands. Any second . . .

"Go away!"

"No!"

He was trying to pry me loose with his free hand, but his other hand still held the club.

"This has nothing to do with you!" he shouted above the rain.

"It has everything to do with me! How can you destroy yourself and expect me to go on?"

"You'll go on."

There was a terrifying clap of thunder, I didn't know how far away. In my panic I let go. He tried to run away, but came up against the lake. This time I dug in with my fingernails.

"Give me that club!"

He held it out of reach. "You don't understand!"

"You're right, I don't understand. Let go of the club!"

"I won't let you do this!"

"Do what? Live?"

"I won't let you die too!"

"Well, I will!" And I got hold of the shaft of the club. I didn't have the strength to pull it away from him, but then he didn't have the strength to pull it away from me.

"I'm not afraid to die!" I shouted, staring into his dark eyes. But I was. I was so afraid I no longer felt the wind and the rain, the muddy grass beneath my feet, the cold metal of the club.

But I did hear the thunder. An enormous roar. And then a great streak of lightning, with branching bolts and an even louder clap of thunder a second later. The lightning was only a mile away. A few more strikes before it would sear our hearts together.

Ben and I stared at each other in silence for an infinite moment, both of us with determination and fear in our eyes. But what was he afraid of? Not death, I thought, but life. And what was I so strongly determined about? To hurl the club away? Yes, certainly a moment ago I wanted nothing more. But now? Maybe in this infinite moment I was actually determined to die, just like Juliet, with the shortsighted stubbornness of a great love. I don't know.

There was a steady low rumbling far away. Then I heard the rain beat against my poncho. The rain. But where was the thunder?

"It's over," Ben said, not with disappointment or relief, but like an anchorman just stating a fact.

He was no longer holding the club with all his strength. I took it from his hand and flung it into the lake. Then I turned around three hundred and sixty degrees. Nothing but black sky. No sound but the rain and my own desperate breathing.

What now?

Ben wasn't looking at me at all but staring into the distance, his hands at his side, lost. I felt so sorry for him.

I laughed, from nervousness and joy, and clapped him on the shoulder. "Don't worry," I said. "There's always tomorrow."

"It took me years to gather the courage to come here tonight. I can't do it again."

"You still love me, don't you? That takes more courage than anything!"

He turned to me and smiled. He was back among the living.

I noticed he was only a few feet from the lake. I put my hands against his chest and pushed with all my might. He fell backwards and rolled into the water.

I suppose he could have drowned, but I didn't consider that at the time. Anyway, the water only came up to his waist.

He spat out a golf ball or something and glared at me with utter shock.

"That's for trying to leave me!" I exclaimed.

I stepped to the edge and gave him my hand. Gullible fool that I was, I thought he was going to apologize, kiss my palm, cry on my shoulder or something. Instead he pulled me in.

"That's for trying to follow!"

We both laughed, working off our nervous energy. Anyway, what was the harm? We couldn't get any wetter. We kissed for a long time, breathing life back into each other.

"I guess I'm just destined to suffer," he said in a defeated voice, helping me out of the lake.

"And I'm destined to make you suffer!" I replied, wiping off the algae. "Let's go back to your place and regroup. Then I'll buy you a hot fudge sundae."

"Did you bring money?" he asked, Mr. Practical even at a moment like this.

"I'll pay you back." And I took his wet, muddy hand, and the electricity that flowed from his body into mine shook me to the core.

⊙ ⊙ ⊙

Often since then I've wondered what if the storm hadn't passed, and lightning struck closer and closer? Would we have gone through with it? Would we have had the nerve to stand still on the soaking grass as the dark clouds of our destruction approached? Would we have had the courage to fling the club away and run like hell? I think he would have held on and died. I think at the next loud thunderclap I would have let go and lived. But only the Heavens will ever know for sure.

~~A pair of starcrossed lovers take their life~~
Shakespeare

A pair of starcrossed lovers take back their life
C. Marlowe